The Price of Friendship

by

Brian Kirkland

authorHOUSE®

AuthorHouse™ UK Ltd.
500 Avebury Boulevard
Central Milton Keynes, MK9 2BE
www.authorhouse.co.uk
Phone: 08001974150

©2008 Brian Kirkland. All rights reserved.

No part of this book may be reproduced, stored in a retrieval system, or transmitted by any means without the written permission of the author.

First published by AuthorHouse 11/11/2008

ISBN: 978-1-4389-1334-6 (sc)

Printed in the United States of America
Bloomington, Indiana

This book is printed on acid-free paper.

Chapter 1

Max Reynolds edged forward in the line of people which was inching its way towards the Continental Airlines check-in desk 34/35 at Terminal C, Logan International Airport, Boston. He had been used to the routine of long distance traveling, his job taking him to many parts of the world through numerous international airports…but never before though had he felt so nervous and never before had it been so important to make the flight. He was more aware of what was going on around him than ever before and it all felt so different. He wished he could scream to the heavens and dash to the nearest exit. He felt the slow, steady trickle of sweat running into the small of his back and he feared that this may be just another way in which he would be caught out when he reached the desk clerk.

He double checked the number he had scribbled on the small slip of Hilton Hotel note paper which was crumpled in his hand, he read it to himself again and again trying not to raise attention…WX2390… WX2390….he knew that he had no need to memories the number but it was all he had and he was clinging to the non-descript piece of paper as if his life depended on it.

He had been sent to the hotel and told to wait for the next instruction two days earlier. Having sat and waited by the phone for two days, barely able to sleep or rest until the call came. The phone had eventually rang and the noise was deafening to him as he answered in a blind panic.

'Who the hell are you?' He had screamed into the hotel phone 'What do you want from me?'

The sinister voice on the other end of the phone was cold and calm and the instructions were crystal clear;

'Be at Terminal C and present yourself to the Continental Airlines Desk before 3pm today' had been the opening line of the instruction

'Quote the following booking number …WX2390 and you will know what to do from then AND under no circumstances let the package leave your side, for even a split second…..we will be watching you…but you will not know who or where we are'

He had checked his watch… 1pm and although he could see the airport and hear the planes from his hotel room, time was of the essence to make the check-in time…he knew only too well the consequences of not meeting these latest set of demands.

There was just enough time to ascertain which flight was checking in at Desk 34/35 on the hotel internet service before he left his room and he knew from that point that he would be traveling to Newark Airport in New Jersey……. but he was sure that this would not be his final destination. Newark is a hub for Continental airlines and he could be connecting to anywhere in the world from there. Where the hell was he going and the package…how did the package fit into the deal? Too many unanswered questions.

He would only find out his final destination when he quoted out loud, the number…WX2390… to the desk clerk and even then he had no clue what would await him when he got there.

Max looked up from the piece of paper in his hand, patted his pocket to make sure his passport was safe and instantly became annoyed that the elderly lady in front of him had not moved at all, why was it moving so slowly? He knew it was moving at the same pace it always moved but to him is seemed like an age from the time he joined the line just behind the elderly lady. He had examined the people in the queue very carefully before choosing to place himself between the elderly lady whom he thought to be fairly inconspicuous and the middle aged business man who appeared to be completely pre-occupied with his array of electronic gadgets. It was unlikely that he would raise any attention and it was also unlikely that either of these individuals would be the person reporting back on Max's movements. That was at least the thinking behind his decision.

He gathered his thoughts and prepared himself for the checking in process as the desk came closer.

The desk clerk was a young black woman, probably in her mid twenties, easy on the eye and looking very professional and extremely well groomed in her Continental Airlines uniform. She seemed very pleasant as she wished the person in front of Max a good day and a nice flight as the young man went off towards the departure gate. That would be the next challenge for Max after getting through the booking process….. to get through the security screening and then to the gate. He noticed from the badge on her jacket lapel that her name was Lucinda.

'Good Afternoon Sir could I see your passport and travel documents', asked Lucinda

Max parked his hand luggage roller case directly in front of the desk and handed over his passport. He felt his voice crackle as he explained that he had no documentation with him but that his booking reference number was…..WX2390. Lucinda entered his information into the computer and within a seconds the tapping of the keys on the computer keyboard was interrupted by the printing of Max's documents…..at last, the moment of truth where was it to be?

'Do you have any luggage to check into the hold Sir?' asked Lucinda

His nervousness had been temporarily replaced by anxiety whilst he awaited the printing of his boarding pass and then all of a sudden with the mention of the word luggage he a feeling of panic well up inside.

'I erm...I have no luggage to check today...er just cabin luggage,' stuttered Max.

'Could I see your hand luggage please Mr Reynolds. We have an airline policy regarding the maximum weight and size of luggage to be stored in overhead bins, especially on transatlantic flights' ....Transatlantic ??? The word hit him like a slap to the face!!. Was he going back to Europe from Newark?? His head began to spin and he was not sure what to do or say next. He could hardly ask where his final destination was!!! But he had to keep his composure and his bag must not leave his side...at all costs.

'Certainly', he replied 'I weighed it myself before leaving the hotel and I am sure it is not oversize,' Max added.

'Even so, if you wouldn't mind placing the bag on the scales we should be able to send you on your way in no time Sir,' interjected Lucinda.

Max took a deep breath and held it whilst the scales registered the weight of the bag....Max could not even look....

That will be fine Mr Reynolds, said Lucinda 'A little on the heavy side but I am sure we can accommodate an extra pound or two' She smiled and offered Max his boarding passes. He let out a breath of air which was loud enough for Lucinda to raise an eyebrow in his direction as he hurried away towards the security check point.

One more hurdle overcome he thought to himself, He was visibly sweating now and droplets were running across his eyebrows. He decided to find a restroom to clean up before he braved the next step .....Security.

As he walked into the restroom, he looked at the boarding passes for the first time....

Boarding pass number One:
Departing Boston 1755
Arriving Newark 1900

Boarding Pass Number two:
Departing Newark 2035
Arriving London Heathrow 0915

After cleaning up and regaining his composure, Max walked confidently to the relevant security check point. He had confirmed the presence of the package he was instructed to carry and made sure that it was neatly wrapped in several layers of clothing. It was entirely possible he thought to himself, that the contents of the package could cause alarm with the security officials as they screened his bag. This was his next fear and one which increased in intensity as he handed his boarding pass and passport to the first of several security officials still to be negotiated before he could finally sit down and try to settle his nerves before the flight.

His documents received no more than a cursory glance from the security official, a diminutive elderly man of Hispanic origin and a very serious disposition.

What would he do if the inspectors did ask him to remove the package from his bag? Running was not an option and he could offer no explanation as to what was contained within the package. He tried to settle his nerves a little by recalling that he had often concealed extra wine and spirits in his luggage as well as food items local to the area he had visited such as Biltong (a local form of dried meat/jerky) from South African and local cheeses from Italy and Holland. All these items had got through the security check with no problem but that was before the onset of increased security measures post 9/11.

Suddenly and without he found himself placing his bag on the conveyor and removing his shoes to do the same with them. For the second time in less than half an hour, the deep breath…. as he was waved through the walk through metal detector and radar device. No alarm signal. Of course there wouldn't be thought Max as he turned to stare directly at his bag as it passed through radar. He flashed his boarding pass to the security officer who had waved him through.

The conveyor stopped as two members of staff scrutinized the monitor which revealed the contents of the bags passing through the machine. Max could swear that his heart missed a beat before the belt eventually whirred back into motion and the security officer's attention was drawn to the next bag and then the next and so on.

His eyes closed and his shoulders relaxed just a little as he grabbed his bag from the conveyor and lowered it to the ground next to his shoes. He put his shoes back on and headed towards Gate 26.

Max Reynolds was on his way……a journey he had known nothing about a mere two hours earlier, on his way now to a destination he was very conversant with but had no clue why he was going there on this occasion and all he felt at this very moment in time was an overwhelming feeling of relief that he had managed to get the package through security and he was free to board his flight. He knew nothing of what was to happen next and he was almost too tired to care at that very moment. Just let me get on the flight, rest and regroup he thought to himself…..he just knew that he would certainly need all his energy, alertness and guile for what was surely to come.

As he lay on his back across three seats at the departure gate with his bag across his stomach, Max took the first relaxed breath of the day and closed his eyes for just a moment in an attempt to reflect on the day's event so far. He could hear the loud speaker messages inviting people to board various flights in the gates surrounding Gate 26. People were moving around the departure lounge, expectant and exiting conversations between family members on their way to a family holiday, cell phone conversations and people making conversation and exchanging experiences everywhere. All of the normal sounds a person expect to be part of but they were noise and distraction to Max who felt that he was alone in a crowded room with only his thoughts and fears for company. Reflections and thoughts as well as fears and trepidation for what was to come flooded into the space he tried to create in his mind. To make any sense of things he would have to take his thoughts back to that night in Boston which seems like a previous lifetime but in reality is still less than a week ago……

Chapter 2

'Your table is ready Sir,' said the waitress, smiling as she ushered Max and his colleague to their table.

He had dined many times at Legal Seafood in South Shore Mall, not the most fashionable of the restaurants in the famous Boston based chain, but unbelievable food and a super reputation in the Southern suburbs was good enough for him.

Max found himself in and around the famous old city of Boston on a regular basis and he preferred to stay in the suburbs or even further a-field, if at all possible, finding it easier to relax outside the city and also it gave him an anonymity which was not always possible at many city centre establishments. Not that he avoided the city centre and on occasions when it was necessary such as working or dining with clients and colleagues he had 'done' most of the more well known and famous places.

Boston was a very impressive place steeped in American history and a thriving business metropolis. Max had no problems getting the right people together in this old city since everyone was keen to travel to Fen way Park home of the Boston Red Sox and the oldest baseball park in the country or the New England Patriots stadium in Foxboro. Both very successful sports teams with enviable records and popular venues.

Max and his old friend Chuck Moore, who was CEO of a medium size New England venture capital firm, made their way to a corner table which overlooked the bustling cocktail bar where a selection of fresh oysters were being prepared for the bar menu customers. Chuck was a client although it never seemed that way since they had been friends for as long as either of them could remember. They got together whenever they could and both knew exactly what each would order to eat and how good it would taste. The usual air of relaxation which normally took over at this point was strangely missing and it appeared to Max that Chuck was unusually pre-occupied.

Oysters for appetizers followed by the largest of the lobsters selected from the tank followed by a slice of world famous Boston Pie was normally enough to make sure the two old friends were fit for nothing after the meal but slumping in front of the TV in the lobby at the South Shore Sheraton Hotel.

As they settled down to order all hell broke out. A high pitched screech broke the casual ambience and followed by an almighty crash directly behind them. The 'out of control' roar of a vehicle engine was accompanied by the sound of breaking glass and screams of blind panic as the car careered through the huge plate glass window and crashed to the ground, wheels spinning in mid air and the deafening squeal of free spinning wheel bearings and a high revving engine.

Max threw himself to the ground by sheer reflex and he felt Chuck land on top of him as crockery, glass and tables flew directly over their heads landing somewhere in front of them.

Hit the floor and stay down...just stay down...then what?? Wait for the screaming to stop? Wait until the screaming stopped and the sirens began signaling the arrival of the emergency services? What was a person supposed to do next?

Max freed himself from beneath his friend as soon as his senses allowed him to make any sort of decision; he very quickly checked that neither he nor Chuck was hurt.

'I'm OK…..just a bit shook up' moaned Chuck as Max leapt forward on top of the mess and debris. Water was cascading down from the sprinklers in the restaurant ceiling and people were screaming. Panic had set in immediately throughout the restaurant and Max slipped and stumbled over the broken glass and tables. He could just make out through the haze created by smoke and water that the black car had torpedoed into cocktail bar with the rear wheels still spinning and steam or smoke was coming from the front end of the car. It seemed like one of the waitresses was pinned against the shattered mirrors which had once been a feature on the wall behind the bar counter, her head and arms seemingly wrapped around one of the front headlights. *What a crazy mess! How can this be happening?!* Max shook his head and brushed the dust out of his eyes and hair as he looked all around him. Craning his neck this way and that, he instinctively stumbled towards the waitress he had seen a few moments ago. The restaurant had been full with guests and the couches for people waiting had also been full when they had entered the restaurant earlier that evening.

The waitress was dead and there was one other person trapped underneath the front wheels of the car….dead also… Max was quite sure. He had experienced much worse during his time in the military but that really was another time and place. It was at least 20 yrs ago and although Max kept himself fit and looked after his lean 6 ft 3 frames as well or better than most 40 yr olds, his reflexes were not what they used to be and he was aching from where he had hit the ground and threw his arms over his head. He quickly snapped out of his reverie and he found himself reaching for the car and trying to force open the front door. The front passenger door was already open so he tried to climb over the front of the car to reach the driver's door. As he pulled at the door handle he became aware of a man alongside him who was also heading towards the car with a dining chair raised above his head. He crashed the chair through the car window and called out for help as he reached into the car through the broken window. Directly behind the man with the chair were two paramedics climbing over the rubble in his direction and behind them he could make out the flashing blue lights of the emergency vehicles and the sound of sirens soon filled the air. He couldn't help thinking that they had arrived very quickly but he had to admit that he was very glad to see them all the same.

Max turned away from the car leaving it to the paramedics who were upon him in a second, he made his way back to find his friend. On his way back to where their table had been, he noticed a number of people gathered outside on the sidewalk who appeared to be being treated or consoled by the emergency services and he wondered if Chuck was amongst them. He decided to check inside before he headed outside and he picked his way through the people rushing out and the paramedics rushing into the restaurant.

He called out to Chuck in the steamy, now dust and water filled atmosphere as he neared the corner table position. He could see his friend propped up against the wall with his head slumped into his chest. Chuck seemed to be sitting very still considering the mayhem going on around him and as he got closer he could see the shimmering red stain on the front of Chucks light grey jacket. *Shit! Shit! Shit! Please let it be a flesh wound or someone else's blood..*

Max threw his arms around his friend and as he lifted Chuck's head, his entire body and mind froze in an instant at the sight which confronted him….

Chuck had been shot.

There was a very clearly defined bullet hole right in the middle of his friend's forehead. A small stream of blood had exited the bullet hole and the shimmering red stain had poured down both sides of Chuck's nose and down both cheeks forming the stain Max had seen from a distance moments earlier on the front of the grey jacket.

The Price of Friendship

Max let out a scream for help as he fell to his knees and hugged his friend close to him and rocked backward and forwards crying uncontrollably. He knew there was nothing that anyone could do for his friend, but he continued to cry for help as the tears poured down his face.

'Let go! Please let go Sir! Let me see where the blood is coming from', pleaded the paramedic as he tried to prise Max away for his friend.

Max eventually let go and the paramedic let out a gasp as he saw the small circular hole between his patient's eyebrows…

'What the……We need to get this man out…This is a gun shot wound!!' The young paramedic exclaimed, stating the obvious. Max hauled his friend up and threw him over his shoulder with strength he was surprised he had. He staggered towards the open window and they both fell out onto the sidewalk. A large crowd had formed outside and a large burly man who appeared to be looking for something to do grab Max's head and cushioned his fall as he hit the ground. Chuck's limp body fell against the man's legs and he toppled over almost in slow motion. Someone else broke away form the crowd which was now being held back by a cordon of cops and he and the burley man managed to lay Max and Chuck down on the ground.

It was unclear to the men who was hurt and who was not and they called out to the paramedics for help.

Max very definitely knew who was hurt and he knew that his friend had not been hit by anything other than a carefully aimed bullet. He rolled away from the heap on the ground and he sat bolt upright staring, wide eyed back at the restaurant.

Why did…who did…what the hell had just happened? How do I make sense of it? Chuck! Oh my god Chuck! Who would want to do this and how the hell did they manage it?

Something took over Max's thinking and without hesitation he headed back into the restaurant, climbing over the rubble and through the opening where the window used to be. Voices

13

were calling after him but he kept going right back into the dust and the damp building. He reached the car in no time at all and as he peered in through the passenger door which he suddenly remembered was already open when he first approached the car he saw no-one inside. No driver, no passenger and the only signs of life were the three men trying to extract the waitress from beneath the front of the vehicle. The crushed woman had already been removed from in-between the car and the mirrored wall and Max was being pulled away form the wreckage.

'It's not safe here Sir, the car could explode at any time'…he noticed flames licking around the hood of the car and he spun around and scrambled away from the wreck.

Max Reynolds just knew that his life could never be the same again from this moment on. He had made his way back to his silver BMW which was in the car park directly opposite the restaurant having refused any medical treatment from paramedics at the scene. He sat in the driving seat staring back at the scene in a daze. Chuck had been taken to the hospital in downtown Boston and Max had agreed to meet the police at Max's house where he and a police officer would talk to Chuck's wife and family. What would he tell Mary, he had known her for as many years as she had been married to Chuck; indeed he had been at the wedding. He had visited their home in Cambridge many times and also their previous two homes in various suburbs of Boston, none of this had prepared him for this visit….how could he face her and what would he say?

Chapter 3

The following day after the horrific incident at the South Shore Mall, Max was sitting in his hotel room awaiting a phone call from the local police. He had spent most of the night with Chuck's family both at their home and then had accompanied Mary when she went to identify the body at the mortuary on Commonwealth Avenue. He had been back at the hotel for some time but was unable to sleep or even rest. After showering and changing he still felt unclean and unkempt as though he was responsible for the death of his friend. He could make no sense of what had happened the previous evening. Initial discussions with the police seemed to indicate that no-one amongst the survivors or the three dead at the scene could be identified as the driver or indeed a passenger from the car which ploughed through the restaurant window at 8.46pm the previous evening. There was no explanation offered for this phenomenon nor was there any explanation for why Chuck had been shot particularly with such clinical precision. Assassination by a very skilled marksman was the official line being used, but no motive or reason was immediately evident. Chuck Moore…assassinated in cold blood…..was the ram-raid a diversion or a means of getting to Chuck? Was the gunman in the car and bailed at the last minute? It seemed unlikely that the car was not some part of the story but how exactly did it fit in? Why would anyone want to get to him anyway? If the incident was all about Chuck Moore then the cost was very high - three lives and untold damage and personal injury. Someone wanted to get to Chuck very badly indeed….if that was the main intent of the incident.

Max had racked his brain long and hard to come up with a glint of an explanation…. but nothing. He knew little about Chuck's day to day business life other than the investment deals they had completed together. None of these, in Max's mind could possibly provide a reason for the shooting….why would they? Financial support for professional sports clubs to fund the purchase and transfer of players from one team to another…. hardly world shattering stuff or reasons for murder!!! Max mainly dealt with rising unknowns and college players who had yet to prove themselves in the major league teams. Young inexperienced players hopeful of achieving lucrative careers in the big time. One-off deals then on to the next.

His head was already exploding with questions and counter questions as he waited for the detectives down in the hotel lobby. He had returned to the hotel to get some sleep but that was the farthest thing from his mind and although his mind was racing his body was existing on adrenaline alone.

It was 3pm and Max decided to go down to the hotel bar to wait for the detective. He informed the receptionist where he would be and the he sat at the bar to think and to drink…. just a little to relax the mind, of course. There was no-one else in the bar, not surprising considering the time of day and the bar tender Carl seemed pleased to have someone to talk to as he slid a glass of Jack Daniels and Coke across the bar counter to Max. It tasted good and was gone well before the ice had time to dilute the strength of the drink. The phone rang behind the bar and Carl obliged. He handed the receiver to Max and backed away to the other end of the bar counter.

The Price of Friendship

'Mr. Reynolds, you don't know me but I know you, I already have the advantage' said the voice on the other end of the line. Max was surprised by the tone of voice which was very clear and assertive and not at all what he was expecting to hear.

'I know why Chuck Moore was killed and I also know why YOU will be the next target' Max almost dropped the phone as all the muscles in his body seemed to tense simultaneously. He began shaking with fear and was unable to speak.

'I also know that you are being followed and it could happen at any time, before you even think of speaking you must listen to what I am about to say and listen good'

The woman's voice became agitated and the speech much quicker.

'Do not speak to anyone…. and I mean anyone… until I give you permission to do so…and I do NOT give you that permission.'

Max found his voice and stuttered in no more than a whisper 'who the hell are you and what do…' He was cut off before he could finish…..

'Shut the fuck up and listen!! If you fail to follow my instructions you will be killed, you have to understand that' snarled the woman.

'Now…this is what you must do….

After the most incredible, not to say frightening, 'phone conversation of his life Max, fled the hotel before any detectives arrived and without explanation to anyone. Carl called after him but before he had even finished the words 'Mr. Reynolds….' Max was gone.

He resisted the temptation to run but he was walking very quickly towards his car in the lot behind the hotel. He had to get away from the hotel before the police arrived without drawing attention to himself. The instructions were quite specific and although he had no idea who had given the instructions or even why he did want to stay alive. He gunned the engine of his Beamer and pulled away with the slightest wheel spin towards the exit. As the security beam lifted he could have sworn Detective Barnes was in the car which was entering the parking lot at the same time. Max wondered whether he had been spotted and he decided that it didn't matter…he had no choice but to get to the viewing platform at the top of the Prudential Tower in the financial district before the last lift went up at 5pm. Traffic was awful but Max had made it in time as he pulled into the underground parking lot, searching for a place to park close to the lift.

He made it to the top of the tower in good time and he stood by the East window amongst the crowds, people were donning the headphones and listening to the audio explanation of the view which they were seeing across the city.

Who was he looking for? He had no Idea…. 'I will find you' the voice had said 'You just be there' Well he was there….. and he was petrified. His legs were weak, his breathing fast and he wanted some answers.

Where are you… where the hell are you? I'm here just as you instructed, where the fuck are you.. whoever you are? Stay calm and keep your wits about you Max said to himself, and he calmed himself with the thought that he had no choice but to be there!! Just bring it on he thought to himself let's see who you are and what the hell is going on. Why am I a target?? It made no sense or reason.

This place was a major tourist attraction particularly for first time visitors to Boston, mainly because it was difficult to appreciate the layout of all the attractions in the city from street level. Max himself had been brought here by Chuck. *How ironic he thought…* many years before and he remembers being impressed by what he had seen.

'Hey fella!' an elderly man was looking directly at Max and he assumed he was talking to him

'How's it goin? Awesome view, don't you think?' Continued the man.

'Its not my first time' replied Max 'but…Yes it sure gives a person a great perspective of this great city' Max was just making small talk but was really thinking., *is this the contact, who is this guy? Just be cool Max…...be cool.*

'Lived here my whole life….raised a son and a daughter here and now I have to leave…going to the sun …Florida or the west coast…the weather here…that's what drives folk away.….

It seemed as though the old man was going to continue the detail of his life story right there and then…he could not be the contact… Max had to move away so that he was free to move quickly or just be available for the meet.

Max edged away from the man without continuing the conversation…but he continued talking,

'I have a package for a Mr. Reynolds, you wouldn't happen to be Mr. Reynolds now would you?'

'Errr…well, I… '

Before Max could even answer, the man pushed a package, the size of a shoe box into Max's stomach with a little too much force than was comfortable and as Max bent over with the force, the man disappeared into the crowd of people. Max straightened up and stared in sheer surprise into the crowd.

The man was gone.

There is only one way out of here and that was down the elevator……Max rushed to the elevator.

There was a line of people waiting for the next elevator. Max quickly inspected everyone in the line but he saw no-one who looked like the old man. He must still be here, Max ran around the four sides of the viewing corridor, searching frantically for anyone who resembled the man…there were too many people to be sure and he approached two or three people who could have been him but all of them stared indignantly back at Max as he nudged or spun them around.

As he completed a circuit of the viewing corridor he found himself back at the elevators.

No answers….just a box inside a plastic bag!! He had the opportunity to speak to the man but never took it…what was the package all about anyway, he thought.

Max looked down at the box which he had kept squeezed into his stomach since it was unceremoniously dumped there by the old man. A very non-descript package, inside a plastic carrier bag which was folded over and secured with tape. Max ripped away the tape and looked inside the white plastic bag. He took out the cardboard box which was the size of a shoe box but had no external markings, just a brown cardboard box comprehensively sealed on all edges with scotch tape. The package weighed about five or six pounds and was solid and stable thought Max as he shook it from side to side.

He took another look inside the plastic bag before he replaced the box back into the bag. There was an envelope.

The note inside was clear and concise,

Do not open this package, keep it with you at all times, we know where you are and we know whether the package is with you. You have been checked out of the South Shore Sheraton and all your belongings have been moved to room 236 at the Hilton Hotel, Logan Airport. You will be contacted again soon.

Chapter 4

Max boarded the Continental airlines flight and settled into his seat, nervous of everyone around him and speaking to no-one.

As the flight touched down in Newark, Max could just see the Manhattan skyline on the other side of the Hudson River in the distance as he peered through the window. He wondered when he would be back on US soil again as the pilot announced their arrival at Newark International airport at 5pm local time. The temperature in New York was 60 degrees and the sun was getting low as they made their way off the plane. Max was required to change terminals to connect with his international flight to Heathrow and he quickly made his was to the monorail. The transfer was uneventful and he experienced no difficulties passing through security for the second time. Although he was pleased not to be detained or stopped by security officers, he did wonder more and more why he hadn't been. What was in the package which was so important, worth killing for but could not be seen by the best security technology in the world? It was just one of the unanswered questions which continued to burn away in Max's mind and he continued to muse whether he would ever find out what was in the package.

What does it matter as long as he gets it to its destination? Was London its final destination and if so what then for him? Would he be allowed to return as soon as he had completed the delivery?

Max decided he had to try and second guess his captors and consider some contingency plans. It was highly unlikely that he would be allowed to just go away and be forgotten when this was all over so he would needed to think about what he would do to save himself and could he possibly avenge the death of his friend. Why was no-one asking questions about the killing... then again, maybe they were. How the hell would he know since he had been 37000 ft in the air for most of the time since the incident? His thoughts turned to the shooting and he became melancholy and sickened as he reflected on the most bizarre night of his life.

He would have to try to find out why Chuck had been killed in order to make any sense of his own part in all of this but being stranded or in transit was not the easiest position from which to start digging for information. He cursed his luck and also his predicament as he tried to figure a way out of this mess.

Six hours and fifty five minutes later, Max was de-planing with the rest of the passengers at Heathrow airport. He had no idea what to expect as he approached the terminal building and although the Atlantic crossing had been reasonably smooth and uneventful, he was extremely tired. He had been too anxious to sleep and had used the quietness to think rather than sleep, now he regretted not forcing himself to at least take a nap.

The plane was almost full and it took a long time to pass through the security checks at London. People were shuffling forward like zombies towards the check point and as Max approached he repeated to himself the address he been told to quote to the security official as the place he will be staying for at least the first night of his stay in the UK. Security had tightened considerably since 9/11 and Max was acutely aware of what was required having passed through many airports in various countries since that fateful day in 2002.

Entry into the UK and indeed most of the western European countries was a much less complicated process than entry into the US and Max had always been amazed at how easily people traveled between European counties. The European community was so much more flexible and liberal than North America and traveling form country to country was so much easier since the Berlin Wall fell and the west became truly integrated.

Max had been born in London but his family immigrated to New York in the early seventies when his father set up an American office in New York. He never returned until he was in his thirties and had lost contact with all of his family. Being brought up in the States, he was a naturalized American and proud of it. It was strange to be back in the United Kingdom under such strange circumstances. He edged his way into the arrivals lounge not knowing what to expect. He had checked the package repeatedly throughout the flight and once again in the men's room as he passed through baggage claim. He had not forgotten the promise that he would be watched throughout the journey and although he hadn't noticed anyone following him he knew they were there and he had treated everyone as suspicious since…..well, since forever it seemed.

Max had been to London a number of times in recent years and on one occasion in 2000 he had spent several weeks in the capital city working by day and seeking out family history by night. His father didn't approve of the practice of going backwards as he called it but his roots had intrigued Max although he had very little success tracing them. During this stay he met with some very influential people in UK sports and he would like to think he had also made a few friends. He stayed in touch albeit on a much too infrequent basis, with Dave Spencer, who had helped Max to get used to the differences between doing business in the US and the UK. His help had been invaluable and without it Max would never had been able to complete some of the better deals he had managed to. Dave was a freelance agent who spent most of his time negotiating contracts for professional soccer stars in the English premiership but had teamed up with Max on more than one occasion to arrange pre season tournaments and overseas tours. They first met in San Diego whilst Manchester United, the most famous and successful team in the English Premiership, were on a North American tour. Max had taken some clients to watch a game and Dave had arranged for them to meet a number of the Manchester stars and Max had returned the favor when they reached the Boston leg of the tour. They became friends over time and had similar interests and beliefs. They both represented organizations who strived to encourage transatlantic sporting events and were continually impressed by the way in which sport transcended many cultural and political boundaries.

Dave lived with his wife and two children in London and Max had visited once whilst on an extended stay in the region. He felt that this may well be a bolt- hole should he need to disappear at short notice. He felt sure that he would remember how to get there if he ever needed to. The number was in his cell phone.

The sign said 'Max Reynolds' in large red letters and the man holding the sign was staring straight at Max as he exited the customs hall. *Back into the game* thought Max as he wondered whether he should trust this man or not. *Did he really have a choice, he pondered.* The holder of the sign was a huge beast of a man, tall as well as bulky with a military style haircut. He was casually dressed in khaki slacks and a plain blue shirt but there was nothing casual about his demeanor or body language as he approached Max and held out his hand…not for a hand shake but in order to take Max's suitcase.

'Welcome to London Mr. Reynolds!' announced the man,

'My name is Frank and I will be your driver' he continued. Where exactly are we driving to? Asked Max engaging eye contact with the man but not releasing his grip on the suitcase

The man looked surprised, almost human as his forehead wrinkled and his head jolted ever so slightly backwards in surprise.

'Well, my delivery document tells me to take you to Intercontinental Hotel, Hyde Park corner in central London, but I can double check with the office if you have a different destination in mind' the driver explained.

Max was confused and irritated but it was obvious that the man facing him was just as he had said....a driver to take him to a hotel. Max was a little embarrassed to have instantly judged him but he consoled himself with the thought that he was fast getting used to being suspicious of everyone and with good reason, he had to stay alert.

He declined the offer to carry his case and the two men walked briskly to the car park without further conversation.

The drive to the hotel was slow and laborious in the west London traffic and both men felt awkward as the miles passed by slowly. Max was almost getting used to not knowing what was going on and he sat back just waiting to see what would happen next. He knew he had to make a phone call to his office in the US as soon as he could to ask his assistant to carry out some checks into Chuck and he also had to make contact with Dave in London...no-one could know he was making the calls and he was trying to work out how he was going to make them. The other priority which was part of his contingency was to make sure that he was traceable. He could do very little to protect himself until he knew more about how Chuck fitted into the picture but he could leave a trail so that he was traceable.

The car pulled into an underground garage, beneath the Intercontinental Hotel and Max eased forward in his seat, preparing to get out.

Chapter 5

Charles 'Chuck' Moore was the all American boy. He had graduated from Harvard University with honors and with the ease normally reserved for the wealthy and the privileged. He cruised into a post with a prestigious law firm and quickly made partner in record time. There was no doubting Chuck's ability and he had always worked long and hard to succeed. His rise to fame, although quicker than could normally be expected, was not entirely unexpected. He had a natural drive with a sense of ambition coupled with an uncanny attention to detail. He was humble and likeable and a pleasure to work with, those around him found it hard to argue that he did not deserve it.

Chuck Moore was bright and intellectual. He had always wished that he could have been better looking and that he had more classic features. He had always had that 'lived in' look like someone else's brother or uncle. He was medium height, and medium build. His hair was black and made up of tight curls and it always looked as though it was clinging towards the back of his head due to his receding hairline. It was greying now and although he had a distinguished greying of the temples he had sharper than normal features which detracted from the better of his features. He worked hard to make sure he was always well groomed but could never be considered handsome. He had married his high school sweetheart and Mary was an attractive blond cheerleader when they met and Chuck had wondered what she saw in him. To this day he still felt that one day she would find her 'real' beau and leave him. She had vowed to never leave him and had always been good to her word. He was glad and honored in the early days and then their relationship had developed into a deepening friendship. They had decided very early on in there relationship that they would wait as long as they could before starting a family, neither really interested in becoming parents . Chuck's career was their priority which soon became an obsession but Mary had not minded the long hours and endless 'compulsory' meetings and parties since they had agreed a specific life plan and by the way… the lifestyle was great. Nice homes, great holidays and a rapidly increasing little nest egg was building in the form of a shrewd investment portfolio….managed by Chuck, of course… Life for Charles and Mary Moore was pretty damn good and they were happy. When their daughter was born, their blessed life was complete.

Chuck could not remember the exact date that all of that changed for him but he remembered every detail of what happened as if it were yesterday.

The law firm where he had started was a very highly respected practice and they had the pick of the Boston Universities well before graduates went to the market looking for placements. Their clients included a number of Dow Jones heavyweights and referrals were their only form of marketing and advertising. The envy of many larger law firms, they had no problem attracting lucrative clients and many of their cases were publicised to very good effect. As a new partner Chuck was required to increase the client base as well as the earnings of the firm and the targets were tough and demanding. Chuck was an excellent lawyer but he never really saw himself as a career lawyer with someone else's company. Over a number of years, he developed some good relationships with many influential people in the New England states. He satisfied his yearning to set up his own company a few years later specialising in venture capital deals.

He became an expert in developing and managing customer relationships and as the size of his business increased he spent more and more time concentrating on keeping the clients satisfied and leapfrogging the smaller guys to get to the big boys. He inevitably came into contact with some less than scrupulous business start ups and also some less than desirable individuals but his reputation allowed him to bypass what he considered to be bad deals with bad people and his business integrity remained intact…or so he thought.

His world fell apart on the day that he said 'Yes' to Sam Deans.

The sun was huge and spectacular as it rose above the hazy line of the horizon. It was impossible to say where the line of the sea stopped and the sky started as Chuck looked out over the balcony of the shore side apartment overlooking Herne Bay on Cape Cod. He had spent a glorious day and night with an amazing girl introduced to him less than seventy two hours earlier by none other than… Sam Deans.

Although the stunning beauty of the view deserved a better response, Chuck held his head in his hands, tears were welling up in his eyes again as he was filled with both horror and a fearful remorse which disgusted him.. He dare not look back into the bedroom and he rubbed his eyes again and again as he tried to come to terms with what had happened.

Sam had put temptation right into Chuck's lap and watched as he took the bait. He had provided an alibi to ensure that Mary would never suspect and Chuck was grateful for the opportunity to experience the exotic and stunning beauty of the girl who accompanied Chuck to the luxury apartment . He had never experienced such explosive passion and sexual ecstasy over and over again. She was pleased and happy to pleasure Chuck in any way he wanted and he wanted it so much. At any time throughout the last 24 hrs, he would have given anything to have more and more.

He had slept for a few hours only and when he woke, still drained from the exertion and the ecstatic pleasures he reached across the bed to steal another touch of her perfect firmness and she lay still, not responding to his touch. He nudged her still body gently whispering her name. It was only when he turned her head towards him that he saw his own belt pulled tight around her throat and her eyes and mouth contorted with the horror she had been through…she had been strangled.

Chuck threw his head into his hands and leapt from the bed as some sort of delayed reaction. He began to wretch and shake as he backed away into the bathroom. He slipped as he reached the tiled floor of the bathroom and threw up violently as he hit the bathroom floor. The force from his scream splattered his vomit all around the room.

Shocked and stunned, he started to weep as he tried to wipe his mouth with the back of his hand. Shaking and shuddering he wanted to scream out loud but the sound was instinctively forced back as he scrunched his face up tight, hoping that it was all a bad dream

The image of her startled face continued to become etched on his mind as he stared into the dawn mist rising over the bay. What a paradox…..a living nightmare of massive proportion with such a backdrop of splendour and natural beauty. He heard a sound as though someone was opening the door of the apartment. He couldn't see the door from where he was standing so he couldn't be sure but a wave of panic came over him. The two men ran into the bedroom and threw Chuck to the floor and pinned him down. As one of the men held him down the other man wrapped tape three or four times around his mouth winding it around the back of his head and the same around his wrists and ankles so that he could not move. Chuck made no attempt to defend himself or fight back, he felt the blood running from his left eye which had burst open when he hit the floor. He lay on the cold tiled floor of the balcony as they dragged him into the bedroom and rolled his limp body up against the wall. He found it difficult to breathe but hardly cared at this point, whether he could breathe or not.

As soon as Chuck was secured, the men started to move around the room very efficiently and seemed to be following a well rehearsed plan. Firstly, they took photographs all around the room and of the dead girl as she lay spread eagled on the bed. The girl was slipped into a body bag and as one of the men cleaned the bathroom and replaced all of the bedding, the other man wiped down all surfaces in the room removing fingerprints and began to vacuum the carpet and wipe down the curtains and the walls. Lastly they cleaned the balcony and closed the sliding doors and drew the curtains shut. They knew exactly what they were doing and the whole operation was completed in minutes.

The two men lifted Chuck and carefully laid him on top of the freshly made bed and he could hear them leaving as quietly as they had arrived….. Click…the apartment door closed and they were gone.

Chuck was hurting all over. He dared not move a muscle. His body was in suspension, his muscles exploding with the pain and burn which accompanies this state of stillness and intense concentration. He had to be still, very quiet and very still.

Was it safe to move, could he risk it?

Max interrogated himself, he wanted to try to move but the fear that had overcome him forced him to lie motionless for what seemed to him to be an eternity. Finally he overcame the fear and since there had been no noise or movement for some time he forced himself to move his arms. They were free to move as were his legs, the tape had been removed and he had been too afraid to notice……He slowly removed the tape from around his mouth wincing with pain as he peeled it away form his face. His hand brushed against the dressing which had been applied to the cut on his left eye. *How did that get there??* He opened his eyes for the first time for some hours.

The room was spotless. Everything was in its place, clean and tidy. He forced his aching body into a sitting up position and peered in the direction of the bathroom which had also been cleaned. The aches and pains of the attack and also the exertion of the last 24 hrs were coursing through his body and he could feel every bruise and bump. The extent of what had happened made absolutely no sense to him.

He was rubbing his head and stretching his legs as the phone rang. It rang six or seven times before Chuck plucked up the courage to pick up the receiver which was sat on the bedside table.

The officious voice announced that there was a large envelope marked 'URGENT' left at the security office and the man leaving the envelope had left in a hurry declining the offer to be let into the building.

Chuck only had on his underwear and the white dress shirt he had worn the night before. He quickly pulled on his pants which he found positioned carefully in the trouser press...*how did they get there?*

He combed his hair with the fingers of both hands trying to look at least respectable enough to face the security guard.

He managed to contain his curiosity long enough to get back into the apartment before he ripped open the large brown envelope. Photographs spilled out of the envelope onto the floor as he stared in horror. Time seemed to stand still as Chuck Moore realised what this was all about.

He could not help himself from frantically skipping through the pile of photographs one by one, throwing each one away from the pile as soon as he saw the sickening images. There were images of himself and the girl in various compromising positions and also images of him looking in horror at the dead body and there it was again ...His belt tied tightly round the girls throat...the horror ....he had forgotten that his belt had been used to strangle the girl......

The perfect set up...Adultery was bad enough, Mary would leave him for sure, but just for extra security the girl was dead and he was in the frame for her murder. In such a surreal situation, he might has well have committed the murder himself......the set up was complete and life, as Charles Moore had always known it, had just ceased to exist.

Chuck decided at that very instant to distance himself from this place and to find somewhere to go, to think this through. Whatever he did next would surely shape the way of things to come. He wondered when he would hear from Deans, the bastard, what did he want from Chuck? They had done some significant business together and both of them had done well out of the exchanges. His mind went straight to the most recent dealings which he had wanted to know more about before confirming the backing of his organisation. He had capitulated at the eleventh hour more than once and eventually, they had managed to reach a settlement after Sam had reluctantly agreed to several clauses upon which Chuck had insisted. Sam had wanted to finance a very high risk import/export division to his growing empire and he was not prepared to take the funding form his own business accounts. Chuck had insisted on quarterly reviews and had reserved the right to pull funding if targets were not met. This meant that the accounts would be under scrutiny from a third party auditor in addition to his own people. The investment was substantial and this kind of surety was slightly unusual in deals of this kind. However, he doubted that setting him up in this way could have any effect upon what was already in place.

Chuck was not sure whether he should go home or not. He lived in the affluent western suburbs of Boston but currently found himself 50 miles away on the Cape Cod peninsular. He could easily check into a hotel and wait for the next move or make contact immediately with Sam Deans...that's what he would do…go and see Sam at his 'weekend office' in Newport, Rhode Island. He decided to pick up some spare clothes from his own office which he knew would be deserted at this hour on a Saturday morning and head directly to Newport. It was a 60 mile drive back to Boston, and about 40 miles back to Newport, time to calm down and plan how he was going to open the discussions with Sam.

Chapter 6

Newport is essentially a tourist town now, having re-invented itself after years of loyal service to east coast fishermen as a lucrative fishing port.

As he entered the bustling harbour area he decided to make sure that Sam was in a position to receive visitors because the weekend office was a getaway bolt hole for Sam and his senior Executives (for want of a better description) and they regularly met up for fishing and hunting weekends. There was no guarantee that Sam would be there, although since the suspicious death of his third wife earlier in the year the grapevine placed Sam as almost permanently in residence at his luxury harbourside property and certainly at weekends. It was also towards the end of the summer season and the whole area was still teaming with tourists and wealthy visitors from 'up north' in Boston and 'down south' in New York State. The local residents normally started to return to their homes and retirement properties just outside the harbour and the town as the tourists start to leave in late September. Sam would most likely be there if the tourists were still around.

Chuck could just see Sam's car parked next to his house as he peered over the high security wall having taken a risk by parking next to the wall and climbing on the roof of his own car. He was not exactly sure which one of the four houses contained within the security wall was actually Sam's but he knew that he would recognise the Bentley. He climbed down from the wall and drove down the hill towards the security gates. Although he had never been to Sam's place before he had an open invitation which included the security code for the gate…he never thought he would ever be using the code under such circumstances or even at all if he was honest ….doing business with Sam Deans had always been a bit risky but until now he had not realised just how risky. Chuck had decided some time ago that he would gradually distance himself from the dodgier of the deals. He didn't need the business now but there was a time when Sam's money was a life saver for Chuck's newly formed business. Maybe the Sam Dean's merry-go-round had found out that Chuck was planning to pull out…now that might be a motive for murder.

Chuck parked in front of the large entrance to the house and walked up to the tall columns which stood tall and stately on each side of the arched wooden door. He didn't need to knock the door or even press the bell to attract attention because the huge door opened as he approached.

'Chuck Moore, as I live and breath!' The booming voice of Sam Dean filled the air "Come in! Come in! Take a load off" he continued

It was all Chuck could do to keep his aching fists by his side, his overriding desire to swing for the man who was ruining his life was almost too great.

He followed Sam tight lipped and without uttering a sound into an impressive hallway, a large ornate spiral staircase rose from the centre of the hall and wound its way up to a second floor presumably where the bedrooms were.

Sam was carrying a crystal whisky glass and the ice chinked as he walked briskly into the large drawing room. He was casually dressed and he didn't look like man who was expecting visitors but the next words he uttered belied his appearance.

I was kinda expecting you…… but not quite so soon, you seem remarkably well for a man who has been through what you have, am I right?' he started to laugh out load and reached out to put his arm around him and Chuck could contain his anger no longer. He threw his hands up in the air to deflect Sam's on- coming arm. Both men stepped back and Chuck yelled 'What the fuck is going on Sam, the apartment, the girl….I can't believe you can be so fucking casual…where is the girl…what have you done with the girl…?'

'Stop right there mister….' yelled Sam in return, 'You come into my house and you start yelling and waving your arms around, I thought you would have realised who you are dealing with here…I have no idea what you are talking about…what damn girl are you….'

When anger and confusion collide as at that very moment, the mind can go into freefall; Chuck's lurched towards Sam grabbing the older man by the collar and slammed him up against a wall. The whiskey glass went flying and a surprised Sam Deans threw a wild punch in the general direction of Chuck's jaw. It landed square on his cheek and the two men fell to the floor yelling and scuffling.

A man like Sam is never alone and Chuck found himself being pulled away from the fracas by a huge black bodyguard type character, who slung him across the slippery floor with no apparent effort. He picked up Mr. Deans, brushed him down and headed towards where Chuck had landed to finish the job…

'Leave him alone Marcus! I can deal with this'

Chuck covered his already thumping head with both arms and curled up on the floor, waiting for the blows to arrive. It never came and once again Chuck had survived.

Sam Deans was sitting on the corner of a low table brushing himself down and laughing

'Mr. Moore, I cannot believe you attacked ME! Sam Deans…!! I should have you beaten and then force you to apologise' he called chuckling to himself and shaking his head.

Marcus had fetched two fresh glasses of whisky and he handed one to his boss, the other was in his huge outstretched hand, he offered it to Chuck as he picked himself up off the floor.

'You need to understand a little about how a man like me remains in a position of power…..There are only winners and losers and I will ALWAYS be a winner. I always have to be one step ahead…one step ahead at all times and be prepared to crush anyone who gets in my way. Simple rules and easy to enforce, so what about you my friend? Do you want to stay on the winning side? Or do you prefer the life of a loser? I would have thought the answer was easy enough considering the delicate predicament you find yourself in' He roared with laughter poking fun at Chuck and even Marcus allowed himself a smirk.

It was too much for Chuck to take in and he had no idea what he was supposed to say. He took the whisky and downed the amber liquid in one gulp. The taste hit the back of his throat and he winced at the burning sensation as he regained *some* composure at least.

This whole situation was hopeless was the first thought which flooded into Chucks mind, there can be no way out except to play ball with this monster and his goon. Chuck was intellectually superior to his opponent and that he felt would be his only weapon. How he could use that weapon he had no idea but he knew that he must gather his thoughts quickly and quietly come up with something to buy himself time and give nothing away until the time was right.

The immediate panic was over as two more heavyweights stomped into the drawing room. Sam waved them away and Chuck could not help noticing that both men were armed with automatic rifles and wore what looked like combat gear. What had he gotten himself into he thought, this place was like a fortress yet he had had no problem getting right to the door and Sam himself had let him in…….

Deans continued, 'We are going to become good friends Mr. Moore, you see if we don't. You are the lucky winner of a place in my organisation and I am sure you will be very happy in your new role.'

He continued maintaining the slightly jovial tone to his voice and yet Chuck knew that there was some serious shit just around the corner and he steeled himself to deal with it. He would have to be calm and collected until he learned what he needed to know. He had to be seen to be playing ball at least until he could work out his next move.

'For the record, I have no recollection of any girl or apartment and furthermore I will overlook your earlier indiscretion…not many people get to throw a punch at Sam Deans and live to tell the tale…well the tale will never be told. I have no idea why you have come to my house but I am very glad that you did because it saved my friends here from 'inviting' you to join me. I have a business proposition for you which I am sure you will be very interested in.'

Chuck had taken a seat on the arm of a leather chesterfield couch directly opposite where Sam was perched on the coffee table. Both men looked a little disheveled and the three men watching this little sparring session all looked on from the other side of the room. The room itself was very stately with wood paneling adorning the walls and ceiling. The overall décor was very impressive and in keeping with the rest of the house but it lacked that lived-in feeling and there were no signs of human habitation except of course for the four men at whom Chuck was staring.

'I will give you a minute to reflect on my offer whilst I go and clean myself up'

Sam Deans left the room and as he closed the door behind him Marcus took a position between Chuck and the door. He was a huge man and solid. His muscles were visible through the black suit and there was no doubting what Marcus did for a living. Chuck felt a cold chill down his spine as he remembered how close he had come to a beating from this most monstrous man.

There was little that Chuck could do except formulate how he was going to say YES to this incredulous 'offer'. He had always stayed just on the right side of the law in his financial dealings. The tax man had probably been his greatest adversary to date but he felt that this was all going to change in the very near future. He felt that he was on the edge of a precipice and he had no way back and no way forward…there was only down… into the world of Sam Deans…whatever that meant.

His host returned within a few minutes apparently refreshed and had on a complete change of clothes. He instructed Marcus to burn the pile of clothes in the hallway, 'they were soiled with the scent of fear' he explained and Chuck knew that this poetic license was for his benefit. He sat at the large polished table and gestured for Chuck to join him. A projector screen appeared from the ceiling at one end of the table and one of Dean's men closed the heavy curtains with a remote control from across the room. Another of the men turned on a projector which had appeared from in the ceiling behind them.

Chuck watched in silence, no-one was pressing him to say anything and he was comfortable with saying nothing YET he knew his time would come and he had to muster his wits and think clearly.

Two faces appeared on the screen; a man in his mid thirties probably, handsome and clean shaven. The man's features were what you would expect from a classic film star and his smile revealed a perfectly formed row of sparkling teeth. His jet black hair was parted just left of centre and his olive coloured skin completed the picture of a wealthy, confident and well groomed individual.

The other face was that of a woman about the same age and as stunningly beautiful as the man was handsome. Long flowing blonde hair arranged around as near perfect a face as a plastic surgeon could achieve. The looked like the ideal couple and if the images were not in the form of mug shots you would have expected to see the Hollywood hills in the background.

'These two people are trying desperately to get a foothold into my diamond smuggling operation out of South Africa' announced Sam.

Chuck was surprised by the blatant declaration and even more so by the honesty and the obvious inference that he knew that Sam even had a diamond smuggling operation!

'This cannot be allowed to happen and you and I are going to make sure they are stopped before they even get going' Sam Deans was used to giving orders and he had created no room for discussion in or around his statement. This was what was going to happen and Chuck was sure that he was just about to find out how.

The man on the right goes by the name of Dirk Botha and he is the son of the legendary Johan Botha who has been moving drugs from various South American sources to the United States via South Africa for as long as anyone can remember. Johan Botha knows all the right people…and enough of the wrong people to ensure that his empire and subsequent wealth continues to rise at an alarming rate. Dirk, the son had fallen out with 'Daddy' and has decided to go it alone with the help of his partner.

Deans raised his eyebrows in disgust and shook his head with a sarcastic tut ….. He continued ……

'The entrepreneurial Mr. Dirk Botha has decided that he would prefer to be into precious gems…particularly diamonds. Now everyone who is involved in the international drugs community knows where they stand in the pecking order and although you may not believe it Mr. Moore, there is plenty of supply and more than enough demand to go around. So we all have our sources and our routes to market, everyone is happy until someone starts to get greedy and then 'the community' makes that person go away, so to speak. Diamonds on the other hand, are a different story.'

Drugs and diamonds and smuggling and…Chuck was getting very frightened and wary of where this was going. How could he be expected to assist in 'stopping' anything from happening in this world he knew nothing about?

'To move on', continued Deans. 'The little lady to his left is Dirk's partner… in crime and life… and she is the reason behind his decision to leave the drugs community and enter into the up and coming world of diamonds from Southern Africa, Botswana to be exact. She has probably never been to Botswana but she definitely knows a man who has. Sources say that he has been romantically involved with another South African who is a Director at Orapa Mine in Botswana. You need to concentrate very hard and get all of these people in your mind Mr. Moore because it may be the difference between getting this right and making a deadly mistake…shall we proceed…

The image on the screen changed and another man's photograph joined the two already up there.

'This is Dirk's brother ….Johan junior, who has NOT fallen out with 'Daddy'… but is stirring up trouble for little brother. Johan junior is two years younger than his brother and an altogether different proposition. You could say he was a chip off the old block following in his father's footsteps. The only thing in his way to the family fortune is big brother Dirk. Now then, Johan junior is a wicked and ruthless individual and usually gets what he wants.

Deans' sarcasm laced with a strong displeasure of all of the people on the screen was becoming more and more obvious.

We have no interest in this family rift and we have no desire to help or hinder any of the relationships within this very significant family. What we are interested in, is the effect it may have on MY desire to grow my diamond movement activities' The tone became a little more angry, the voice was showing signs of some cracking and the word 'we' was being used freely…

Chuck knew that if he had any chance of talking his way out of this one it was gone with the definitive introduction of the word 'WE.'

'Where do you fit into this puzzle I hear you asking yourself' Deans had calmed down a little and was quickly back into character. 'Well I need an intelligent, respected member of the financial community who is not known to the…shall we say; underworld community to be the front man in a deal or one might even call it a scam involving Dirk Botha and partner and their aspirations of personal wealth. I intend to not only make sure he gets the independent financial backing that he requires but I… sorry 'We'… will make sure that neither he or his whore are able to trade in anything precious again!!' His tone of voice was serious, somber and final.

Chuck was completely out of his depth and he wondered what this nonsense about a scam was really about and what language this madman was speaking. This world was not for him and he was beginning to feel the physical effects of blind panic in the pit of his stomach. Before he could make any comment, the screen changed he was looking at himself in bed with the beautiful, beautiful girl making love in a way that he would never forget.

'My apologies Mr Moore…. I'm sure I don't need to remind you what is at stake'

The shock tactic completed the job, Chuck felt physically sick and the panic he felt inside was immediately visible to all in the room…he knew he was at the mercy of this madman and his crazy plan.

Mary was his bedrock, his very existence depended on the deep love and friendship they had always shared and he could not risk losing all that they had built up over the years they had been together. She would never forgive him and even if she did then he had the small matter of a murdered girl to deal with.

Before he could regain his composure the image of the screen changed to show a dead girl laid out on the same bed.

The sheer horror which this series of images conjured up in Chuck's mind was just too much and he jumped to his feet, rage had taken him over and he grabbed the chair next to him with both hands and raised it above his head. He had caught everyone in the room by surprise, including himself, as he flung the chair into the projector screen tearing it from the ceiling. He made a mad dash towards the door as more of a protest than a serious attempt to escape because even in this state of rage, it was obvious that he was completely at the mercy of this impossible situation…. and how stupid had he been to put himself in this position. He felt a blunt thud in the throat and he sunk to his knees grabbing his throat and gasping for air. An expert blow from one of the guards had stopped him dead in his tracks and he squirmed on the floor looking at his attacker for help.

Eventually Chuck began to regain his breath and he slumped onto the luxurious carpet hunched over his knees with he buried his head deep into his two open palms holding back the tears.

'Well then Mr. Moore…shall we get down to business… we have no time to lose' It was as if nothing had happened and Chuck became acutely aware of the seriousness of his predicament.

Sam Deans went through the details of his plan and with each sentence Chuck became more and more amazed that this fool actually expected this incredulous plan to work. He kept taking sips of cold water which he poured from a cut glass decanter on the table which had amazingly survived the fate which had befallen the projector screen and two glasses of whisky. The water helped him to regain full breathing capability but he was still unable to speak, which was just as well he though because anything he could possibly say now would only make things worse for him…if that were possible.

The plan basically required Chuck to front and fund a scam which would ensure a delivery of diamonds (which would be made available by Sam Deans' organisation) got into the wrong hands as far as his would be successor, Dirk Botha was concerned. The wrong hands in this case, were to be the particularly ruthless Jacobus Du Preez a freelance dealer from South Africa. Sam thought that the irony of the foolish contender for his crown in the American market being brought down by a fellow countryman was too much to resist. Sam had been introduced to Jacobus in 2002 by a mutual friend. The two men had talked about the advantages and the risks involved within the 'industry' and he had thought that Jacobus could be his way into the South Africa. He had not realised at that time exactly how he could use the DuPreez connection but the situation had soon presented itself. If everything went according to plan, Sam would get rid of his challenger without raising a fist and also open up a future South African supply route.

So much for the future of the Sam Deans empire ...... Chuck began to consider his own future and it
   looked far from good.

Chapter 7

CHUCK SPENT THE NEXT TWO weeks under constant surveillance from Sam Deans. He knew this but still he went about his daily business trying to act as normal as possible and although everyone around him noticed a difference in his personality no-one said anything directly to him. After all, he was the boss and the provider and had always been the reliable and consistent one. He managed to deflect any references to his behavior by pleading temporary overwork 'Soon be coming to some quiet time; he would say or 'gotta keep on top of things when the clients are busy…there are quiet times and busy times; well, this is the busiest'. No-one believed him but they all went along with the explanations. Everyone of course, except his beloved Mary.

Rows flared up where none existed before, the relationship was taking an enormous strain and friends and family became worried about Chuck and about the marriage. Chuck began to think he was going to go mad waiting for the call from Sam Deans and he just wanted to get it over with. Sooner rather than later, let's get it over he repeated to himself, whatever it is. He had not seen Sam Deans since the day at his home in Newport and he had no instructions except to just wait. Well he was waiting and waiting was not easy. Although he was told to make no contact with anyone in the Sam Dean's organisation under any circumstances and to act normal he knew that nothing would ever be normal again.

It was just like the start of any other day as Chuck parked beneath one of the huge glass fronted buildings in the financial district of Boston. The onset of fall had started to bring out the autumnal colours and driving through the western suburbs into work was becoming an extravaganza of colour. Fusions of flame red and blazing yellow was taking over the greens of summer. The Mass Turnpike was still bumper to bumper with vehicles but it takes on a whole new personality in the fall. There is no slow drift in colour form greens to browns to reds, the brightest and most extravagant colours just seem to flash straight into view as if the colours were made up on an artist's pallet and then splashed directly at the trees and bushes creating new and unique combinations of colour as they paint the leaves. Every year brings a new experience of what can be achieved by Mother Nature as the flora takes on incredible changes hour by hour and day by day, until the leaves fall to the ground giving way to frost and snow. Stunning combinations and unreal hues are everywhere. The New England fall is the busiest time of the year for tourism as visitors flock to the area from all over North America and indeed form all around the world and…. they are never disappointed year after year. Although the best of the best is much farther north in Vermont and Maine, the entire east coast region became a spectacle and a unique memory to those who live there as well as to those passing through.

The beauty of this particular fall season was completely lost on Chuck Morris for the first time in his life. He was completely pre-occupied and he had been distracted from the reality of almost anything else for ever it seemed but it had only been two weeks and three days. He was consumed by the nervous expectation and fear of what all his senses were telling him would inevitably go wrong. All previous feelings that he could actually pull it off were long gone. He was convinced that when the call came he would be going into an impossible and very dangerous period of time which he had come to believe could only have a bad ending. He had considered running, leaving the country either alone or with Mary but where could he hide? No-where...that was the inevitability of it. He could only run for so long and then he would be killed or slammed in prison for murder and with no wife to support him because of the trap which Sam Deans had set and of course his own weakness and naivety in taking the bait and Oh! How he had taken the bait. If it were possible to turn back time what would he have done? This question had crossed his mind many times in the last two weeks and one of the most difficult and confusing issues to him was the fact that he could not honestly say that he regretted his time with Sandy. That was the first time he had admitted to himself that he even *knew* the girls name let alone think of her. He had been responsible for her death as if he had killed her with his own hands and she had to die for the sake of some sickening financial deal. Yet even with all of the repercussions and the deadly effect this might still have on Chuck and those close to him, he could not bring himself to regret the time they spent together. He hated himself as much for this as for the fact that he had put so many people at risk.

It was just like any other day except for this day would be the day of reckoning for Charles Chuck Morris and as he exited the lift on the 24th floor he saw the familiar figure of Sam Deans getting into the same lift he was just about to leave... Sam gently grabbed Chuck's arm and led him back into the lift against the direction of the people alighting at the 24th floor. They were alone in the lift and Sam Deans pressed the button which took the lift back down to the lobby level. They descended the skyscraper lift shaft in complete silence and as the doors opened at the bottom revealing the tiled floor of the lobby Chuck Moore knew this was the start.

They crossed the lobby and Sam guided them to the main doors of the building where a black Mercedes with blacked out windows was waiting with the rear door wide open. They climbed into the back seat and the driver sped off, out of the shadow of the large building and into the bright sunlight of an east coast fall morning.

Sitting in the back seat of the vehicle, they were separated from the driver by a blacked out screen just as most of the city taxis leaving the airport he remembered. He had always thought that this was a poor way for visitors to get their first view of this fantastic city, he remembered feeling a little intimidated on his first day in Boston many years earlier. In Chuck's case on this day in this car, he could not even see out of the windows. Although he had not been kidnapped he strained to take note of their every turn and tried to plot their route as if he had. He knew the city as well as anybody and felt that he could get a rough idea if he concentrated carefully enough. The journey was short enough for Chuck to make an educated guess that they had traveled only a short way out of the city and it sounded from the traffic noise and the sounds of the surrounding area that they were traveling on the freeway probably inland away from the coast and probably north because most of the freeways south would pass near or close to the coast or the estuary and he knew there to be plenty of tourist traffic. His assumption was correct and within a few minutes they were pulling off the freeway. They had reached their destination.

Neither man had spoken a word throughout the ordeal so far and even as Chuck was ushered out of the car there was no discussion. Sam stayed in the car which sped off joining the rest of the busy daytime commuters and once inside Chuck was asked to take a seat outside one of the many meeting rooms on the ground floor of the large new building. Everything seemed to be made of glass, large glass windows looking out on the busy Route 1. The casual furniture at reception and in the corridors were all made of glass in some form or other and even the meeting room doors were smoked glass emblazoned with swirling logos and room numbers. Chuck was sitting outside

The Price of Friendship

Meeting room No 12 and the logo read Chichester Suite in Italic letters. When he was finally shown into the room, he was faced by three other people who were sat around a large polished wooden meeting table. The first non-glass item he had seen since he had arrived. The three people were obviously waiting for something or someone and they looked to have been working for some time as evidenced by the empty coffee cups, the disheveled nature of their clothing and the many documents strewn around the table. There were several files and binders piled up on the floor next to an attractive blonde lady who stood up as he entered the room. She welcomed Chuck to the meeting and he recognized her as Mrs. Fiona Botha, partner of Dirk Botha. He had first seen that face on the projector screen in Newport and subsequently on the many photographs and documents he had received through the post since that day. The two men sat either side of her, he had not seen before and he realized that was very likely to be the case as they introduced themselves. All he could remember was that they described themselves as financial consultants for Mrs. Botha; he never even tried to remember their names even if they had said their names.

Chuck sat at the table and was offered coffee from a pot which was stewing on a small glass side table...back to the glass them he though to himself. The coffee had obviously been brewing for some time and he declined the invitation politely.

What was he doing there he asked himself, could he really pull this off....he needed to be calm and collected and above all detached in a very professional way he knew what to say and how to say it..

Chuck had rehearsed the next half hour in his mind over and over secretly praying that he would never need to put it all into practice. The atmosphere was quite surreal and although Chuck knew what should happen he had not been told where or when, but now found himself right in the middle of this plot of intrigue. He remembered his lines well enough to convince those around the table that he represented a secret investor and he presented his credentials just as he had been instructed. The discussions and the negotiation went on for almost an hour and Chuck was amazed at how close his instructions had been to what really happened. Almost word-for-word he thought to himself… they had prepared him for all eventualities and he could not help but be impressed… and a little suspicious as he closed the first part of the deal, shaking hands with Mrs. Botha before signing on behalf of his benefactor.

The car was outside to meet him as he left the building. Chuck let out a huge sigh and his head dropped into his chest as he closed his eyes tight and run his hand through his hair. It was only then that he noticed he was shaking and sweating. Beneath his charcoal grey suit jacket, he was soaked to the skin and as he climbed into the car he was aware that he was being watched from the building and just managed to maintain his composure as the car door closed behind him and the driver sped off.

Sam Deans was very pleased and he congratulated Chuck on an excellent job as he reached out to shake Chuck's hand as he got into the car.

'Well done my friend, very well done it went just as we thought and you played your part perfectly'

Chuck looked directly into the man's eyes and growled 'I am not your friend and I never will be. Never, ever address me as your friend again…'

Sam reeled a little and then settled back into the large seat shaking his head but without saying a word.

Some time later, the car pulled up alongside the lift in the underground parking lot where Chuck had been picked up. Chuck climbed carefully out of the car trying not to look at Sam Deans as he rushed to the lift doors. He drew several breaths of parking lot air as the car pulled away and quickly disappeared into the concrete background.

Chuck Morris didn't go back to his office; instead he went directly to his car. He slumped into the luxurious leather of his BMW and was overwhelmed by the happenings of this extraordinary day. He felt like crying or screaming or something to release the extreme pressure which had built up in his head. Instead he started the engine of his car fastened his seatbelt and drove out of the garage without a backwards look. He suddenly realized that he was not sure when or even if, he would be back to the office or the business he had built from nothing, so carefully and so methodically he had planned and built his business at the same pace as his life. Everything was in place for a bright and rewarding future, the ground work had been done and he was on the way to success doing something he knew he was good at.

I cannot let this wreck everything I have worked for…I just can't…I have to stop this happening.

As he drove through the business district traffic in downtown Boston, one thought kept banging away at his brain like a hammer……*Now they know what I look like and who I am….I am no longer unknown to the underworld as Sam Deans had so eloquently put it…I need to find a way out of this.*

Chuck drove remarkably carefully in the circumstances, he desperately wanted to gun the Beamer and race away but something was telling him not to raise attention to himself, to keep it all together and he was doing just that. Traffic was heavy and he crawled out of the city along route 2 west into the suburbs. He drove past the tree lined avenues and the shingled older houses as he had done so many times until he reached the interstate crossing and into Cambridge.

He was heading home and it was only 3pm. It was not unusual for him to be home so early but in recent weeks the longer the evening, the more arguments there were and he tried to avoid contact with everyone by going out again almost a soon as he had showered and changed. The traffic had thinned out as he negotiated the numerous curves. A large black Lincoln Town Car was holding up the traffic a little as it pulled out of a narrow road and joined the main stream of cars heading back towards the city. Chuck was day dreaming a little but as the car passed alongside him, his heart suddenly missed a beat. He stared at the car in his rear view mirror.....was that the car he had just got out of...It couldn't be.....why would it be... he decided he was becoming paranoid and although he was tempted to swing round and follow the car he shook the brief suggestion off as nonsense and he continued on through the leafy suburbs to his home.

Another two weeks went by before Chuck was again called on to play a part in this interminable charade. It had taken him days to get some form of normality back into his daily routine after the first episode in downtown Boston. People who cared about him were still wondering what was behind his strange and unpredictable behavior and those who were used to working with the consummate professional just couldn't seem to come to terms with the new Chuck Morris. His business was starting to show signs of strain as several key clients were getting frustrated at Chuck's unavailability and unreliability. In reality, Chuck had set himself up by being too available to key clients at short notice but that, he believed, was the key to building good partnerships and getting a good reputation especially in the early years. He could easily become a liability to his own business and the corporate vultures were circling. Chuck knew this only too well and he also knew there was no-one he could confide in and nowhere to turn for help. He was alone in an impossible situation yet he had to find some way out or at least find a way to limit the damage it was causing to his personal and work life. He had thought of nothing else and had almost confessed to Mary, his wife, on more than one occasion in the last few days. Not that easy.....Not that easy at all and although she had always been his rock and he was indebted to her for so much. He could find no way to predict how she would react...and how she reacted would be crucial to whether he told her or not. He had though it through over and over again always coming up with the same outcome...he always found a way to convince himself not to tell her. Probably more out of cowardice than anything else but…How could he possibly do it to her? No! Just play the game until he found another way. Every time he went through it all he continued to conclude that he was still alone, very alone and at the mercy of madmen.

The details of the scam had not been lost on Chuck and he had considered a number of ways to get ahead of the game and maybe put himself in a better position, from where he could maybe, just maybe find a way out. He knew that the movement of the funds could be done without suspicion, although he had never succumbed to the illegal tricks of the trade, he was fully aware of how they worked and let's face it even fully legal dealings sail very close to the wind at times. He despised the thought that he was deliberately flaunting good practice but he recognized that there was too much to lose to worry unduly.

He had made sufficient funds available in a special account to cover any losses he may incur and he had also brought forward several investments together in a portfolio which can be paid directly to Mary in the event of anything going wrong. This was designed to short circuit death duty and could not be traced to Chuck, Sam Deans or anyone else for that matter.

All of this was financial risk management but now he had to consider much more serious damage limitation, he had to find a way of sharing the risk. He was isolated as the financier behind the deal and Sam Deans was completely disconnected. He could make each side aware of the other's intentions but he considered this far too risky and hardly likely to succeed. Alternatively, he could make sure things were seen to be going along as planned but make sure that he had an exit strategy. A low risk strategy which should have a high probability of success. Easier said than done but the more he thought of how this would turn out, the more he realised that it was very unlikely that he would be left alive…a frightening and very sobering thought but even if the racketeers were happy to leave him alive he had no doubt that Sam Deans would soon cease to have a need for Chuck Morris after he had played his part.

Even if he was left alive he would be at Sam Deans mercy for ever. It called for drastic measures and he knew just the man to help him develop a strategy.

He would create an opportunity to spend some time with his old friend Max Reynolds as soon as he had carried out this next requirement.

The car arrived as before and although Chuck was just as nervous as ever there was a certain feeling of resignation creeping in to his actions. He had been well briefed and he knew what was to come. He would be meeting with the infamous Mr. and Mrs. Botha and if all goes according to plan, they would be signing the plans for transportation of £2 million worth of diamonds from the mine in Botswana to an undisclosed location in South Africa. Funds would be transferred to an independent receiver in Botswana to cover the initial purchase of the diamonds and then they would sit in South Africa awaiting clearance for the next phase of the process. The next phase would be where the danger would increase exponentially.

Chuck completed his meeting with very little difficulty although he had felt a little edginess at the sight of six people on the other side of the table two of whom were obviously armed where he had only expected to see the Botha's and their investment goons. Sam Deans was very uneasy with this unpredicted level of man power and he could see no reason for anyone to be armed because there was no actual cash changing hands and there was no need for heavy handed tactics. Chuck was much less concerned because he always feared the worse anyway.

He returned to his office after the meeting and tried to act as though everything was normal. However hard he tried it was not possible to be normal and everyone around him knew it. What they did not know was that Chuck Moore had just made the largest investment of his life and he had covered the risk in such a way that if it all went wrong then they would all be out of a job. The contract for delivery of five million dollars worth of un-cut diamonds was in place and his name was all over the deal. He had tried to argue that he could use a pseudonym and still pull it off, but Sam Deans was adamant that the success of the scam relied upon Chuck Morris using his own identity and the identity of his company was the very reason that the scam would work. Now that the first payment had been made the diamonds would have to be sampled and qualified by the buyer. Chuck had read this in the terms and conditions of the deal, but he had no idea what it meant or he could only hope that it would not involve him. He had no idea when he would be required again but he had already decided that he needed help and now was the time to find it. It was probable that the first shipment and this 'qualification process' would take some time before anyone would need to see the financier again. This should give him time to put an exit plan together whilst everyone in the underworld was busy doing what they do. He knew he would be taking a risk in involving anyone else but he had nothing to lose and if he truly believed it may be his only chance.

There was nothing unusual for Chuck's personal assistant to call Max Reynolds directly on his cell phone and invite him out to dinner. On this occasion Chuck decided to call Max and find out when he would next be in town. After a few minutes of social chat and catching up, they agreed on a date and a time and Max agreed to make the booking and let his friend know where it would be as soon as he knew. It all seemed like the most normal thing for two friends and colleagues to be doing and although Chuck felt serious pangs of guilt and uncertainty, he also had an overwhelming sense of relief. If he could only get some help his plan might just work and the way he saw it, what had he got to lose.

Chapter 8

The weather was cold and brisk and although the forecast said heavy rain coming across from the Mid west over the next few days, the sun was shining and people mingled and rushed around the city streets in overcoats and scarves. The dreaded North East winds which whipped the East coast around this time of year were strangely absent and the relief was evident on the smiling faces of the wrapped up Bostonians. Chuck weaved his way through the traffic heading towards the city as he skirted the financial district and headed south on route 1. He had rehearsed his discussion with his old friend Max Reynolds to the point of boredom and as he kept telling himself there was no way of knowing how Max would react to the dilemma facing him. Chuck hated himself for putting his friend at risk but his own life had degenerated into a veritable scam since the last time they had met. Everything had changed, Chuck felt a desperation which he knew would be recognized and appreciated by Max. They had shared many secrets before and there was a bond of trust which was one of the reasons he was approaching Max in the first place. He knew Max to be very intuitive and also a most intelligent and resourceful individual, he recalled the way Max had gotten himself out of many a tricky situation both commercially and personally, he just knew that

Max was the man to help. He was also financially astute and would at very least be able to find any faults in Chuck's exit plan. However he would soon realize that for the plan to be successful he would have to be involved on a personal level and that point of realization would be the time when Chuck would know whether his friend was in or out.

Chuck arrived at the Legal Seafood restaurant on South Shore Mall early and took a seat at the cocktail bar. Max rolled in, late as usual and the two men were shown to a corner table and they sat down to enjoy their meal.

Chapter 9

THE DIAMOND BUSINESS AND THE country of Botswana have been booming since the discovery of diamonds in 1967 and it has been nearly 40 years of constant growth for this model of democracy in Africa. Botswana boasts one of the highest per capita incomes on the continent, more than $4,000. The income is 10 times the per capita income when Botswana gained its independence from Britain in 1966 and there are major plans to continue expanding.

But if it wasn't for diamonds, Botswana -- which is landlocked in southern Africa -- would still be just a cattle outpost in the bush. That would be a difficult life in a country that is about the size of Texas and has only about 10 square kilometers of irrigated land.

In a deal that may have seemed a little unfair in 1969, the government of Botswana signed a 50-50 deal with De Beers, the global diamond giant, to explore and mine all of the country's diamonds. As a result, the nation's economy has quadrupled in the last four decades and it boasts the highest standard of living on the continent.

Botswana draws much of its income from the sacks and sacks of diamonds mined from the Orapa Mine in the country's northeast to the Botswana Diamond Valuing Company sorting facility in the capital, Gaborone. In the sorting facility, 10 floors are filled with tables laden with diamonds of every shape and size that will be sorted, graded and certified before being shipped to the De Beers diamond centre in London, England.

Orapa Mine is the largest open cast diamond mine in the world and amazingly, employees sift through millions of dollars worth of diamonds with minimum security presence. There are closed-circuit cameras but everyone goes about their business as though they were sifting coffee beans and not precious stones.

There is a level of trust amongst all of the stakeholders in the diamond industry in Botswana which sets it apart from most , if not all of the independent African countries. Wealth and political stability are fused together in a way which suggests it will last for at least as long as the availability of diamonds.

This picture of an ideal world does not, of course, exclude the presence of organised crime altogether.

Small amounts of diamonds are regularly stolen from the mine in Orapa and the sorting facility in Gabarone by a highly organised network of people on the inside and the outside of the organisations involved. It takes many months to secrete away small shipments of diamonds without raising too much suspicion so when it is time to release these to the outside crime networks they are extremely valuable and sought after. Meticulous planning to the finest detail ensures that the right gems are made available at the right time and of course at the right price. There are numerous layers to such a crime network and the people at each layer have no information or details regarding any other layer. The members of staff who are risking their livelihoods are well paid and they are required to stick to very strict rules and they are never ever allowed to ask questions. They receive simple and direct instructions and immediate payment from third fourth and sometimes fifth parties, ensuring the necessary distance between the different layers within the overall operation.

The Price of Friendship

Dirk Botha and his partner, Olivia were visiting their new found friends in the executive housing complex which was just two miles south of the expatriate housing area in Orapa, Botswana.

Dirk had never been to Botswana before although he had heard much about the opportunities the country presented from business colleagues and friends in South Africa. Olivia had visited many times and it was to her old friend Geoffrey De Jong's home they had come to spend a peaceful weekend of bonding and relationship building. Maybe a mini safari in the great Kalahari or simply relax and enjoy the peace and quiet. Dirk had been told that this was just necessary and the Mr DeJong was the right person to speak to and he would be receptive to any ideas. Olivia had also insisted that they try to make friends because the business of smuggling diamonds was a very dangerous and tricky one and to have a friend watching your back was essential. She, of course, already had an intimate relationship with Geoffrey and although she realised she was taking a big risk by introducing the two men, she knew that the risk was a necessity in the circumstances. The stakes were very high and mere relationships were secondary. Olivia was a very attractive lady with film star looks and a personality which attracted anyone she pleased but beneath the polish and shine was a ruthless, hardened woman who would stop at nothing to get what she wanted. She and Geoffrey were not completely in agreement with this little soiree in the desert but as usual she had won the case because he adored her without consideration for sense or reason. You might say that she just had a way of doing that to people.

The weekend was successful because of what had to be discussed was discussed and they also managed to have a full and eventful time in the Botswana bush. They even had a tour of the mine which was extremely interesting and strengthened the resolve of both Dirk and Olivia. Actually seeing the way in which their fortunes were being prepared was bizarre in the extreme. To think that one or more of the people sorting and packing could be on the payroll and even some of the gems they had seen being mined and sorted could soon be in their possession was very bizarre indeed.

Dirk had to admit that he had warmed to their hosts by the end of the weekend and he had a good feeling about doing business with his new found friends. He hadn't realised that Olivia and Geoffrey were such good friends and was impressed by her choice of business partner. He had been too drunk or too entangled in the events of the weekend to notice the times they had sneaked away together and they had played such an exact game of chance that he had no suspicion that they were lovers. In fact he kinda liked Geoffrey and hoped that they would get to know each other better. He had no idea how well they would get to know each other in coming months but sweet, beautiful Olivia did.

The private airfield was deserted as they arrived to board the Lear jet which would take them back to the private airstrip at Jan Smuts Airport in Johannesburg. The flight was less than an hour and Dirk and Olivia chatted non-stop from take off to landing. They were enthused by prospects presented by the arrangements they had agreed over the weekend and both had to admit that the private wild and wonderful side of Africa was very much still alive in Botswana. As they drove from the air strip back to their home on the outskirts of Johannesburg, Dirk pondered on buying some land with his new found wealth and having his own game reserve deep in the bush. Olivia on the other hand was concentrating her mind on the next steps of the deal and wondering how she would eventually manage to get both Geoffrey and Dirk out of her life for ever….as soon as they had served their purpose.

When the call came for Dirk to meet with his father and brother the following day he allowed himself a wry smile. They could at least have waited a few days before confronting him with what they would undoubtedly consider to be a betrayal.

The Price of Friendship

He was barely back from Botswana and they were already lining up to have a swipe at the prodigal son. His senses told him to play the game just as he and Olivia and, indeed, Geoffrey, had agreed but something inside him was telling him to get at least some enjoyment from the situation. Probably better to go with the sensible option at this stage there would be plenty of time to gloat and he was sure going to make the most of it then. His personal satisfaction would be all the sweeter for perfect timing and this was not the time.

Johan Botha built his empire around a basic model not dissimilar to the way in which the old gangsters operated during the prohibition era in the United States. The sheer terror which shook the heart of many American cities and yet also made a lot of people very rich was a simple, yet effective method of control. If you are 'IN', your entire family was in and your friends came from within the organisation. There was no way of being released from the rules and codes set up by the individual gangs and the only way to leave a particular gang was by way of a wooden casket. Violence was the choice method for solving disputes and gang leaders had no idea of what the entire business looked like or how it operated.

Johan Botha had a very small inner circle and they made sure that Johan's orders were carried out to the letter. Mistakes were not tolerated and controlled each area of the business and they had no jurisdiction in each others area of business. Johan was not a young man anymore but he ruled with an iron fist and he was feared. He had contacts at all levels of the law enforcement pyramid right into the heart of the South African Assembly and, some believed, into the President's office. Such was the power and autonomy of his organisation that he was protected by the very people that he was stealing from. He was not the only leader of organised crime in the country but he was considered to be the biggest and most established.

This was the belief of the majority of people in the 'industry' but there are always exceptions to the rule and there was a contender to Johan's crown by the name of Jacobus DuPreez who was beginning to get a larger than acceptable share of the market. As in the Americas and Europe the drugs community in Africa was very much a known entity and even the authorities knew who was who. They could not make any significant inroads to stopping the movement of class A drugs but they were allowed by the drugs community to be seen to be successful in making a few insignificant busts…..just for the cameras of course and to make the general public think that there was some form of law and order. In reality, of course, the laws and the orders come from within the drugs community and politicians and law makers were simply pawns in the overall game plan.

Precious gems are in much shorter supply than drugs and it is a more complex operation. Gem stones from the mines are sorted in different locations and are much more traceable. The amount of gem stones arriving at diamond cutters for preparation which are illegal is traditionally a small percentage of the total and this creates substantial problems for would be smugglers to get market share. The major players are very different to those involved in drugs. Johan Botha had not been seen as a major player in this area but if his son was getting involved in the precious gems game, specifically diamonds from Botswana, then Johan had to know that he was not being backed by Menheer DuPreez. If he was in league with Du Preez then this could have a detrimental effect on the balance of power in Southern Africa. Dirk had repeatedly shunned lucrative positions within his father's inner circle and he was still alive only because he was a Botha. This may well be a step too far….. even for a Botha.

Chapter 10

Dirk and Olivia made their way to the offices of J.Botha Enterprises Pty overlooking Sandton Square in Sandton City just outside Johannesburg. The central business district of downtown Johannesburg had long since been declared unsafe and many corporate offices had relocated to the more salubrious area of Sandton City in the 90's. The stock exchange moved from its world famous Commissioner Street location and this signalled a mass exodus out to the suburbs for many corporate and international company head office facilities

Johan Botha took offices in the area as soon as he could and secured some very valuable real estate into the bargain. The offices were very new and modern in design and he was perfectly placed to watch the world go by. Sandton Square was re named Nelson Mandela Square after the very first public statue of Mandela was erected in the square in 2004 but locals and those who use the area regularly still call it Sandton Square..... and that was where Dirk and Olivia had been summoned. Dirk was used to the overbearing and controlling manner of everything his father did but Olivia was much less accepting and he worried that she would want to enter into a game of one-upmanship with him and this would get them nowhere. On the few occasions that they had met before, this had been the way things had gone. It was obvious that they would never be friends and Dirk was not sure that Olivia should be at the meeting at all. However, as always… what Olivia wants Olivia gets and she had insisted on being present.

Johan was more than comfortable conducting his own meetings but he always insisted that one of his inner circle was present. Wherever they were and whatever they were doing, if they were required to be present that's exactly what they did and sometimes the notice was very short indeed. On this occasion just Dirk's brother and Johan were present and that was just as Dirk had expected.

After the initial pleasantries were over, Johan got straight to the point,

'I wanted to see you for a couple of reasons', He began

'First and foremost I am most disappointed that you continue to disrespect me by refusing to join the business and secondly, in your enthusiasm to ridicule me I hear that you are planning to do business with Jacobus DuPreez, He continued,

'You are well aware that I cannot allow this and if you persist you will be seriously risking your protected status….. if you understand my meaning'

Dirk showed no signs of fear or even displeasure, his demeanour was calm and relaxed,

'Once again your spies are wrong. I am working completely independent of you or any of your competitiors or friends for that matter. I can't see how anything I am working on will have even the slightest effect on your business and …'

His father interrupted,

'It is not about what you think or what you want Dirk, it is about what I know…..and I am reliably informed that you are planning to move diamonds from Botswana to Europe under the Botha name and I know that you do not have access to the funds for an operation of this magnitude. This is why you will

need the help and probably guidance of an existing network…
enter Menheer Botha'

'Sorry father but you are wrong on more than one account and I am not prepared to discuss this matter if you are not prepared to listen',

The atmosphere in the small office could be cut with a knife as a tense and nervous Johan Botha rocked back in his chair. He was a tough looking man with a very long face and broad pronounced features. Typically Afrikaans in appearance and the guttural sounds with which he spoke English was a dead giveaway that it was not his first language. He reverted to his native Afrikaans as he swore loudly at no-one in particular,

'Bliksem!' Bliksem!' he yelled and his chair launched itself onto the floor with a load clunk as he stood bolt upright and stared at Olivia with that stony glare.

'You, my dear have made a very big mistake. My sons are my property and I will have them. I will not allow you to fill his stupid head with nonsense about smuggling diamonds. He could not do this alone and by the sheer fact that you are here…uninvited and unwelcome…along with the fact that the contact in Botswana is a very close friend of yours and we all know how close don't we….'

She stood to protest before he said anymore but Johan's oversized hand waved in her direction…

'But my dear…BUT' He continued in a load echo of a voice

'This nonsense will stop and it will stop right now!'

There was a moments silence before Dirk rose calmly to his feet and, taking Olivia gently by the arm, he headed for the door. Johan junior had been too quiet to this point and Dirk showed no surprise when he rose quickly from his chair and stood between Dirk and the door. They stared uncomfortably at each other and then as if it was always the plan…..Johan junior pulled out a 0.38mm revolver and placed it firmly against Olivia's forehead.

Time seemed to stand completely still as Olivia froze, her eyes were wide with surprise and shock and she was shaking like a small child.

Dirk noticed two very significant things in an instant; the gun was fitted with a silencer and Johan senior had closed the blinds.

As he looked around moving only his eyes and not his head, he could see Johan senior casually walking away from the window and in their direction. He began to light a cigar as he casually walked across the room. Dirk began to panic as he realised the seriousness of the scene and as he glanced at Olivia who stood statue still, arms and legs rigid with fear.

A single 0.38mm bullet blasted into Olivia's brain.

She careered backwards, in a surreal sailing motion hitting the wall with a sickening thud. Blood gushed from the back of her head and she slithered down the wall like a rag doll falling in a heap on the floor. The bullet buried in the wall directly behind her and the resonance of the blast pierced the air. Johan Jnr quickly turned the gun onto Dirk who had sunk to the floor beside his beloved Olivia and suddenly the two men where once again staring uncomfortably into each others eyes.

There was no time to protest or even make a sound the suddenness of the action by Johan Jnr was befitting of a clinical professional assassination.

Dirk almost wished that his assailant would just pull the trigger…

'Do It!'! He screamed

'Just do it! My life is as good as over anyway!'

Dirk Botha turned away and emptied the five bullets from the barrel of the revolver onto the carpeted floor directly in front of his father. He turned to leave and looking back at the horrific mess he had created facing his father he whispered in a low growl,

'That is the last time I will kill for you, we have people for this…but you still force me to do it'

The Price of Friendship

He was waiting for an explanation but none came. Johan Snr. turned away and as his sons stared at the imposing figure of the 'great' man he strolled casually towards the window whilst making a call on his cell phone. He looked out over the busy square as he arranged the clean up of this tragedy as if it were another day at the office.

Dirk woke up the next day his eyes swollen from sleep deprivation and many hours of uncontrollable sobbing. He was completely bereft at his loss and clueless as to what to do next. All he could see was Olivia's limp form slumped on the floor in his minds eye and all he could hear were the parting words of his father ringing in his ears,

'She was bad news 'Dirkie' boy...bad fucking news. The bitch was making a fool of you and you know what is even worse than that Eh? Eh? She was just about to make a fool of me and that my son is not a wise decision.

'Before you go asking too many questions or challenging what just happened, you should be grateful to your old man for saving you. Not only was she fucking everyone who could do her a favour, including your new friend, Mr De Jong but she had no intention of taking you along for the ride after you had fulfilled your usefulness....'.

'Oh Yes! My son! **Your** brother just did you one big favour!! You owe him.....big time! I will be taking charge from now on... I have decided to see where this diamond smuggling business might lead'

It was all gone now, thought Dirk, the dream of escaping the family, the dream of going it alone and being someone in his own right. Of course he knew about Olivia's lifestyle...did they think he was so stupid? It didn't matter it just didn't matter! In the scheme of things he had never considered it to be all that important. She was an incredible person and so full of life and that just comes at a price...a price that Dirk was prepared to pay... but his father was not. Who gave him the right to decided who should live and who should die? A monster, thought Dirk as he mourned, not only Olivia but the life she could have offered him.

Right at that moment in time, Dirk Botha had no idea what to do next and he didn't really care. The future just didn't exist in his mind he could not think of anywhere he had to be or anyone he had to do He felt desperate and desolate, probably the most lonely he had ever felt in his life.

If time was such a great healer then let it start to heal. He had plenty of time.

Within days of the killing, Dirk was receiving so many calls from people he had never heard of…all asking to speak to Olivia. The answer machine memory was full and still the calls kept coming in. He ripped the phone off the wall and threw it across the room, yanked the cable from the socket in the process. He smashed Olivia's cell phone to small pieces in the same fit of blind rage.

Chapter 11

The Intercontinental Hotel on Hyde Park corner seemed extremely busy for a mid week, thought Max Reynolds as he entered the lobby. He headed directly to the reception desk as he had been instructed and sure enough he had been booked in for two nights. As he signed for his room key he couldn't help thinking that two days in room 222 might be all that he knows about his immediate future. The fact that he knew he was under surveillance and that awkward feeling of not knowing who was watching him still influenced his every move. As he made his way to the elevator he constantly scanned everyone in his view trying to recognise anyone who he may have seen before in the last few weeks or days. This had become an all consuming habit and on more than one occasion he thought he had seen people more than once. Whether it was true or just a figment of his imagination, he had no idea but he continued to create a mental picture of so many people in his mind. One particular recurrence was bothering him more than most, the old man on the flight who sat a number of rows behind him and seemed to be taking an abnormal interest in his movements during the flight was also in the same line at customs and he could swear that he was following him. Of course it could be his imagination, but his obsession with being suspicious about everyone and everything around him had heightened his senses way beyond circumstance and sheer chance. This was a new life for Max Reynolds and he was having to think on his feet, go with the flow and make it up as he went along.

He had decided even before he got on the flight that he needed to create a retraceable trail and he also had to at least make contact with the only friend he had in London…just in case he needed help. He would have to be very careful how and when he made contact but make contact he would and soon.

Max had also tried desperately to work out why this was happening to him. He had run many scenarios through his mind and examined them each and every way but he had concluded that he simply didn't have sufficient information to make any sense of it. Chuck Moore had been shot and from then on his entire world had turned upside down so it seemed obvious that there would be some link between Chuck and this nonsense but how and why, remained a complete mystery. He would have to find out more and quickly.

Room 222 in the Intercontinental Hotel was typical of many city centre hotels in the UK. Maximum use made of minimum space with all the creature comforts of home and 24 hr room service. The décor was plain yet tasteful in an old English kind of way. Well trodden wall to wall carpets covering wooden floorboards which have been in place for so many years that floor is naturally uneven and the wooden sash cord windows overlooking incredibly busy streets. The room was big enough to be comfortable and satellite TV and video games were advertised on a small card positioned on the bedside table. Max placed his suitcase carefully on the bed and carried out his habitual routine of checking the box inside the case, making sure it was still there and hoping that he may notice something about it that would help to identify the contents.

Moments later he sat on the edge of the bed, no wiser as to the contents or the reason he even had the damn box. The ritual was the same each time and he hardly knew he was even

The Price of Friendship

doing it anymore. The outcome was always the same…nothing! He could never summon the courage to just open the fucking thing, what harm could it do and then each time he considered it; the risk always outweighed the benefit. The contents of the box could hardly solve his problem anyway…No! Better to just follow the instructions to the letter and then make sure he had a good exit strategy.

He decided to call his friend Dave just to let him know where he was and promise to visit whilst he was in town, even if he never did meet up…..in fact he hoped he would never have to…

He had not been too surprised to find that his cell phone had been blocked early that day when he tried to make a call from the airport. He decided then to buy a pay-as-you-go version but had seen no opportunity to do so since arriving in London.

He tried to call directory enquiries from the phone in the room but it was dead. He tapped at the button on the handset but there was no dial tone. As he replaced the handset on the cradle there was a loud knock on the door. Max was startled and he dropped the phone as he spun round quickly towards the door. The knock came again and he found himself standing very still and silent hoping it would go away. He snapped out of the trance and stumbled towards the door, it suddenly occurred to him that he needed to know who was there and why.

He opened the hotel room door to find a small message lying on the floor outside the room. As he bent down to pick up the note he felt a thud to the back of his neck followed by a sharp pain and then just darkness.

When he came round he felt a thumping pain in his head and even though he thought he had opened his eyes he still couldn't see. There was tightness around his head and over his eyes…… a blindfold.

He tried to call out, but no sound came out of his mouth… he was gagged.

He struggled to free himself but his hands were bound and he fell to the floor. A strong pair of arms picked him back up and sat him back on the chair. The sticky tape which had served as a gag was ripped unceremoniously from his face and he winced and screamed at the same time.

'I am sorry to hurt you Mr Reynolds but it was necessary in the circumstances and if you could just remain calm and still I will try to explain why you are here. The blindfold will have to stay for your own good, I am afraid and the less you say the better, I simply removed the gag to help you breath.'

The voice was familiar…or was it? Everything happened so fast and Max was panting to catch his breath. The sharp pain was gone but the thudding still echoed in his brain.

Calm down Max…just…. breathe slowly and be calm…this could be it…be calm and do as they tell you….

The accent was English and there was just no way it could be anyone he knew…Max could sense that there were at least two people in the room and he thought he was still in the hotel room. The smells and the sounds….Yes! He was sure he was still in the hotel room.

'You have to take over from your friend Mr Moore'

The voice continued and the mention of Chuck was enough to raise alarm bells in Max's brain. He shuffled uncomfortably in the chair and tried to remain calm to hear the rest of this shit!

'Mr Moore was unexpectedly removed from a very delicate operation and it has become necessary for you to continue what he started. In the circumstance you will not be told any more than you need to know and if you follow our instructions you and your family will be allowed to live'

There is nothing like the stark reality of a really bad situation to bring a person down to earth. Max began shaking and the more he tried to hold the tears back the more they welled up behind his blindfold. He was more afraid than he had ever imagined a person could be. The fear and the desperation had reached a climax in his mind and he felt he was losing control.

A sharp blow to the side of the head soon stopped the shaking and once again he was placed back on the chair. Max was weeping now and he had to make a supreme effort to regain his composure.

'So! Mr Reynolds! What's it to be?'

There was the voice again....

The tape was removed from his wrists as he began to settle in the chair rubbing his wrists and stretching. Max was hurting and struggling to be calm but he managed to address the voice as best he could,

'What do I have to do?' He murmured.

'Now that is what we wanted to here. The next few days we need you to be alert and ready to follow our instructions .Please don't have a change of heart because we are very serious people and there is no time to screw around, so please take advantage of the hotel facilities, relax and enjoy for the rest of today and maybe tomorrow, and we will be along to collect you as soon as the next phase of the plan kicks in. ...so take your time and be ready'

The room was empty in less than two minutes and Max removed the blindfold and looked around the room. The sound of the London traffic hummed in the background but as he rubbed his eyes all he could see was yet another set of four walls containing him within this awful nightmare.

Max slept well despite the excitement of the morning. As soon as they left him alone he slept, the tiredness of the flight and the 5 hour time difference was enough to make him take to his bed and he slept like a baby for several hours. When he woke it was evening in London and he considered going out for a walk to clear his head. He knew he would be followed and his every move would be watched even if he did manage to get out of the hotel. It was ironic that he was being kept alive at a time when he felt so afraid. He was probably safer now than he would be at any other time in the days to come. He decided to try the phone once more before he left, although he knew it would not be working.

It felt strange to know just a little more about what was happening but at the same time he felt he knew nothing. He still had not found out what his friend Chuck had got mixed up in, but he *had* found out that whatever it was…it had got him killed.

He also knew that he was now the one in the firing line but he had no idea why it was him and how he was going to avoid the fate which had befallen his friend.

The Hotel occupied a large corner plot within walking distance of Mayfair, Pall Mall and Horse guards Parade which Max remembered walking down towards Buckingham Palace the first time he had visited London. He had headed to Europe for the very first time with his girlfriend of the time. They did the whole tourist bit; Palaces, Towers, Museums and Churches. Riding down the Thames on an open top boat on a rainy summer's day tested their youthful exuberance to the limit, but they were happy and contented and life felt good. Heady days and exhausting nights of passion and pleasure all seemed so far away from the stress and pressure he felt as he headed down the stairs to the reception. He decided to buy a sports bag of some sort so that he didn't have to leave the package behind when he went out. He felt extremely nervous leaving it in his hotel room for the few minutes it would take him to buy the bag from the hotel store. He chose the stairs over the elevator preferring not to be incarcerated for a moment longer and he could see all around him from the open staircase as he descended to the ground floor…. Max had always wondered why the English referred to the 1st floor as the ground floor…the differences in language and terminology was something that had always interested him for some strange reason and he always made a point of trying to find out the why's and how's behind it all.

The Price of Friendship

Max returned to his room, packed the box into his new bag and headed for the street. It was a weird and uncomfortable feeling to be out and about and he was surprised that it was allowed in the circumstances. His main objective was to find a way to discretely make contact with Dave, to leave a message at least…his first attempt to leave a trail.

Without walking too far he came across an internet café and thought this would be his first opportunity. He walked into the modern open plan building and headed for a desk top station. How he was going to find an email address for his friend he wasn't sure and he may just get a phone number or even confirm the address. He took a seat and fumbled in his pocket for a credit card to set up a temporary account. The moment he started his Google search, he felt a presence behind him and a chair was pulled up next to him. Max froze and his hands hovered above the keyboard.

'There is no need to panic Mr Reynolds, my instructions are quite clear and this falls way outside those instructions. It seems you cannot be trusted so I am going to have to ask you to return to the hotel and stay there….Now'

Max didn't even see who it was. He never turned around to check and he had no intention of doing so until he was sure the coast was clear. He stood outside the café staring into space annoyed at himself for making such a schoolboy error…he would have to be much, much smarter than that… he scolded himself as he retuned to the hotel. H e headed straight for the bar and downed a large Jack Daniels before the ice even had chance to stop crackling in the glass…

'Another one please' called Max to the barman who had engaged conversation with a couple who were sat at the other end of the bar. Two shots of amber nectar could do no harm he decided as he settled down on a bar stool to enjoy. The barman looked a little familiar to him as did almost everyone in the room; Max thought he was slowly going out of his mind. With all the extra effort he was putting into trying to remember every face and every voice tone he heard his brain was spinning and his eyes ached as much from the effort of it all as the recent blows to the head he had received at the hand of his captors.

The whisky tasted absolutely wonderful and much better than usual. The relaxed state of mind it created was very welcome and for the first time in ages, Max decided to let himself relax…. just a little…just enough to relieve a little tension. His mind wandered, back to the car crashing though the restaurant window in Boston where this all began for him……there must be something he could remember that would shed some light on what this was all about. And how the hell was he going to make contact with Dave the nightmare soon returned to the forefront of his mind and he pushed his third drink away from him….. now was not the time to let anything come between himself and his senses. He was annoyed with himself not for the first time tonight and he returned to his room striding up the stairs two steps at a time with purpose and focus.

The night went very slowly, Max had slept all afternoon and wasn't tired enough to sleep, the classic mistake when experiencing any kind of jet lag, he knew better but couldn't help himself and now he was paying the price. By the time day broke, Max Reynolds had decided not to sit back and wait for the next move to happen… he had a plan.

The night porter had left the rental car keys inside the morning post bag. They were sitting on top of the post and Max retrieved them on his way to a very early breakfast. He sat down for breakfast and half way through and with food still on his plate he made a visit to the bathroom but instead he headed down to the parking lot in the basement of the hotel. Soon, he was heading out of the city on a mission.

Max headed west out of the city following the A4 towards Richmond, in search of the address the night porter had left in the envelope which contained the car keys. The risk of involving the night porter seemed worth it although the £300 'tip' was not easy to part with. Porters and the hotel concierge are well known for their confidentiality and what always impressed Max was that they never asked questions. Just what he needed. The traffic was heavy and he was getting more anxious as the journey progressed. He decided not to call ahead preferring to surprise them when he arrived.

Dave Spencer lived in a large Edwardian style property deep in the prestigious and very expensive Kew Gardens area of Richmond. Opulence and wealth was evident all around and although he passed many poorer areas and terraced rows of pre-war houses on the way out of the city, the western suburbs of London had impressed him the first time he visited and he was no less impressed the second time around. He was driving a Ford Mondeo, an average, run of the mill sedan, just what he had asked for, which actually looked out of place in these parts…he hoped that his choice of vehicle would not turn out to be a mistake.

The porter's final act of favour was to secrete Max's bag the night shift room identical to the bag he had on the back seat of his Mondeo…..the one which actually contained the mysterious package which was the root of all this intrigue and subterfuge. As was the case in most such establishments, the hotel had a number of rooms reserved for shift workers and Max felt reasonably comfortable about the arrangement at least until he returned to the hotel. The presence of an identical bag might buy him some time if he needed it later. He thought that if he became separated from the package during the next few hours he could direct an enquiring person to the identical bag to buy him time to get back into position. The big risk he was taking was to be away from the phone in his room. He knew he had limited time to do what he needed to do but had to make a move and soon.

Luck was certainly with him as he pulled into the tree-lined drive leading to Dave's large home. There was a car coming the other way and he could see his friend at the wheel. They pulled up alongside each other and exchanged greetings. The surprised look on Dave's face soon turned to one which beamed a welcoming smile and the two men got out of their cars and shook hands warmly and energetically.

Max had rehearsed what he would say but the words just seemed to spill from his mouth and he could see the worried look on Dave's face who visibly tensed as he heard the words,

'I am involved in something which pretty damn amazing and I may need some help, I hope that it doesn't come to it but can I hide out with you for awhile if I need to…possibly at very short notice…I wouldn't ask if I wasn't desperate…'

'No problem., me old 'mucker'…No problem at all you should know that, Shelia will be pleased to see you and we may find time for a few beers and a Ruby Murray!!'

'Just you be careful …and don't bring the old Bill round.' Dave laughed and stared a little uncomfortably and too long into Max's eyes

'Never know what they might find eh?' Dave laughed out loud and wagged a disapproving finger in Max's direction.

No need to worry on that count 'mucker' explained Max 'nothing illegal just a tricky business deal which could go either way' he continued.

The two men exchanged a few more word and then, luckily for Max, Dave excused himself explaining that he would soon be late for a meeting at F.A Headquarters in London

'People to see and money to make' He exclaimed as he climbed back in the Bentley and sped down the drive towards the main road.

Max was uncomfortable and he knew then that this would have to be a very last resort and he would need to find another way out if possible. There was something not quite right about the conversation he had just had, Max could not put his finger on it but the feeling was real and not very nice. He knew he had to get back to the hotel and fast, his attention turned to the journey back and he checked the package was still on the back seat of the Mondeo and followed in the tyre tracks of the Bentley.

The drive back into London was going reasonably uneventful until Max had an uncanny feeling that he was being followed. A strange nervousness came over him and although he tried to put it down to the stress he felt, he checked again and again in the mirror. He was definitely being followed. The car behind had stuck very close to him round the last three turns and kept coming close and then pulled back to a safer distance. The nervousness he felt soon turned to fear and he found himself holding back the panic. He started to pull away and the car kept accelerated in response. Max slowed down and the car did the same. Max decided to lose the following car.

He slammed the accelerator down and swerved out of the inside lane and in front of a white lorry which was attempting to over take. The driver of the lorry hammered on the horn and screamed obscenities at Max

He looked in the mirror and…there was the red Mercedes…. right on his tail…

How am I going to lose this bastard! He knows the roads better than me and this fucking car will never get away! Shit! I have to lose him! What the fuck does he wan? I must lose him!

Max was going over 90mph and still accelerating. The speed limit was the last thing on his mind and whatever speed he went he couldn't lose the Mercedes. He slewed the Mondeo off the road at the next junction and almost lost control as he careered onto the embankment, slid down the grassy bank and thumped back onto the road. Pulling up sharply, tyres skidding and brakes squealing he spun his head round to check for the following car and the moment he did so the red Mercedes smashed into the back of him. He jolted forwards and the air bag exploded into place pinning him back into the seat. The sound of crunching steel and the hissing of boiling water was all Max could hear as he rolled out of the car onto the wetness of the grass verge. He rolled away from the car clutching his chest, slipping and sliding into the buckled crash barrier. Every part of his body hurt but all he was concerned about was the chasing car. Max eased himself up against the steel of the barrier and peered back through the smoke and steam towards the red car. He stumbled towards it and as he approached the back of his car he heard a loud bang accompanied by a scream then nothing. He was startled but instantly recovered his balance reaching into the open door of the mangled car. The driver was slumped across the passenger seat and there was blood everywhere it seemed. He stared in amazement and shock… at the gun in the dead man's hand, the barrel was still jammed inside his mouth.

My God! He shot himself! What the hell is going on?! I don't understand… Why did the crazy bastard shoot himself?

The crash had attracted a great deal of attention and there were people arriving already. Two cars had pulled over on the exit slip road and several people were running over to where Max stood. .A middle aged man who had leaped out of a large white van was already making a call on the cell phone as he ran.

Max panicked, he grabbed the bag from the rear seat of his crumpled car and sprinted away from the crash as fast as his aching legs would go. He darted into the some woods directly in front of him. He saw nothing and no-one as galloped through a bunch of trees and down into a valley in the middle of the woods. He couldn't feel the pain in his body, just the swishing and creaking of the branches as he crashed through the woods. His heart was thumping and felt like it was ready to burst out of his body. He ran for what seemed like ages but he knew he had to stop soon, just for a minute to catch his breath, but the rush of adrenaline wouldn't let his body stop moving. Down the ravine and into the next bunch of trees he went. He saw a light up ahead in the distance and as if on auto pilot he veered off in a different direction for fear of being seen. Eventually the need for oxygen to re-fuel the brain forced Max's body to slow to a jog and managed to regain some of his bodily senses, just enough to force himself to slow right down. He fell against a dry stone wall on the edge of the woods. His chest heaved and he panted madly as he lay in the mud and leaves. The sharp, jagged edges of the wall were cutting into his arms and neck as he struggled to catch his breath, Max Reynolds was in deep trouble and he just couldn't believe the shit he was in.

This mess just seemed to get worse and as he lay in the woods in complete shock he suddenly realised that he had to get back to the hotel and quickly…. He stood up and brushed himself down and amazingly his bag remained intact on his back. The straps of the bag had dug deep into his shoulders and he rubbed them wincing with the soreness as he placed the bag down on the ground and stooped down beside it.

This was the reason behind all of the mayhem; this fucking pile of canvas which concealed, God knows what! Max began to open the bag and he vowed to himself not to stop until he knew what was in the box……enough of this fucking nonsense he scowled to himself.

There was confusion all around the two cars at the crash site, as the paramedics removed the dead driver of the red Mercedes and carefully placed the stretcher into the back of the ambulance. A policeman was calling for assistance on his radio explaining the scene he had found; one driver missing and another dead in the strangest of circumstances. The fire service had been and gone having put out the fire and left the mangled mess for the local car recovery service to remove. The cars were already off the road and the only disruption to traffic was the speed of the cars passing by as they slowed down to allow the occupants of every vehicle to rubberneck at the accident site.

The message coming back to the policeman was that the Mercedes was registered to a private company and the Mondeo was a rental, which had been issued to a Mr Phil Brown, a porter at the Intercontinental Hotel, Hyde Park Corner. The officer decided to start with the Mondeo and he headed into London to begin his investigation.

Chapter 12

Sergeant Jones approached the reception desk at the Intercontinental Hotel and asked to speak to Phillip Brown. He was informed that Mr Brown was on the night shift and would not be available until 6pm. After speaking to the hotel Manager, Sergeant Jones returned to his car with Phillip Brown home address written in his note book. Brown was actually sleeping in the shift bedroom at the hotel and he was woken up by a knock on the bedroom door and the sound of the hotel manager's voice outside the door calling him to open up and he let him in.

'The police have been here looking for you just now, something about a car crash involving a car that you rented last night'.

'Jesus!' Exclaimed Brown,

'Well whatever it's all about I suggest you get home sharpish, I have sent them to your house to divert their attention away from my hotel, I would also thank you not to bring them back here if that's possible,

Phil Brown had no idea that this would be the day he would lose yet another job. He couldn't have known what was going to happen that afternoon as he slept in preparation for his shift.

He rushed to get dressed and raced home through the London traffic. He desperately tried calling the number of the mobile phone he had sold to the American the previous evening because he needed to know what had happened before he spoke to the police. As he drove he realised that he hadn't really broken any laws nor done anything which most hotel porters were renowned for however, too badly wrong but any trouble with the police was almost certain to lose him his job at the Intercontinental so had to find a way of staying out of this mess. He knew there would be plenty of questions and he had no answers

Max answered the phone which was ringing in his jacket pocket. He said nothing at first preferring to find out who was calling, he knew it would be the porter but he couldn't be too careful. Soon the two men were talking at the same time neither man really understanding what the other was saying

Thirty minutes later Max was sitting in the back seat of Phil Browns car and he was shaking and shivering with shock. He suddenly began to feel all of the mental and physical and pain coursing through his mind and body.

Phil Brown had pulled up alongside Max who had bundled himself into the car like a drunk falling into a taxi cab. The car was moving very slowly into a narrow service road and Phil Brown was chattering nervously about what had happened. Max had explained about the car chase on the phone moments earlier and it sounded like his new associate was trying to explain a story which he had worked out in his mind as he drove over. Brown pulled up sharply and he banged on the steering wheel with both hands as he realised that there was no way his story would work. The two men sat considering the facts and although there was very little Brown could do to help his employment situation he really didn't want to be involved in a police investigation. His record would come rushing back to haunt him and if there was any suggestion of a transgression of his parole conditions he would be right back in prison. He had no idea why Max was in this situation and didn't really care except for the fact that he was already implicated. There must be a way to get them both in the clear.

Max was still entranced and he didn't even look bothered about the seriousness of it all. Brown had been rambling on about options and alternatives and Max never heard a word. His eyes were transfixed on the canvas bag on his lap and he hadn't uttered a word since he got into the car. He was completely absorbed and more than a little confused by what was laid out before him on top of the canvas bag.

In the background he could just hear the ranting of Phil Brown's voice but it was an annoying noise interfering with his trance-like state of mind, like the buzzing of a mosquito in a person's ear. The real noise in the foreground was the drumming of his heartbeat and the swishing sound of the traffic passing by.

Max Reynolds was looking at a human hand. It looked as though it had been severed unceremoniously as evidenced by the crushed and flattened area where the wrist used to be. It was wicked mess with tendons, arteries and veins sticking out of the wrist socket, like some surreal waxwork. The hand was clenched in a fist and the finger nails had dug deep into the flesh at one time probably just before someone or something had tried to prise the hand open. There was something inside the clenched fist which made it look larger than it should and as Max peered closer at the hideous body part without daring to touch, he could just make out the shape of a small soft cotton sack tied at the top with a silk tie of some sort. The ties had come lose and as he peered closer through the gap of the fingers of the hand, he saw the sparkle of what looked like diamonds. There seemed to be one large stone and many smaller ones in a package the size of a tennis ball The sickening churn in his stomach was becoming more violent and Max began to feel light headed. He felt the cold clamminess of his skin and the beads of sweat coming out of his skin and settling on his forehead. He failed to understand any of this but the whole scenario took a twist for the worse when he recognised the large gold class ring on the third finger of the hand…this was the hand of his friend Chuck Moore……

Max was shocked and horrified by what he saw. He felt the retching action of his stomach and throat the sickly acid taste of sick as it passed into his mouth and he turned his head to the floor heaving and retching. As the heaving passed he wiped his mouth on a handkerchief and stared back at what his sudden burst of courage had revealed. He was amazed that he had eventually plucked up the courage to open the package and the courage he had found in the face of such absurd adversity over recent days. His life had changed beyond all recognition and he could hardly remember who he used to be. He had learned very quickly to think on his feet and had managed to stay alive when he had never needed to before, in fact in a way that the old Max Reynolds would never have dreamed of being able to do. This new macabre twist had taken him completely by surprise and he was stunned. Quite what he had expected to find, he had no idea but it certainly could never have imagined this.

Max looked up from the spectacle which lay out on the seat next to him to find that Phil Brown had not only ceased his incessant rambling, but he was staring in horror at what lay on the back seat of his car.

'In the name of God…He exclaimed 'What the fuck is that? And why is it….

Max grabbed the canvas bag and laid it on top of the items which had attracted Phil Brown's attention.

'Shut Up Just Shut the fuck Up! I need to think' He cried

Max tried to concoct an explanation in his mind but none came. What was he supposed to say? There seemed to be no way to explain, no way to express in words what had happened. There would be an explanation for all of this but he had no idea what it was and he dare not conceive a good enough reason for the most recent events. How could he think of drawing anyone else into the awful nightmare?

'I am sorry Mr....Whatever- your- fucking-name is....but I am going to have to ask you to get out of my car and take that little lot with you' Explained Brown as he stabbed his finger in the direction of the bag and leaned across the back of the drivers seat to throw open the rear door behind him. As he gestured towards the door in a most insistent manner, he continued,

'I don't know what you are into, nor do I care but I have just lost my job and the police are looking for me and that is just about as much as I can handle right about now so if you don't mind ....'

Max's shoulders dropped just a little as though he was resigned to being alone in his nightmare with no idea what was to follow. He gathered everything together and stuffed it back into the bag. As he forced the contents in, he felt an envelope lying on the bottom of the box which had contained the hand. He hadn't noticed this at first, maybe the shock of what he did find diverted his attention from looking for anything else. In an instant he decided to leave the envelope just where it was for the moment. Things were bad enough already and now was not the time to make them worse, he thought to himself.

'I understand' said a tired and weary voice which whimpered out of Max's mouth.' I am sorry to have dragged you into this' he continued ' but I swear I didn't know what was in this package and I had no idea who was trying to run me off the road'

'I can't explain and I can only expect things to get even worse so I will go' Max closed the box and zipped up the canvas bag in readiness to leave the car. He slid across the back seat of the large black car; he felt a hand on his shoulder.

'Listen, I will take you back to town and drop you off close to the hotel. If you need to get to a train station or an airport I will take you there, but I can't help you any more than that'.

Max was grateful for the offer and he settled back into the seat for the ride back to London.

As they drove he tried to cast his mind back to that night in Boston when he and Chuck had met up for dinner. The mutilation of his friend must have happened after the shooting whilst he was lay in the rubble of the restaurant, Max remembered carrying his friend out to the sidewalk and laying him out in front of the paramedics. It was all such a blur but it was still hard to imagine not noticing a thing like that.

This was crazy!! What did it matter when or how it had happened? The fact remained that it had happened and now he had to find out what it all meant. The hand, the diamond and the envelope. whatever that contained...He needed to get back to the hotel and gather his thoughts more carefully to see if he could use this new information to help himself.

As they approached the Hyde Park area, Phil began to speak,

'I will let you out on the east corner of the park and you will need to walk the rest of the way. I can't afford to be seen at the hotel just now, so I will say my goodbyes now. I've seen nothing and I know nothing so if the police ask...you haven't seen me OK?!'

Max nodded and closed his eyes to compose himself for the next Chapter of this horror story. They had pulled up at a red light and suddenly the passenger door flew open and a burley man leapt into the car. At the same time the back door was flung open from outside and another man planted himself next to Max.

Drive! The man in the front screamed 'Drive!!'

As Phil hit the accelerator and the car surged forward Max threw himself out of the car and he rolled into the road clutching his bag. The black car had pulled away and as it swerved to avoid the on-coming traffic, Max ran in the other direction towards the hotel. He dodged the stationary traffic which was waiting for the lights to change and he disappeared into the morning crowds.

Max made it back to the hotel in double quick time. He launched his tired and battered body up the stairs and dashed into his room, slamming the door behind him. He rushed towards the phone to check for messages…there were none. He looked around the room quickly and efficiently searching for any signs of anyone or anything unusual, nothing. Once he was satisfied that he was alone and maybe, just maybe he had got back without being missed, he hit the shower.

He sat on the edge of the bed wrapped in a towel reflecting on how the day had turned out…so far and what he had learned about the mess he was in. The first step of his exit plan had been to find Dave and this would provide him a place to hide if required, well he did find Dave but something wasn't right and he didn't feel at all comfortable using that route. In fact, he wished he hadn't taken the risk at all because things had deteriorated immeasurably since he left the hotel. It had, however provided him with the courage to look inside the dreaded and infamous package and what had that done for him? Well, he was absolutely sure that Chuck had been involved in some way with stealing or smuggling diamonds or he had been set up. In either case he had been killed as a result of his involvement and the evidence of his death was very important to someone. A person could survive the severing of a hand but there was something symbolic about the hand and what it was grasping, presumably just before it was severed. Proof of the kill as well as the bag of the finest diamonds it was possible to imagine. At least it was obvious why he had been warned not to open the package. Well, fuck that! thought Max, he needed to know and he was glad he did. Whatever information he had could only be useful to him as he planned his escape.

The envelope! He suddenly remembered the envelope.

Max opened the canvas bag and rummaged through the box until he found the envelope. As he opened it a key fell out onto the floor and there was a note. He read the single side of paper and as he picked up the key he allowed himself a sickly grin, almost a smile as he realised ...*Unbelievable! Fucking unbelievable!*

The smile left his lips and he shook his head slowly, unable to fully comprehend the full implications of what he had read. His eyes scanned from the key to the note and back again and as he stared at the key he knew that he had to get back to the US......... and quickly. He wrapped the note paper around the key and buried it deep inside his wallet.

Chapter 13

THE PEACE AND QUIET OF a regular work day at the London office was suddenly thrown into turmoil and confusion for DuPreez. All caused by a single phone call. It sent him into a violent rage. Carla had to duck to avoid the table lamp as it flew across the room and smashed against the wall just next to the door. She scuttled out of the room closing the door behind her in one quick, well practised motion. She knew better than to be anywhere near him when he was in this mood she had seen more violence and anger in the two years she had worked for this maniac than she cared to remember. If the pay wasn't so good and the benefits weren't so awesome she would have left long ago. She would stay as long as it took to build up enough money to leave and then she would be long gone. The entire experience had frightened her but for the sake of a secure future for herself and her children; she had stayed through the tantrums and violence. On more than one occasion her mother had begged her to get another job but she stoically and stubbornly remained in the post…just for a few more months, then she would be set.

The voice on the other end of the phone was understandably angry but managed to speak in a normal yet sarcastic tone. Although the irritation and the anger were peeking through the awkward silences he continued to ask for an explanation for the disappearance of a set of Kruger Diamonds. Oh! and by the way, there is the small matter of the down payment we wouldn't want to forget that now would we? The large value of this consignment meant that a substantial deposit had already been paid in good faith

The voice on the other end of the phone with whom he was pleading for more time to find out what had happened and with whom he was promising on the life of every member of his family to resolve this matter, was none other than…. Meneer Johan Botha.

Where was the boy? What had happened to Dirk the deal had been set up Olivia and the fool Dirk Botha, suddenly he was talking to his greatest adversary…..something had gone horribly wrong and he was right in the middle of it.

DuPreez left the office that afternoon pledging and promising himself out loud, that someone was going to pay for this. He had made a promise and his reputation depended on finding out what was going on. That meant recovering the diamonds and making sure that anyone even remotely connected with the disappearance was punished…but first and foremost to get those diamonds back before the shit got any deeper. There could be no loose ends and when he unravelled the mystery…. and he would….then the world would know that …DuPreez was not a man to be tricked or fooled around with.

'No calls, No messages ….I will not be contactable by anyone, for any reason until I get back…..And I may be gone some time…' Explained DuPreez as he headed for the door to leave.

'Bur Mr DuPreez, I…….'

Carla noticed the shoulder holster and the gun nestled in the leather pouch as DuPreez threw his jacket over his forearm and stormed out of the office. She cut short her response and feared the worse as she flopped down into her chair, hoping that he would be back…for her own sake and that of her children.

The Price of Friendship

Johan Botha wanted HIS diamonds and DuPreez had not even realised that they were bound for him or even that they were ready for delivery. Olivia and DeJong had set up the slow but necessary process of secreting small numbers of the gems away and DuPreez had expected that to take some time before any were available to him to broker in the market. Of course he knew about the recently mined 'special rocks' which had raised so much attention but they would be guarded far too heavily to be considered a viable option. No-one in their right mind would attempt to steal such high profile stones. Organised theft relied upon slow and steady movement of small stones that's the way it had always been and no-one risked rocking the boat. Sure, richer deposits can be found but none had gotten as far as the black-market, certainly not to his knowledge and certainly not from Orapa. It would be madness and compromising to the organisation in place. It would have to be someone who doesn't understand the delicate balance of the organisation.......

Maybe the bastards had double crossed me....Maybe they had ignored the time honoured rule...and gone it alone....If it had been Johan behind the deal all the time ,he would know the rules...If it had been Johan's scam then why had Olivia and Dirk insisted that he was not to be told?. I need to get in touch with DeJong as soon as possible ..... If anyone knows it will be him.

For the second time that day, DuPreez was stunned by the content of what he had considered to be a routine phone call... He had made the call to Jeffrey DeJong only to find that his cell phone was diverted to voice mail. A subsequent call to his home revealed that Mr DeJong had been killed in a car crash the previous evening, under suspicious circumstances....

Since this information had come directly from a relative at DeJongs home he had to accept that it was true. The net was closing in and DuPreez had few options left to find out what had happened, His relationship with DeJong was never the strongest but he would have believed what the man had told him and he was sure that he would have told him what was going on…if nothing else, in the hope that he would be able to get some payback from the transfer of information. There was a high value placed on accurate market intelligence and there was also a code to follow, call it honour amongst thieves of you like but it was really about networking and making sure that a person can put themselves in the line for new information before the next guy. The apparent lack of places to look led DuPreez to take a chance with a call to his contact at the office in Gabarone. The DeBeers operation in Gabarone was always in the loop for information regarding new developments and certainly any activities which were happening at Orapa Mine. The call may be a long shot and also a little more risky than he would have liked but 'needs must' at a time when he felt isolated and vulnerable. This was about survival as much as anything for him and although he was a survivor and a seasoned campaigner, he had seen much in twenty years in the 'business' and he was well aware of the dangers associated with failure.

He managed to find out that there was no 'official' record of a so called 'Kruger set' of diamonds but if there had been a significant amount of interest in 'a significant find' it was well below the radar of the authorities which normally meant that it was all the more interesting to several parties. It was always sensible to verify information with at least one other source and DuPreez had to consider is next move very carefully.

He gathered information in very small pieces from several sources and by the end of the day he had constructed a possible picture of what 'might' have happened. The Diamond had indeed been mined at Orapa Mine and the normal routine of small amounts and often had been overruled it seemed. This opportunity was too good to miss and a plan had been formulated very quickly to make the diamonds disappear. No-one seemed to know who put the plan together but this was only to be expected, no one person ever knew all the details of the plan, this was fundamental to its success and this was normal and accepted by all the people in the chain. What was not normal and did not follow convention in these matters, was the speed at which the theft had taken place. It was very risky to miss out the 'safety steps' in such a plan and it seemed that more people than normal seemed to know that 'something' was going down. It also appeared that everyone he spoke with suspected that someone 'new' was in the frame for receiving the goods. This was unheard of and although no-one seemed to know who the new person was and even how reliable the rumours were, there was so much conjecture that the entire network was twitchy and people were going underground fast. DuPreez had found out as much as he could without drawing too much unwanted attention and whilst he had thought that Dirk Botha was the new kid on the block and now his father seemed t have taken control he still could not explain why the goods had not been delivered. He considered the fact that he was being set up and he also began to suspect the fact that Johan Botha might know more than he was letting on. He headed back to his office to check some information and on the way he would have to find a way to call Mr Botha's bluff if he wanted to get to the bottom of it all.

Back at the office, DuPreez pondered his next move and he felt that he had no option but to risk a meeting with Johan Botha. The only way he could do that was to make Botha believe that he knew where the diamond were and he was ready to make a trade.

The strategy was certainly high risk but he would at least buy himself some more time. The longer Botha waited for some feedback the more impatient he would get and impatient men are sometimes prone to do unpredictable things! Botha had to believe that DuPreez knew where the diamonds were or what was the point of keeping him alive? DuPreez had to convince the infamous and very dangerous Mr Botha that he was in a position to make a trade in order to buy sufficient time to find as much as he could regarding the real whereabouts of the damn diamonds! The apparent disappearance of Dirk and Olivia was picking away at DuPreez's mind continued to evaluate his dilemma and he hated loose ends. There was peace again in the office as he rocked back in his large leather office chair and closed hi weary eyes to think. Carla had been gone when he got back to the office and he had diverted the office phone to the answer service as soon as he returned. The Victorian building was home to a firm of lawyers, two insurance agents and in recent months the upper floor had been renovated to accommodate a residential letting agency. No-one really knew or cared what business DuPreez's carried out from his three offices on the second floor. Such was the anonymity of a bustling city centre location.

He was unable to speak to Johan Botha that afternoon though he did try. He had steeled himself for the lie as he waited for Botha to come to the phone but he was told that the great man was in meetings and was not to be disturbed. DuPreez knew that he was probably being made to sweat a little and he also knew that he would not be the only person who was looking for the Kruger set. He knew Botha would have several packs of hounds searching for the same elusive prize and the first one to come in with the goods would be the only one who would be recompensed for their time and efforts, what's more the eventual victor would be the only one who would be safe.... as well as rich...maybe!!

He decided to check into a hotel close to the office for the night and as he walked the two blocks down Mayfair, his cell phone rang in his pocket.

The last place he wanted to be for a discussion of this sort was in the street surrounded by commuters and shoppers. Botha however was not prepared to wait for a more convenient time and he insisted on having the discussion right there and then. DuPreez kept him talking until he could duck into a Starbucks on Oxford Street where he perched on the edge of a bar stool looking out into the city street through the large window.

The Price of Friendship

I have located the goods and I am ready to talk to you about the next step, he explained to Botha in a firm authoritative voice

'Is that so, well I am relieved to hear that and these next steps you talking about, what is your proposal?'

The negotiation had begun and the two men arranged a meet with a minimum of talk... DuPreez bought himself 24 hrs and that was as much as he was ever going to get. He had to move fast.

Chapter 14

Dave Spencer had reluctantly agreed to collect Max from his hotel, but agree he did, and it was obvious from the tone of his voice that he considered this to be a big favour and Max was confused and a little nervous at his friend's response. He recalled that there was something a little odd about their earlier meeting and he decided that Dave's reluctance was more than a little suspicious even then. He would have to be very careful. He needed to get to the airport as discreetly as possible and this was his best chance of achieving that end. He hadn't told Dave anything other than the fact that he wanted to meet urgently and he would explain what it was all about when they met. His friend pulled into the hotel pick up parking spot bang on time and he was alone in a car which definitely was not the Bentley. Before he had chance to get out of the vehicle, Max was alongside with baggage, tapping on the trunk of the car gesturing for it to be opened. His friend duly obliged and as Max climbed into the Ford, or whatever it was… he sensed an uneasy atmosphere and he felt apprehensive and worried.

'You are big trouble my friend…big trouble' exclaimed Dave

I have been contacted several times by God knows who, warning me not to make contact with you. I knew you were in town way before you made contact and I have been warned off in no uncertain terms!'

'I have no desire to know what is going on and I have even less desire to get involved. We have been through some stuff together and we have got away with some dodgy deals but this is something quite different and I am not happy that you involved me' he continued

'I guess from the fact that you have your baggage that you are still running and I am sorry that I will not be able to take you to the house…you must understand that I cant take that risk, I am already too close and I will not be able to help you any more.

Before he could continue Max eventually managed to get a word in,

'I appreciate you coming over, I really do…..I just need to get to Heathrow or even Gatwick and I will be gone. I had no Idea that you were at risk and I can't tell you how sorry I am. I would understand if you say no but I am desperate.'

To both men, this conversation was the strangest they had ever had. It was like they were complete strangers, adversaries' even, avoiding eye contact and keeping each other at a distance. The stand-off made them, nervous, uncomfortable and scared and the sooner they parted company the better. Max was frightened and saddened for himself and now his old friend. Dave was downright angry but he didn't want to turn his back on his friend completely, one last act of kindness and then he was out of it. He prayed he had made the right decision to turn up at all and he just wanted this meeting to be over and quickly.

Dave began to drive and before very long, Max was sure that they were heading for Gatwick. They headed west out of the city and as soon as they reached the M25 motorway, Dave hit the gas and the car lurched into life. They were both very uneasy and small talk was just not on the agenda, the two friends stared out of the windscreen directly ahead, almost

The Price of Friendship

willing their destination to come closer to them as they sped down the outside lane of the motorway.

Max was inside the comparative sanctuary of Gatwick Airport Terminal 1 in no time and he didn't look back at the car which was heading back into London. That was the most sickened and remorseful Max had felt throughout this entire course of events in recent weeks and he hated himself for ruining a perfectly good relationship and for what? He became very angry which overcame his increasing fear and anxiety. He would make someone pay for this and he knew just who that someone would be. The tables were just about to turn for Max Reynolds and as he stood in the line at the ticket desk, he could hardly wait to get back on home soil. The next available flight with seats to spare was the United Airlines xxx which did not leave until early the next day getting him in to Boston at 2pm the following afternoon so he had to find somewhere to stay overnight. He was amazed that he had managed to elude all of the people who would obviously looking for him so far at least and although it pleased him he was still acutely aware of the need for alertness and discretion to avoid attention in every move he made. The Hotel had several rooms available and Max checked in for a single night under a false name and paid with cash. He needed somewhere to hide more than somewhere to sleep and although he was extremely tired he felt that the levels of adrenaline would keep him going and he doubted that he needed sleep. Max Reynolds was becoming accustomed to an evasive life of subterfuge and self preservation.

It must have been about 2 am when Max was woken by a subdued knocking on his bedroom door. It was the sound of a person trying not to be heard by anyone except by the occupier of the room. Max was half awake, in that zone where a person is not asleep but not fully awake either. He very quickly scanned the room, reviewing his security situation. A third floor window, a very small bathroom and no closet, just an open rail on which to hang clothes. Nowhere to hide and no escape route he concluded and not for the first time he found himself wishing he had a gun. That would be his next purchase as soon as he reached the States he decided and then he heard the tap on the door again.

Max stood staring at the back of the door and then crept towards it with the intention of checking who was out there. Suddenly and quite unexpectedly a slip of paper appeared from underneath the door and it lay invitingly on the floor directly in front of him.

Confusion and indecision flooded into Max's mind. He stooped down slowly and deliberately keeping one eye on the door. He grabbed it and snatched it away from the door as he backed away into the room. He recognised the signature on the bottom of the note before he even read the content. He opened the door and happily but still guardedly, allowed his visitor into the room.

Germaine Fulton looked more like a huge, ebony statue of a famous person rather than the real deal. He had been so famous and instantly recognisable in the USA particularly in his heyday as a linebacker for the New York Giants it would never have been a surprise if there was a statue erected somewhere in the southern states of America, from where this giant of a man hailed.

'Mr David…. he believes you could use some protection ….it would be my pleasure' boomed the massive man in a voice as low as he could possibly muster.

Whispering was just not possible for a man like Germaine Fulton; he would never have needed to whisper during his illustrious and sometimes controversial career so why would he know now it was done?

Max hugged his unexpected 'intruder' warmly as much from relief as anything else and for the first time in many weeks a smile spread across his face. There was no doubt that he was pleased to see his friend but there was a tinge of sadness in his heart as he recalled the way his career had ended. Max had been representing a young player looking to break into the major league having had an amazing final season at UCLA when they first met. Germaine was an established player in the NFL and he took a shine to the new rookie Max had introduced to the team. During the draft before the season of '94 Germaine spoke up for the rookie on more than one occasion. Max was grateful and they formed a friendship of sorts, always good to have contacts in the right places. Germaine's career came to an abrupt and savage end when he was badly injured in a play-off game in '97. He never played again, at any level and because he was not a native New Yorker he returned to New Orleans a broken man and as they say…the king is dead…long live the king, Germaine Fulton became history before his time.

Max had helped him do some promotion work across the USA and Dave had used his services to help develop the new up and coming Grid Iron Football League in Europe. Between them, Max and Dave they had helped this awesome athlete back from the brink of obscurity.

Now here he was….. willing and able to help out an old friend….

'It's pay-back time….' Roared the big man, as they broke from their embrace.

Max stepped back to inspect the big man,

'Two hundred and fifty pounds…solid and a little grey in the temples… but you still cant get a shirt collar big enough to look right round that beast of a neck!'

Both men laughed and shared a high five which nearly broke Max's wrist!!

'I am not sure what Dave has told you but really, I am trying to be discreet and low key so I appreciate the offer but I just wouldn't want to drag you into my mess' Max was writhing inside as he risked hurting Germaine's feelings but it had to be said.

'I don't think you realise the mess you are in buddy'

Max couldn't hide the look of surprise and expectation on his face and he could see a serious and worried frown appear across the big man's forehead.

Dave can't help because he's too close to it and it would be too risky, but I can and I fully intend to…. so let's moving we have no time to lose and we can talk in the car.

Max was amazed and intrigued by what he had just heard and rather than putting forward a decent argument, he found himself packing up his belongings and following Germaine out of the door.

This is crazy. I have a plan and this can't possibly be helping, I need to get out of the country and I have a plan, .why am I being taken in by this man.

They climbed into the taxi cab which was waiting at the rear of the hotel and headed back to the M25 bound for Gatwick Airport. The journey took about 30 minutes which was plenty of time for Germaine to fill Max in with all that he knew.

It turned out that Dave had been 'got at' much more seriously than Max had thought and by the time he had approached Germaine, he totally feared for his life. His wife had been threatened and also his son who started studying at University College in central London. Germaine explained that someone was really serious about following Max but there seemed to be a good reason to keep him alive, at least until they got what they wanted. What Germaine and Dave could not work out was…what were they looking for and why. Dave had contracted his friend Germaine, to 'accompany and protect' until there was no longer a need and he was paying handsomely for the service.

Max was overwhelmed and also very frightened. He had never thought he would be in need of protection and when Germaine eventually placed the .38 automatic into his hand and closed his fingers around the handle of the gun squeezing Max's fingers underneath his own, he was glad that he did have friends. The gun was just a gesture because there was no way Max could get through the airport security with a gun. He placed it back into the huge paws which Germaine called hands.

The change of plan was intended to confuse and also buy some time. Max and Germaine were booked to travel to Boston via Chicago on American Airlines the following day. Whoever was following him would have to monitor at least two flights now even if they had kept up with the plan changes. Two separate flight bookings following two routes back to the US and a bogus hotel reservation was not the extent of the confusion they were planning to cause. Max was humbled by the extent his friend and ex colleague were prepared to go to protect him and something deep down in his sense of self preservation made him a little nervous…he still needed to be very, very careful and a little sparing with his trust.

As they left the M25 and headed towards Gatwick North Terminal, Max still had a firm grip on the canvas bag and he was surprised that Germaine had not made any comment as to the contents considering that he seemed to know so much already. They went directly into the terminal and took a row of comfortable seats each…they were settling in for the night preferring to stay out in the open for the seven hours or so that they had to wait until check-in time the following morning.

Sleep was not an option and Max spent yet another night forcing himself to stay awake and alert.

Check in time came and went and they boarded the xxx flight to Chicago without incident. Max had an exit row seat in row 18 and Germaine was at the rear of the plane. They never made any contact with each other throughout the flight and believing that they were relatively safe at 30,000 ft on a half empty plane, they both allowed themselves the luxury of a little sleep. They disembarked at Chicago O'Hare International Airport, casually and discreetly still making no contact with each other and travelled separately yet in sight of each other between terminals to catch the connection to Boston. Then it all changed.

Max was walking about 10 or so people in front of his minder so that Germaine could keep sight of the people around him, when suddenly he heard a volley of automatic rifle fire, immediately followed by screaming and yelling from the hysterical travellers. The noise was deafening and sickening and everyone either threw themselves to the floor or hid behind something...anything they thought would protect them. Security and Police uniforms were everywhere in seconds and guns were drawn high in the air and now official screams joined the melee and confusion.

'Everybody, Down!!!' No doubt that the calls were coming from the police or the security personnel

'Take cover! Everyone! Take cover!!'

Max hugged the canvas bag close to his chest and dragged his roller suitcase flat along the floor as he crouched and covered his head with his free hand. He couldn't see Germaine but he knew he was there, he started to scramble through the screaming people towards where he expected his friend to be but he couldn't see him. He decided to sit tight and as soon as he could, make his way to Terminal C where their connection awaited them.

Another volley of fire and this time the screams sounded like people being hit by the bullets. The ear piercing screams and wailing was almost louder than the gunfire. Sirens went off and the sprinkler system sprang to life. There was water spray everywhere and it turned to a mist as it hit the floor and the windows. The combination of noise and water and mist was as surreal s it was frightening as if this was not real at all just the set on a disaster movie.

Two or three men were slung to the ground and numerous police officers pounced on top of them like a football pile up. More screams and shouting.

The Price of Friendship

'Freeze! You bastards!! Lose the weapons and put your hands behind your back!'

The instructions were unnecessary and impossible to carry out because the men were buried beneath a pile of officers and the guns had skidded across the polished tile floor. Paramedics pushing wheelie stretchers rushed past where Max found himself lay on the ground and he strained to see where they were heading.

The sirens stopped and the screaming slowed, the volume of noise was getting quieter and more subdued. Screams turned to more sporadic shouts until it started to die down into loud chatter all Max could hear was the sound of broken glass, luggage trolleys and suitcases being righted. Men, women and children were weeping and crying as they gathered up their belongings and brushed themselves down. The smell of fear and the horrified expressions of fright and shock were emblazoned across every face. No-one knew what had happened but there had been so much horror and terror across America in recent years that everyone ALWAYS feared the worse.

Some sort of order was eventually resumed and everyone had to be searched and interviewed as they passed the line of police who stood between them and the exits. Max looked towards the crowd of paramedics and he also feared the worse.

Surely it can't be the big man in that crowd surely not please God make it not be true. Not another killing for nothing; please say it's not true...

As soon as he reached the line of trolleys, slipping and sliding on the blood stained floor, his heart began to race and his hands were clammy as he lurched into the crowd looking for Germaine.

He wasn't there, no sign of him on or off the trolleys...

'Thank God! Thank God!' Max cried out load and took several deep breaths to compose himself. Looking around he still couldn't see Germaine in the crowd, he called his name but nothing. Time was moving on and he had to make the connection. Maybe Germaine has gone ahead and they may meet up at the gate. Max made his way through the red tape and security delays to Terminal B gate 53 hoping to see Germaine waiting for him. The underground train was full to the doors and as every train arrived at the boarding station more people crammed onto an already full carriage. A security nightmare thought Max as he bounded up the escalator to the gate area having survived the crushing bodies on the train. He was alert to everyone around him as he walked briskly through the concourse looking for his departure gate, the terminal was very quite and almost eerie in contrast to Terminal A where all the action had made everyone frightened and nervous. He looked out for Germaine in the stores and the indoor cafes and bars as he walked hoping that the big man would leap out to surprise him at any time. But again nothing. He reached the departure gate and took a seat in clear view of all oncoming people.

A young woman took the seat next to him and they sat down at the exact same time. Their arms brushed against each other and they both reacted as if they had offended the other…
'Sorry…' They said simultaneously and they both smiled and chuckled at the co-incidence. The woman was small and dressed in tight jeans and sleeveless shirt revealing a colourful tattoo which adorned her left shoulder. Her long dark hair flowed across her shoulders and although the tattoo could clearly be seen through the fine strands of her beautiful hair, her most attractive feature were those sparkling green eyes shining through a pretty, slightly naive looking smile.

Max looked away as soon as his immediate curiosity was satisfied as he tried to concentrate on the matter in hand, looking for Germaine.

'Looking for anyone special?' asked the woman

Max was a little startled and he must have had an unsettled look on his face as he replied a little too sharply

The Price of Friendship

'Yes, someone very special' Came his brusque and sharp reply...

'I am sorry!' The girl replied' I always put my foot in it you know...speak first then think later. Please forgive me for intruding'

Max realised for the first time that she had an accent, an English accent and his entire body tightened intuitively.

'No No I am the one who should apologise it has been a long and very stressful day, replied Max, and trying to end the conversation before it started. He could not allow himself to be distracted but it wasn't easy.

The woman stuck out a slender, manicured hand in Max's direction as an invitation to shake hands by way of introduction.

'My name is Theresa and I will be assisting your passage to Boston, I do hope we can be friends'

Max froze and stared directly into the stunning green eyes.

'There is no need to worry Mr Reynolds, Germaine was identified by...shall we say...an undesirable so we had to create a diversion to remove him before he got hurt and I will be taking over until you reach your destination. '

'People were hurt back there...even died...'

'Most unfortunate I agree, but I suppose it must have been necessary, 'the end justifies the means'... Mr Reynolds'

'What kinda crap is that?!' Max leaned closer to the woman as he tried to control his temper and muffle his raised voice.

'Where is Germaine? I insist you tell me...and now, young lady...RIGHT NOW!

She smiled sweetly and offered Max a digital camera. As he took it from her he could see a video come to life on it's small display screen...It showed two men escorting a man who could have easily been Germaine, into the back of a car. As the film rolled, he could see Germaine's big face smiling back at him. He mouthing the word 'Sorry' and hunching his huge shoulders

113

apologetically as he climbed into the back of the car unassisted and of his own free will. The car pulled away from the airport terminal as the film clip came to an end and the light faded from the camera...

As he looked up from the impromptu film show, she was gone, he saw her taking a seat across the aisle from where he was sitting and she was beginning a conversation with two small children as they played on the floor.

Max sat back into his chair and let out a huge sigh, visibly blowing out a large breath of air.

What now??? This protection 'thing' is too organised to be a knee jerk reaction on Dave's part....Yes we have been friends for a long time but this!!! No! No! I don't need protection I know what I am doing next I just need to get back to Boston in one piece and I will begin my exit from this freaking' nightmare... Do they know as much as I do? I doubt it .... I am on the front foot now and I just cannot be distracted.....I have to be able to move more freely than this........

Max gathered his baggage and his senses and headed towards the men's room. He felt the piercing green eyes firmly drilling into his back as he walked slowly, following the signs to the nearest bathroom. As he rounded the corner from the gate area to the main concourse he gathered his bag close to him and started to run slowly at first then faster as he reached the EXIT signs directing passengers to the baggage claim area. He could sense that he was being followed and he hoped it was only the English Girl. He felt he could probably lose her simply because he knew the lay of the land and also he was getting used to this game of hide-and-seek. Then he would be free to travel alone and to where he needed to go. There were regular flights from O'Hare and also Midway Airport...plenty of options as soon as he got away.

He raced through baggage claim and outside the terminal building. It was getting dark and he was sure he could lose himself amongst the cabs and coaches in the passenger pick up area. He hid temporarily behind a line of people who were waiting for a transit coach just to check if he was being followed. He saw no beautiful English girl or huge NFL star behind him. In fact, no-one at all seemed to be following him, he suddenly had a strange feeling that he may have actually got away. Now what? His instincts forced to him to make a quick check that the canvas bag was still inside his roller case and once confirmed, Max boarded the transfer coach which was taking passengers across the city to Midway Airport.

They followed I90 south as far as the intersection with I55 where they headed inland from the south shore of Lake Michigan and south towards St Louis. In no time, Max could see the Midway International Airport billboard looming up in the near distance. The plan was to board a flight to Boston as soon as possible avoiding any further delay.

Concourse A if his memory served him right, was from where Air Tran flights departed to many domestic locations within the continental US…..including…..Boston, Mass.

Max was so tired and weary that he needed to rest. He could feel his entire body weakening and each rush of adrenaline took more and more from the reservoir of strength Max felt within him. Two or three hours flight would not do it for him and he needed a good nights sleep to recharge, ready for the coming challenges.

There were seats available for the final flight of the evening to Boston and although Max had to pay full price for the one way flight and he knew he would probably have to take any seat he could, he took the offer enthusiastically. Yet another flight booked and paid for, Max headed for yet another departure gate and yet again, he was tired, weary and trying to stay alert. He spotted no-one following him and he had no unwanted intrusions as he sat awaiting his flight. He boarded with all the other passengers and took his seat like a regular commuter.

Amazingly, Max Reynolds had boarded the Air Tran flight without being followed and he made it to Boston just before midnight, unaccompanied as far as he was aware.

He knew his house would be under surveillance although he still wasn't sure how many different parties were after him….. he certainly knew who was behind the main threat and he knew exactly where he was heading next. He decided to pick up a hire car at the airport, preferring to remain as anonymous as possible for the time being and although he was a native Bostonian he was travelling around his home town like a tourist. He drove his rental with purpose and like a man on a mission, which of course he was.

Out of town, south on Route 93 to Interstate 95 towards Providence, Rhode Island. If he continuing south west for an hour or so, Max would reach his eventual destination…. Newport, where he would be having a, yet to be arranged rendezvous with the man Max Reynolds hoped he would never have to see again in his entire life……Sam Deans.

Chapter 15

It was hotter than usual in Sandton City, Johannesburg, and the heaviest clothing anyone was wearing was made from very thin cotton and it was short sleeved. People, young and old were busying themselves as usual all around Sandton Square. On this day it was noticeable that everyone was quickly passing from air conditioned building to air conditioned building or from shady tree to shady tree. The intense heat was relentless as it beat down onto the glass walled buildings and the shimmering street. The city baked in the heat of the sun and the normally lush, greenness of the custom planted areas of grass and flowers which separated the concrete and glass looked a little tired and straw coloured as it took a beating form the ultra violet rays of the African sun.

DuPreez was in town to meet with Johan Botha and the meeting was sure to be as hot as the weather outside. DuPreez had returned to Jo'Burg as soon as he could from London and had taken temporary residence at a girlfriend's flat in the suburb of Hillbrow. Just a precaution in case Botha was planning to make him disappear any time soon…..as soon as he handed over the goods…not that he had the goods of course but he was still planning to go through with the meeting to find out what he could to help in his search for the gems. A very risky and tricky strategy but one he felt he had no choice to follow because he was dead anyway…unless he could come up with the goods or a good explanation why he didn't have them. Botha would never believe that DuPreez had mislaid or lost the diamonds…no way! His only chance was to get the damn diamonds which he was no closer to doing so he had run clean out of choices.

Out in the open with plenty of people for cover….Sandton Square was as good as any place to meet and as Johan Botha left his office building, DuPreez was already in position sitting on the edge of the water fountain which was in the centre of the main paved area between the office buildings. A few people still braved the searing heat as they sat on the low wall surrounding the fountain swigging on cold drinks and eating lunch time snacks. DuPreez was just another one of them. He had recruited a 'small firearm specialist' which had become the buzz word for a gunman to watch his back and the black man in the shadows watched very closely as Botha walked casually across the square towards the fountain. Botha was flanked, as always by armed colleagues and on this he would not compromise. It was a sad and depressing thought that a man with such wealth, power and influence could not walk alone in public…

DuPreez was ready and waiting and he began the conversation as soon as his 'guest' sat down beside him on the stone wall.

'I am more than curious why these goods are attracting so much attention' began DuPreez 'I am not altogether comfortable with the predicament I find myself' in he continued

Someone is going to be disappointed and that means I will end up dead…I need some assurances and I also need the true value of these items before I deal, think of the highest number in your head and double it!!! I need to disappear a long way away for a long time to be safe…I am sure you understand'

The guttural South African accent got more and more distinct as the sentence went on and by the time the ultimatum was out, only another South African would know that it was an ultimatum.

'Now you listen to me Meneer *Fucking* DuPreez'. Botha entered the negotiation

'The fucking diamonds are mine, I placed the order and I demand delivery before we leave this place and IF you want to leave this place alive...Don't fuck with me Meneer!!'

Botha was way past talking in riddles and referring to his diamonds as goods or item or anything else for that matter. His position was clear and DuPreez was backed straight into a corner...first move!!!

'This is an international issue *Meneer*, there are people just as powerful s your good self who are making the same threats'.

Botha glanced at his colleague and back at DuPreez just quickly enough for DuPreez to sense some sort of weakness or lack of control.......this could be good he thought to himself.

'I am not interested in these imaginary opponents of whom you speak; I will take my diamonds now'

DuPreez started to stand up and a very strong hand slammed him back down onto the wall with one tap on his left shoulder.

'I am dead if I leave here anyway and you will not have your diamonds AND it would be most unfortunate if my guy was to shoot your guy and lots of people panicked in the open air on such a pleasant *fucking* day....'

It was obvious to DuPreez that Botha had no clue where the diamonds were.... First score to DuPreez.

It was also obvious that Botha didn't know who else was chasing the diamonds. If he did, he didn't share the information, not surprising really but he did look shocked when DuPreez mentioned it.

'I obviously don't have the merchandise with me; do you think I am so foolish?? I have to be sure you are willing to pay the current market price and as I said before, these diamonds are hotter than hell right now so make me an offer…'

'One million US dollars was the original value and I see no reason to change that. I will guarantee your safe passage to Europe and at least you will be alive to see your family again. If you turn down the offer you will die and I will still get the diamonds…it will just cost me a little more. So, what's it to be be DuPreez ?? Well?'

'I am the one in the bargaining position and I will accept no less than 2million plus a guaranteed safe passage out of here… I will leave now and I will be back in 24 hrs, same place and time…If you choose to return tomorrow I will see you then otherwise, I bid you good day.'

Incredibly and very unexpectedly…… DuPreez walked away from that place intact and unharmed. It was a stalemate and he had learned enough to stay alive at least. He walked through the crowd just waiting for the gun shot or the attack from behind but none came and the spring of success entered into his step as he made his way back to the parking lot to collect his car.

In contrast, Johan Botha veritably stormed back to his office, his anger and frustration was apparent to all. His first reaction was to have the 'fool, DuPreez, followed, steel the diamonds and kill him. The only reason he was not doing just that is because he was beginning to doubt whether his compatriot even had the diamonds. He needed an answer to this question before tomorrow. He wasn't sure where the foreign interest had come from but he was damn well going to find out. He called together all of his senior people and charged them with an ultimatum of his own…find out who has the diamonds and also who is in the frame to buy them. If he did find out that DuPreez didn't have the diamonds then he would certainly follow through with the aforementioned plan…with the greatest of pleasure.

Botha's loyal lieutenants set off on a 'mission impossible' but set off they did, and they were fully expected to deliver results before tomorrow. A frenzy of phone calls and rushing through corridors ensued and the search was well and truly on. No stone would be left unturned and they would find out something...anything because they had to deliver some information, however small and in some cases however relevant or true. They would of course be looking in all the same places that DuPreez had looked, probably with the same results. It was entirely possible that they would find out even less than DuPreez. When the 'big machine' gets moving the underground gets very deep and impenetrable, much more so than when a well connected individual like DuPreez goes digging. The Botha footmen would wield their strength like using a hammer to crack a nut and in such circumstances information becomes difficult to come by and even more difficult to trust.

DuPreez looked out over Hillbrow from the window of his friends flat. The Hillbrow tower was a renowned landmark and the area around it had always been a hive of multi-cultural activity, even in the days of apartheid Hillbrow always seemed to behave as though it was above all of that. Multi-Cultural and dare it be said multi racial as well. He came from a very Afrikaans background and had been raised to hate and detest anyone without a white skin but DuPreez had to adjust and accept the changes or get out of the country. In very uncertain times particularly during the years immediately following the release of Nelson Mandela, all white South Africans as well as a multitude of 'white refugees' from the old Rhodesia's as well as Zambia and countries further north had to follow the FIFO principle...Fit In or Fuck Off! The considerable infrastructure which was put in place by generations of white rule would serve to sustain the country whilst the new regime took a grip. The economic failure of other independent African states during the twentieth century and the worsening security situation in those countries provided a poor forecast for success but at least the people were free and that meant everything to a nation who had suffered such oppression for so many years.

As DuPreez reflected upon events in the country he loved and he considered a metaphorical parallel with his own immediate situation he feared the worse. He had lit the blue touch-paper with Johan Botha and although he had made some progress in terms of getting information, he still had no idea how to use this newly found knowledge to his benefit. He had drawn a complete blank over the overseas element of the jigsaw and he was now convinced that this was the key to unlocking this mystery. He did have many contacts in the US and also Europe but they were all established in the diamond smuggling world and he had to consider that the suggestion that someone new was muscling in had to be taken seriously but where would he start to look. Botha was the main man in these parts in drugs and gems and he appeared not to be any wiser than DuPreez as to the whereabouts of the Kruger set.

Botha had many enemies and also many friends who held a similar standing in other countries. He knew of a number of people who would like a slice of Botha's empire from overseas. Sam Deans on the East coast of America has always been after Botha's import/export racket but DuPreez doubted that he would enter into the diamonds market…not his style. The other candidate might have been Botha's son, trying to make the old man take notice but as things had turned out, that was a very doubtful scenario. Dirk Botha, the son who would have been most likely to 'defect' had been stopped in his tracks but did he manage to get to the merchandise before he was rumbled by the extensive Botha intelligence network? Although unlikely, the remotest possibility was worth further consideration decided DuPreez, who was fast running out of options and more importantly time. He would need to make the right calls to the right people and fast. He had little to bargain with but except for the fact that no-one seemed to know any more than him he would need to bring as much pressure to bear as possible.

Eighteen hours later, DuPreez sat on the wall surrounding the fountain in Sandton Square waiting for the unlikely arrival of Johan Botha and his entourage. His marksman was positioned exactly as before and DuPreez had planned what was to follow as well as he could in the time available.

He checked his watch and he stared at the ornate digits which adorned the face of his pretentious and extremely expensive Rolex, Botha was thirty minutes late. If he lost the chance to speak with Botha now he was not only lost but very definitely a dead man. It was entirely possible that Botha had exposed the bluff and that would mean only one thing…no more need for the services of DuPreez. On the other hand, Botha may be increasing the tension and expectation by seeing how long his reception committee would wait before they gave up and left.

The answer came swiftly and without warning like a military operation.

A vehicle screeched to a halt in front of the square and two men armed with automatic machine guns leapt out before it had even stopped and fired into the air. Whilst the sound of gunfire was still echoing between the tall buildings and the screams of the lunch-time crowds still pierced the midday air, DuPreez found himself being bound and gagged and dragged across the ground towards the revving car. He was bundled into the vehicle and the two gunmen fired a volley of bullets over the heads of the cowering crowd, just for good measure. The car sped away.

People started to pick themselves up and as they looked at themselves and then each other they realised that no-one had been hurt and no-one had the slightest idea what had just happened. Except, of course, Johan Botha, who was sat in the passenger seat in front of the luckless DuPreez. He reached through the gap between the two front seats in the cavernous interior of the vehicle and jammed a large paw-like hand around the throat of DuPreez forcing his head back into the seat.

The vehicle raced out of Sandton and sped north on Livonia Road and out on the open road, away from the built-up areas.

'Never fucking underestimate me and never ever try to fool me Mnr DuPreez.' Whispered Botha into DuPreez's left ear as he squeezed his throat and squeezed a little tighter. His face was contorted with anger and he was spraying spittle into DuPreez's ear as he tried to control his voice.

In contrast DuPreez was gasping for air against the gag which was tied tightly around his mouth and struggling hopelessly against the huge arms which were forcing him down.

'I know that you don't have the diamonds and I should kill you right now…Maybe we should make an example of you, but first I want to hurt you bad ….God! I want to hurt you, you foolish man…'

'Maybe I should keep you alive just long enough to get the diamonds for me and then I will decide whether to kill you or your family or both…' The air inside the car reeked with the pungent smell of sweat, fear and desperate panic, as DuPreez continued to gasp for the smallest particles of the wretched air just to stay alive.

Botha ripped the gag away from DuPreez mouth and he gasped for a deep breath. The hand was still tightly wrapped around DuPreez throat and he started to choke and gasp for air at the same time. The pressure on his throat was eased just a little and Botha began to speak again.

'The phone in your friends flat was bugged and I heard your pathetic attempts to track down… Sam Deans had to do with this' He continued 'I thank you for the lead and I hope you enjoy the rest of your journey.'

The car slowed very slightly and the rear door was flung open. DuPreez was launched out of the car door and his limp body rolled over and over and directly into the path of the on-coming traffic. He bounced off two vehicles until he finally landed beneath the huge wheels of an articulated vehicle as the driver slammed on the air brakes fighting to control a sideways skid and eventually careering off the road leaving the mangled body behind on the tarmac surface.

The race for the missing diamonds was closing in on Sam Deans and the number of people chasing had just been reduced by one.

Chapter 16

As Max Reynolds drove purposefully and a little quicker than could be considered safe towards his destination, he began to reflect on exactly what was going to happen when he got there. If it all got nasty which it most certainly would, he may *never* return to his life and his family and friends. He couldn't call for help as every time he had tried it had resulted in someone getting killed or hurt. The note which he had found inside the package along with the other horrific contents, lay crumpled on the seat next to him .He had established that Chuck was involved in smuggling racket which had gone horribly wrong and now he thought he knew who was behind it, well at least he knew who had brought Chuck into it. He was on a mission to stop this madness. Too many people had died already and it had to stop.

Max had known Sam Deans way back in the past, a time which he had considered to be another life almost. A time which he would rather forget but life has a habit of throwing bad news right back in a person's face and then it all comes flooding back.

During his time at Massachusetts Institute of Technology (MIT) just across from the Charles River from Boston and right in the heart of the Cambridge district, Max had made several bad choices and one of them was a young girl named Stella. They were both just out of high school and although Max was never going to make it in the world of engineering and science, Stella was a natural scientist and a political reactionary who was pledging to make it big in a world which was at that time, dominated by men as well as solve the problems of the world by making her views well and truly known.

Enter; Max Reynolds, the high school jock who also happened to have a very good brain which helped him to get a coveted place in the world renowned MIT. He had a natural way with the ladies and he found it easy to make friends and influence people. Stella was bowled over by Max's charms and good looks and in no time they were an item. A passionate and fiery relationship carried on for many months until the drugs scene took over. Max was much more level headed than Stella but she became such an influence on him that he was persuaded to use his influence and contacts in sporting circles to obtain some hard core shit and what Stella didn't take herself, she sold on campus for a tidy profit.

Demand very quickly outstripped the supply of the drugs and Max found himself in conflict with a man named Sam Deans. After many painful and frightening encounters with Deans, Max was kicked off campus dishonourably and without achieving any qualifications. Deans simply continued to supply via another unsuspecting soul and the last Max remembers was a scandal breaking in the city which exposed Stella Robinson, daughter of a respected Boston millionaire as an unscrupulous drug dealer who had ruined many young lives during her time at the Institute. She was distraught and Max never found the courage to make contact with her ever again. He had heard that she never really recovered from the ordeal or the drug abuse she had put herself through. He, of course, had fought long and hard to recover the opportunities he had lost and the reputation which had followed him since his exclusion from the college. He had managed to get out just in time, Stella was not so lucky. But

The Price of Friendship

Sam Deans went on to become a very wealthy 'business' man who's dubious past just served to give him the reputation he needed to succeed in the suspect career path he had decided to carve out for himself.

No-one ever said life was fair.

Max had not seen Deans until many years later when they bumped into each other at a celebrity party at Sam Deans' weekend home in Newport. Max had not forgotten the incident at MIT but Sam Deans had no recollection of the ordeal when challenged by Max in public after several glasses of champagne. A very embarrassing encounter and yet another unfortunate incident which Max knew that he would live to regret and maybe this was the time for Max to put things right. He had uncovered a scandal which he should be able to use to blow Sam Deans apart yet he was racing down to the very same place that he had embarrassed himself years before.....by doing exactly the same thing....confronting Deans on his own patch. He needs a better plan his time and he also needs some help.

Max slowed down and pulled off the freeway at the next exit which advertised services. He drove slowly into the parking lot of a Hilton Express and turned off the engine. He was angry from the memory recall he had just been through but he also felt more in control than he had been for some time. Max reached for his cell phone from the outside pocket in his case. He hadn't checked the canvas bag for some time and he needed to make sure everything was still there at the same time.

Max stared into the distance and shuffled in his seat to make himself a little more comfortable and thought out his next move. He powered his cell phone in the cigar lighter socket and within seconds it sprang to life alerting him to all the missed text messages and calls. There were too many to check and he really only wanted a working cell phone because he had decided to call Chuck's wife Mary. It had suddenly occurred to him that he had information about Chuck's death that she may be interested in knowing......also he had his wedding band which she may well appreciate having back. He felt that he may also be able to find out why Chuck was involved in this mess, maybe he had been framed, if he could get some more information from Mary, he could plan his attack on Sam Deans more comprehensively and with a greater chance of success. He wasn't sure how she would be able to help him but he was going to try her anyway. Mary lived within 30 miles of where he was and he would call her and offer to visit, that would give him chance to prepare for the meeting. His heart skipped as his mind drifted back to a time when he and Mary had been much, much closer.

It was not unusual for Max to call Chuck's home phone number and Mary answered the ring almost immediately.

'Its Max Reynolds, how are you doing' He announced

There was a slight delay and then she responded,

'Hey! Maxie, how you doing? I heard you were overseas'

A frown appeared on Max's forehead as he considered her instant reply

'Ya! I was' He responded 'But I am back in town for a while, wondered if you were free to meet up and catch up, you know'

'Sure! No problem' Replied Mary and they arranged to meet that evening.

Max checked into the Holiday Inn Express for the night and prepared himself for his meeting with Mary and also gave some thought to his subsequent attack on Sam Deans. It would be good to see Mary, they had been good friends and she had always been the best company. Although he had no idea how he was going to break the news to her, he knew he had to be very careful and also very cautious. It occurred to him that he was already breaking the promise he had made to himself..... not to risk anyone else's life. He really felt that he needed to make her aware of what had happened just in case he didn't survive his meeting with Sam Deans and he needed some help.

Mary was already sitting at the bar sipping a glass of red wine when Max arrived. He was a little embarrassed at being late but he was sure he wasn't. Mary was at least fifteen minutes early and Max felt good about that, for some reason. She was sitting on a bar stool, side on to the bar as he approached and she looked absolutely spectacular. Stunning! She was a very attractive woman and she was dressed immaculately in a very expensive looking, very low cut, and silver blue dress and as his eyes followed her gorgeous long legs to the floor the black stiletto shoes came into view. Her hair was cut short and very stylish. Her slender body was tanned and glowing. She chatted to the barman and anyone could see that he was entranced…as anyone would be. Wow! thought Max as he reached the bar counter, there was something about a woman so beautiful that made men feel very nervous and for the first time in as long as he can remember, Max was smiling and he wasn't looking around him waiting for something bad to happen as he planted a kiss on Mary's cheek. The smell of her perfume was intoxicating and the giggle of recognition she let out when she realised it was Max was simply exhilarating.

They hugged warmly and walked together towards the hostess to be shown to their table. As they sat down opposite each other, for the first time they really looked at each other. Mary looked confident and satisfied if not happy but there was no sign of sadness in or behind her eyes. Max was shocked as he stared into her eyes looking for something.

'Maxie Honey! Its been too long, how have you been?'

'It's been a tough few weeks!' exclaimed Max.

'I need to tell you what has been happening but let's order dinner and we can talk later,

'Sounds good to me' announced Mary and they concentrated on the menus until they both were ready to order.

They ordered very quickly seemingly preferring to chat. The food arrived and they ate quickly and efficiently as if there was another agenda entirely. They chatted like old friends which, of course, they were. They had spent many dinners and social evening in each others company, not always with Chuck or any one of a string of girlfriends Max had brought along following his divorce. Max and Mary had always got along. They had crossed the line from friendship to 'something more' only once long ago and it was never, ever spoken about. There was something so completely different about this evening. There was a complex dynamic about the evening. On the one hand, Max wanted to tell Mary of the horrors he had uncovered involving her deceased husband and also he needed to try and get some insight into any dodgy dealings Chuck was involved in. On the other hand, there was Mary......She was a remarkable beauty, always had been she could turn men's heads and keep them turned. Without even trying it seemed, her radiance and physical presence was mesmerising and if she was involved in a conversation all heads were turned to her, it was difficult to turn away from her and she had perfected the art of drawing people into her aura. Max had seen her calm down and control many potentially explosive situations with a smile or a polite embrace accompanied by a soothing whisper in the ear, he had also watched as Chuck praised and worshiped this goddess who was his life. She who had decided he was the one and he would be forever in her debt that he was allowed to be with her. It was almost embarrassing to see and Max had commented many times on the strangeness of their relationship. Despite the image which Chuck presented to the outside world, Mary showed obvious love and respect outwardly and so obviously towards her friend and partner. It was obvious to all that they had been very much in love.

Yet here they were in this place on this evening…just days after Chuck had been killed, and she was so obviously flirting with him!! He was definitely flirting with her and he couldn't remember the last time had felt so alive and excited. Max had always found it easy to talk to women and he had his share of relationships and even a steamy, wanton affair during his only attempt at marriage which eventually led to the demise of that relationship for ever. A very bitter divorce had put Max in a different place in his life and for some time he decided

The Price of Friendship

against serious relationships preferring to put all his efforts into building his career. He had always enjoyed the chase and the build up of passion and expectation even in conversation and he could feel the evening drifting amazingly and unexpectedly in that very direction.

He just couldn't help himself and he felt no resistance from Mary. The evening went so well that by the end he couldn't bring himself to tell her the worse and he hadn't learned anything at all about what Chuck may have got himself involved in, in fact although he had thought about his friend many times during the evening, to his amazement he couldn't remember Chuck even being mentioned. There was something very strange about that…Max felt pangs of guilt and he also felt confused and he wondered how Chuck's name would come into the conversation? Max gathered himself and decided to bring his friend's name up and see what reaction he got.

Mary looked a little saddened and the radiance of her smile turned down just a little as Max tried to talk about their friend and her husband.

Mary stopped the conversation dead. She glared at him ever so slightly and forced a smile to her lips and she reached across the table and placed a single, slender finger against his lips as he spoke.

'Maxie….. I really can't think about this right now and don't want to ruin this awesome evening. Can we please drop the subject and go back to your hotel'

Max froze with the sheer surprise of the words he believed, he had just heard. His eyes opened wide with shock and Mary stared deep into them. A mischievous look crept over her face beginning with a cheeky smile and culminating in a deep erotic stare. Max realised that she was still pressing her finger against his lips and he took her hand and as he gently removed it folding the fingers back into her gorgeous hand he kissed each one deliberately and delicately without breaking the trance-like stare.

Max slammed a pile of dollars on the table and without a moment to waste they walked briskly out of the restaurant and headed nervously outside towards Max's car. The excitement was electric, there was no time to consider the 'what if's' or the 'should we shouldn't we's' the eroticism of the moment had captured them both and it was driving them on. Mary tugged at Max's arm pulling him towards her car and she whispered,

'My house is closer…let's go there….'

Max never replied he just smiled and followed as they headed towards Mary's vehicle. The expectation was incredible; Max was shaking and trying to keep himself together like a teenager on a first date. Words escaped him as held the driver's door open to let Mary into the car

She was intoxicating and he caught a waft of her perfume when they brushed close to each other as she climbed into the vehicle. He tried to kiss her but she pulled ever so slightly away from him with a sweet knowing smile, patting the seat next to her encouraging him to join her. As he ran around the car and eased himself into the passenger seat, she planted a huge kiss directly onto his lips at the same time as reaching for the ignition switch, the engine roared to life and she floored the gas peddle, they were away, with Max still puckered up and waiting for the rest of the kiss! She laughed out loud and shuffled into her seat more comfortably as they headed away from the restaurant towards Mary's home. The short drive was almost too much to bear. Thumping heart beats and frustrated expectations of what was to come created a mesmerising atmosphere in the small confined space. Mary drove much too fast and they virtually leapt form the car as they arrived at the house. Mary opened the door and wandered casually into the kitchen, apparently cool and in control of her emotions. Max followed her into the impressive home virtually panting and nervously stumbling across the threshold of the front door.

Mary casually opened a bottle of wine whilst Max stood leaning against the side of the refrigerator, just staring longingly at her awesome presence and absorbing the sexual energy created by her every movement.

They tried casual conversation but nothing was going to delay the obvious and Mary only managed to pour one glass of wine before Max clasped both of her hands to his chest and kissed her longingly full on the mouth. The spell was broken and they both erupted into a frenzy of tugging and pulling as items of clothing fell to the floor one by one. They fell hard against the wall and Max scooped Mary up and carried her into the lounge without interrupting the hard passionate kiss.

He placed her gently onto the thick, luxurious rug and she spread her legs invitingly as he lowered himself down onto her. He was completely under her spell and she felt for his hard member placing it gently close to the opening of her wet and steamy womanhood, he carefully entered her. The unexpected gentleness of his slow yet deliberate thrust sent Mary into an involuntary spasm of pleasure and she raised her hips from the soft surface of the rug pulling him deeper and deeper into her. Time stood still and passion and pleasure took over from the agitated frustration. The erotic frenzy was now in full control and they freely rode the crest of pleasure swapping places and positions like a perfectly choreographed symphony. After the first hard and panic fuelled movement, they started up again as soon as they could, caressing and pleasuring each other with bodies, mouths and minds. Mary was incredible and intoxicating and Max could hardly believe the perfection of every curve of wonderful body. Her energy was amazing and she rode him for what seemed like ages until he gushed inside her once again. They were almost fighting to please each other and each pleasured the other with every part of their heaving and adoring bodies. They made love in the lounge and then in the bedroom and although they both needed to sleep the feel of the soft sheets against their weary bodies caused embrace after embrace and they continued the erotic symphony of passion throughput the night, exploring each other and sharing the ultimate in pleasure and gratification until they could go no more.

Eventually they collapsed in each others arms and fell to sleep, as one.

Max woke from a half sleep and reached an arm across the huge bed patting the sheets, but there was no-one there. He dragged himself to a sitting position and rubbing his eyes and stretching the reality of where he was and what had happened came crashing to his conscious mind like a steam train. He called out for Mary but there was no answer. Looking around the massive bedroom he could see his clothes strewn around the floor creating a trail to the bed and he smiled to himself and allowed himself to fall back into the warmth and comfort of the sweet smelling sheets.

Within minutes Mary came into the room wearing a beaming smile and very little else. She was carrying a tray with juice, bread and a plate of fruit and she sat gently on the bed next to him.

'Hey there, sleepy head! Are you awake?'

Max lay still for a brief moment and then he jumped up grabbing Mary rolling her over passionately onto the bed laughing and roaring like a freed animal. The tray went flying into the air and there was coffee across the room and they both screamed in unison laughing and wrestling with each other. Mary freed herself from Max's clutches and rolled over on top of him still laughing and smiling she lowered herself to his lips and kissed him with all her might and they melted into each other rolling and twisting across the huge bed.

The morning went in a flash and it was early afternoon when they decided to face the world. As they showered and dressed separately their thoughts were as one..........the fairytale evening and consuming passion of the night were all history now. What did it all mean, they looked across the room at each other as if now they were clothed they were ready to face outside world, there was a feeling of deep guilt and regret on both of their faces but also something special, a feeling of longing and friendship. It surely did not feel like a seedy one night stand, they had been too close for that and no-one except Chuck had been betrayed by it all and he was not even alive, so why was the overriding emotion, one of guilt and regret?

There was an awkward and almost embarrassing atmosphere about the way they said goodbye in complete and utter contrast to the closeness and bonding of the time they had just shared. They shook hands for God's sake!! What the heck!! Max stood in the doorway and gazed back at the astounding beauty of the woman he had just bedded so completely and wondered if it was all real. He still had to tell her about the diamonds and the dismemberment of her husband for Gods sake!! How could he go there now? It was inconceivable that they would ever be able to have that conversation. He tried to bring himself back to reality but it wasn't happening for him as he stood half in and half out of the door as Mary held it open for him to leave. The cab was waiting in the drive outside, ready to take him back to the reality of his nightmare situation and all he could see was the perfect form of his incredible Mary beneath her tight seductive clothing as she leaned provocatively against the door he head tilted just a little suggesting she felt just as sad and yet just as expectant as to what was to become of them as he did.

Max cupped her face in his hand and kissed her sweetly on the cheek and they began to speak at the same time

'Err… I will call…..' Stuttered Max…

'No! No! I will call you later today…. I promise', interrupted Mary 'I have some things to do but we will talk later…….be sure and wait for my call' she continued and she closed the door quietly and deliberately with Max backing away.

He turned and walked towards the waiting cab wondering whether they had ruined a perfectly good relationship or whether they had just started up a new one.

A short moment of panic hit Max as he realised that he had left the diamonds in the car outside the restaurant, how could he be so stupid!!! He asked the driver to step on it and braced himself for a very nervous fifteen minutes as they made their way back to the restaurant. By the time they got there he was nervous wreck. The events of the following evening and the tension of worrying about the diamonds was just too much and his body was shaking and he was sweating profusely.

The car was still there…..parked alongside the large white building. There were several other vehicles parked there, probably the lunchtime diners and restaurant staff. Max made his way over to the dark Blue sedan in the distance and fumbled for his keys as he walked. There was no need for keys.

The driver's door was slightly ajar and the window was smashed….there was a neat pile of glass on the floor alongside the car and as he peered beneath the driver's seat where he had stashed the canvas bag he saw nothing. It was gone.

It was if his whole body gave way in sheer panic. His legs gave way first and then his breathing stopped as he slumped to the ground hitting the hard tarmac floor with both knees. He buried his head into his hands and the wave of emotion came flooding out in the form of an uncontrollable scream.

'No!!!' He shrieked

'No! No! No!' It was if he couldn't stop. He was banging his head against the open door as he grabbed it to stop himself falling completely to the ground. A cut opened up on his forehead and the blood streamed to the ground when he knelt. It was all too much for Max and as wept openly, all that he had been through over the last weeks and months went racing through his mind appearing like a picture show of incredible images passing before his mind eye. What would be the next image to appear? Was there even a future for Max Reynolds?

Chapter 17

T̲HE ONLY PERSON IN THE world who knew where he would be at that time was Mary, thought Max as he sat at the bar inside the restaurant. The very place he reflected, where it had all started to go wrong. The barman had recognised him from the previous evening and who wouldn't remember the man who went home with the stunning lady form the bar... He had made some advances himself with no success but he could hardly forget the victor and he was full of envy as he splashed some coke into the ample measure of Jack Daniels.

Max was dabbing the cut on his head with a bar towel and although he had stopped the flow of blood, as soon as he released the pressure, the cut began to swell again and blood from beneath the surface soon appeared and began to drip on to the bar counter. He had his wallet out on the bar counter from where he had taken the key which he had placed there when he first found it alongside the diamonds and the gruesome severed hand of his friend, Chuck Morris. He hadn't had the time or the inclination to remove Chuck's ring from the hand and although he wished now that he had, he still couldn't see himself removing it.

He was playing with the key; spinning in on the bar counter and staring at it is come to rest between the droplets of his blood. There was an irony about the fact that all he had left was the key and he had no clue what to do with it. Less than 12 hrs ago he was hiding a large fortune from GOD knows who and now he was left with a simple key, which he was never supposed to find.

'That looks like a nasty cut, what on earth happened?' The tone of the voice was concerned and a shiver went down his spine accompanied by a ripple of pleasure which brought itself to the surface of his skin as he turned to see Mary standing behind him. He knew it was her because he had made the call, but still she created an air of excitement.

'Leave that' She said pointing to the glass of whisky glistening on the bar counter.

'We need to get that checked out...' She reached out to Max and brushed his hair back away from the cut with her hand.

It took all Max's effort to spin slowly around on his bar stool and face her. She smiled as always, but there was definite frown of concern across the normally smooth perfection of her forehead.

Max was caught in two minds. Whether to challenge her directly to find out what, if anything she had to do with the break-in or to seek refuge with her....give himself time to re-group and gather his thoughts before making any rash accusations. It may have been an opportunity break in; after all, the car was isolated overnight in the parking lot of a well known restaurant. He had questioned the security guard who had seen nothing but that was not unusual. Security was more a matter of satisfying insurance conditions than catching criminals; he had learned this from many dealings with major establishments in the past.

Contemplation was pointless because before he could say a word she had paid the barman and they were walking to the door together. Much had changed since the last time they headed for the very same door a few hours earlier. Much had changed and Max was at a complete loss as to what to do next. Mary called the car rental firm from her cell phone and explained the circumstances. They drove in silence to the medical centre a few blocks from Mary's house. She went first and returned to the car with a nurse who applied a dressing to the wound right there in the car. Max could think of nothing to say as they continued the short trip to Mary's large home, up the drive and around the rear of the property to the decking which overlooked a large pond with exotic plants and a large array of trees planted in a perfect half circle around the pond.

Max flopped his sore body onto a garden chair as Mary pulled open a parasol and wrapped a warm blanket around Max's shoulders. She disappeared into the house to prepare a stiff drink and returned in no time with a tray of two drinks and a dish of savoury snacks.

'Now this time I don't expect to send the tray flying into the air', She quipped, trying to lighten the atmosphere.

'Listen Max, I saw the look on your face in the restaurant just now and I don't understand….what's going on..? ' She looked quizzically into his eyes waiting for an answer.

It was now or never for Max, did he have the nerve and the strength to tell her? He took a large swig from the drink she had put before him and his taste buds were greeted by the familiar taste of JD with a splash of Coke.

Max took her hand and prepared to reveal all.

Mary went through several swings of emotion as Max explained his findings and the predicament he found himself in. She was silent throughout but he could see her holding back the tears at some points and her hand went to the mouth more than once holding back a shriek of horror or anger or just plain displeasure at what she was hearing.

When he had finished, Max sat back in the chair and emptied the glass of whisky in one go. He winced as the spirit passed over his tongue and down his throat burning and glowing as it went down.

Mary threw her arms around her good friend and began to cry. Max returned the hug and they embraced in silence apart from the sound of Mary crying for what seemed like an age. Eventually they parted as Mary turned away and ran into the house. Max was drained and he sat motionless with his eyes closed and head bowed. He had told her everything and now it was too late to take it back. It was 'que sera sera' from here on in, 'what will be, will be and he would have to hope and pray that this woman was true to her word and would help him in some small way to retrieve the diamonds and the contents of the canvas bag.

Mary was gone for some time and when she returned to the deck, Max was stood leaning against the handrail around the side of the wooden decking, looking out to the pond, talking quietly to himself as he pondered and considered what was going to happen next. Mary approached him quietly from behind and when she got close she put both hands on his shoulders turning him gently around to face her.

'I knew that Chuck was getting into something bad and something very wrong. He was acting very strangely and there was no way I could get close to him. I tried Max, I promise you I tried so hard to reach him but he was somewhere else in his mind and the more I tried the more stubborn and defensive he got. It all seemed to happen so quickly and then suddenly, he was gone. I was broken Max you know I expected something bad to happen because of the way He was acting, I always believed he would get himself out of trouble and back into all our lives'.

'I am sorry to ask but you need to think very hard…did he give any indication what he was into? We know he obviously got on the wrong side of some bad people but for some reason he was taken out either by Deans or Botha or someone else completely… I know Sam Deans is behind it somehow but I don't know how to make it all stop. Until it does we are all in terrible danger…I need some help Mary at least to think it through' Max was urging Mary to dig deep into her memory.

She was sniffing and whimpering, very close to tears, but just managing to keep her composure

'I need to show you something' she announced and then she led him into the house.

Max was leaning on a large kitchen counter, both arms were outstretched and he was staring in amazement at a series of photographs spread out across the marble surface of the counter. Mary couldn't bear to look at them again. She had received the photographs after Chuck had been killed and from that moment on she was convinced that he had died as a result of the affair. Maybe a jealous husband or a gangland set up… either way, Mary was convinced that Chuck had contributed to his own demise and she was trying to hate him.

Max placed the key and the screwed up piece of note paper on the counter next to the photographs and looked across at Mary.

'This is it Mary….This is all we have to go on. I must get to the bottom of this and find out who has the diamonds, will you help me?

Mary Moore stepped towards her friend and taking both of his hands in hers she said,

'Max….listen very carefully…I recognise that key!' She was noticeably shaking and her eyes were wide and frightened.

Max gripped her hands tightly. 'Mary, are you sure?' he pleaded. 'Does the note mean what I think it means?'

They were shaking in time with each other and as Mary's fear took hold she turned to Max and a look of impending doom took over her face. She had an ashen colour to her skin and she looked scared and worried.

'I think we should get out of here Max, go somewhere safe while we make a plan to get out of this mess' she was crying as she spoke and pulling away from him the whole time.

Does that mean you will help me? Max asked with a tone of expectation.

'Let's just go hey? I am pretty keen on staying alive!!'

Max swept Mary off the floor and squeezed her tight. She did not respond to his show of emotion, the seriousness of the situation had just hit home for Mary and she was a very frightened lady.

She packed very quickly, just enough for an overnight or two and Max started the SUV in the drive waiting for her. The photographs and the key.......their only link to what may happen next, were hastily stuffed into Mary's overnight bag. She grabbed some of Chuck's clothes and threw them into a bag for Max, and headed out to the waiting vehicle. They had no idea where to go but Max had decided to call at the Holiday Inn Express to collect some things. He guessed that his house was under surveillance and therefore not safe and all he wanted to know was what Mary knew that she wasn't saying and how this would affect them. She had seemed remarkably affected as soon as Max produced the key and she went from scared to petrified as she read the words on the note....

Mary was a very fit woman, she exercised regularly almost fanatically, as much to maintain her exceptional looks as to stay fit but she had been a track star in college and also played competitive volley ball for a number of years. She was ready, fit and willing to save her own life, a life which had been very good for Mary Moore maybe now the time had come to protect her very privileged existence.

She had changed clothes and packed in no time but still she looked like a million dollars...dressed in a tight fitting, dark pants suit and sporting a black baseball cap, her hair flowing from the rear of the cap and the black suit hugging close to her fantastic curves... she looked a stunner in anything she wore... and even better when she wore nothing at all Max thought as he watched her lock up the house and stare longingly at her wonderful home for a moment before she turned away and skipped towards him as he waited, motor running.

They headed towards Max's hotel and then on towards Newport. They both instinctively knew that this was the next place for them to be, they would need to be careful and they would need to be discreet but they knew that the only person who would be able to shed some light on the situation was one Sam Deans.

The Motel had a number of rooms available and Max decided that a ground floor room with front and rear exits would be the best solution. They had both been used to comfort and wealth to a certain extent but now it was all about practicality and timing. It was a whole new ball game for them both with new rules. Suddenly a female socialite with the looks to kill and a sports agent with nothing but a passion to find the truth and stay alive in the process, were about to take on the big boys…….

Chapter 18

Sam Deans was resting in his weekend house, when he received the call to tell him that a deal was on with Johan Botha……. And not just for the chance to make an offer for the Kruger set of diamonds but also a deal was on the table to exclusive dealership for movement of South African diamonds into the US. The caller was one of Sam's longer serving subordinates…which just meant that he had not made any mistakes whilst making sure that Sam became wealthier and wealthier…otherwise he would have been replaced or removed….That was considered pretty impressive in the Sam Deans organisation. Length of service meant seniority and more trust…which often led to more risk for the job holder and therefore less chance of survival, so anyone actually overcoming all the pitfalls were either very lucky or just plain ruthless…. more often that not the latter. This was certainly the case for Charlie 'C' who was on the other end of the phone call.

'What now Boss?' Came the curt request

Sam Deans was amused by the offer and pondered and delayed before he replied

An offer to deal diamond eh? They will soon realise who is in the driving seat!! And the Kruger set are already mine!! How dare they try to sell them to me!! I arranged the deal in the first place……

However…we should not be too hasty. There may be a way to get all and everything…….and all on my terms…we shall see.

Sam Deans was smiling to himself and things were looking up for Mr Deans. His response to the call from Charlie 'C' was typically casual and matter of fact as he insisted on a briefing with everyone present first thing tomorrow morning. In this instance the whole Sam Deans organisation was summoned to the office in Boston. It was customary to meet in the city and although he was relaxed and positive and wondered why he would want to break that mood when he had provided perfectly good transport for all of his people, it was much better to meet in the city. He called to one of the multitude of serving people at his beck and call to make ready to leave for the city early the following day.

Max and Mary had settled into the Motel as best they could and were beginning to prepare for what could only be described as a confrontation with a very dangerous and particularly ruthless organisation.

Neither was really ready, but they were confident that they could at least do enough damage to spoil the party….. for someone. When they considered their strengths there were many; they had the element of surprise and they were very mobile. Since conferring over the implications of the key and the meaning of the note, they felt that they had a major advantage………..They had intelligence which no-one knew they had…..now they just had to stay alive long enough to use it All they needed to do was develop a plan around their strengths. They were feeling upbeat and positive…emotions and feelings which Max had almost forgotten existed.

The drive south was very revealing. Max had discovered that the key actually belonged to Chuck and it fitted a safety deposit box somewhere in the city…that was all Mary knew but she was sure of that.

The note was even more revealing and it had helped them to identity the bank to which the key belonged. Mary had

The Price of Friendship

made numerous cell phone calls to various socialite friends and associates as Max drove. Then, as Max drove and she dug out information from her extensive contacts, they managed to piece all the information together and they were able to identify the location of the bank.

As soon as she had seen the note back at her home, she recognised the pet name which her good friend Cindy had used when she to referred to her 'Sugar Daddy'...Sam Deans. This had spooked her and from that point on she knew that there was real danger.

In spite of the danger, the excitement and pulse rates had continued to rise, the further they drove and the closer and closer that they had got to some real answers to the puzzles and queries they posed themselves. Mary was amazing in the way she had pieced the information together and Max was impressed. He could never have got so close without her and he felt good about his decision to make contact. By the time they reached the hotel they were elated and excited and intellectual stimulation was transformed directly into raw sexual passion as they tumbled through the door entwined in each others arms. Max lifted her roughly up against the wall and she instantly responded ripping open his shirt as he tore at her panties forcing them to the floor. The sex was fast a furious, right there on the floor of the seedy motel room. It was passionate and very quickly over. Over almost before it had begun but it was simply amazing...there were no words to describe how she made him feel as he lay dishevelled and spent on the floor of the budget motel room somewhere in Rhode Island State.

Reality soon kicked in and they got down to the serious business of planning a trip back to Boston to check the contents of the box without being recognised and then re-group to consider their findings before getting to grips with the Sam Deans problem. It was remarkably business-like as they prepared their plan. Hard to imagine the sexual energy between them, but it was there and it was very, very real.

They had decided to remain incognito by staying in discreet motels and keeping a low profile. There was no need to check out of the one they were in and they headed for Boston the next morning engulfed by a nervous silence in the air.

Sam Deans was cruising along the same road at approximately the same time to a destination within miles of each other. The irony was lost to both parties but the time would soon come when they would be in exactly the same place at exactly the same time………..

Mary had just about managed to dress down sufficiently to be difficult to recognise. Her stunning brown hair was a very much darker shade now and it was brushed forward covering much of her face. The make up was heavy and not at all what she was used to and it would take at least a second look to recognise her. They felt that it would be best to go in together because they needed to watch each others backs. Max would have to sign to open the box because the box was obviously in Chuck's name. Max had practised the signature repeatedly and they could only hope that Chuck had chosen a bank at which he was not known, otherwise they were screwed. It seemed like a safe enough assumption and a risk which they had no choice but to take. They had parked close to the bank in Holland Street and although the car was close enough to run to if it all went wrong their escape plan was to separate and meet back at the car four hours later. No-one would recognise the non-descript rental vehicle which they had picked up along the way and four hours would give them both time to change clothes at least and also time for any commotion to settle down around the bank. Any longer they thought, would lead to the car raising more than a little attention, being parked for so long in the same place.

The nerves were taut and the tension was just short of unbearable. Max was visibly shaking and he held both hands in front of him to see the effect it was having, a tremor was obvious as if he needed reminding that it was impossible to steady them. Mary was more taken by the excitement and exhilaration of it all and she shook her head mockingly at her partner in crime as he tried to concentrate on relaxing his nervous body.

They walked into the foyer of the bank as if they were meant to be there, a brief discussion with a clerk led to them being ushered to a Manager's office where they sat waiting for the big moment. Max had managed to convince the clerk of his identity and now it was just the Manager between himself and the safety deposit box.

Again, the discussion and the identity checks were brief and carried out with the utmost courtesy and respect. Max was impressed at the false document which Mary had managed to get at such short notice and he was starting to feel a little more confident as he was shown into a room where he would be able to open the box alone. Mary could hardly hide her frustration at being left behind in the Manager's office and she tapped her foot and drummed her fingers on the desk in an open show of irritation.

Max stared at the safety deposit box. It was a long narrow insignificant metal drawer which had been withdrawn from its runners and it had a loose lid which lay on top of the drawer. A very ordinary object really yet its contents may well represent so very much. Max was almost too nervous to lift the lid almost too scared to find out the contents for fear it may be yet another disappointment. He rubbed his hands together and flexed his fingers like a safe breaker preparing to open an impenetrable safe. He let out a long slow blow of air and relaxed his shoulders as he concentrated once again on the inanimate object which lay before him. He flipped open the lid of the box…...

Before him, lay an array of the most impressive, glittering diamonds he had ever seen. They were in two layers, each diamond nestling in an individual impression like huge egg box. Each layer of diamonds was cushioned by a soft black cloth which lined the box like a dark mysterious shroud. There were at least three huge magnificently cut gems instantly visible on the top row, sparkling and twinkling in the low light and they were surrounded by at least 20 other gems, each just as brilliant and as stunning as the other. Unlike the rough cut diamond which was stolen from him previously, these were perfectly cut and prepared. They looked spectacular. Max was awe struck by what lay before him and when he finally allowed himself to breath….he let out a long slow breath as he gaped at the vision before him, entranced by the sheer majesty of the diamonds. He gently removed the top layer to reveal yet another just as stupendous. He placed the two 'egg boxes' side by side on the wooden table and stood back to admire his work.

The temptation to touch was overwhelming and he ran a finger over the top of the gems touching each one gently and with the reverence they deserved. He tried to fully appreciate their stunning beauty as he stroked and turned them, one then the other until he had made contact with all 48 diamonds. He knew a little about precious gems and he knew enough about the 4 C's, Carat weight, Colour, Cut and Clarity to know that these diamonds were excellent quality. It was impossible to tell with any certainty at first sight but they 'seemed' incredible.

They looked colourless and flawless to the naked eye and they all looked to be 'round' and 'brilliant' which suggested a collection purely for investment.

That is of course assuming that they are genuine!! He couldn't even contemplate that option, they had to be real…. they just had to be.

Max nervously pressed the buzzer to raise the attention of the Manager who was standing outside the door of the small security room. He walked in and Max asked for a small container or box which he could use to take the contents of his box away. The Manager frowned and peered at the safety deposit box trying to decide what kind of container to choose. He checked that his customer was actually asking for a container big enough to contain the entire contents of the safety deposit box and when Max answered in the affirmative, his frown deepened and as he turned to leave the room he brought Max's attention to the document wallet which was attached to the rear of the safety deposit box.

Each time the box was opened a signature had to be added to a list on the outside of the wallet and inside the wallet would be any documents which related to the contents of the box and a record of transactions.

Max could hardly draw his attention away from the glittering gems. Eventually, he did so and when he emptied the contents of the wallet onto the table, one eye still on the diamonds, he revealed a number of formal documents relating to the diamonds and as Max read the details his jaw began to drop in amazement with each document he read.

The Manager had left the room to look for a container and Max had locked the door from the inside as he concentrated on the documents. The authenticity of each individual diamond was proven with each report he read. Every diamond was genuine. The very last document he came across was a gemmological appraisers report summarising the value of each diamond.

It is a popular misconception that diamonds are valuable because they are rare. It is a fact that there are enough diamonds in the world to fill a cupful for every man, woman, and child in the planet. The reason they are so expensive is because strict controls are placed on the quantity of diamonds produced for sale worldwide. Well, either the strict controls had been circumvented or the person who gathered this collection together had done so over a very long period of time which was highly unlikely.

The value of the diamonds which were laid out in front of Max Reynolds was a few cents short of $50 million.

Max carried the aluminium container carefully out of the security room towards the Manager's Office and took a deep breath as he prepared to enter. He hadn't had a great deal of time to consider what to say to Mary or rather how to tell her what was in the deposit box. It was way beyond her expectations he was sure of that. They had talked endlessly about what might and might not be in the box and what they would do in each eventuality. They had concluded that it was useless to speculate and anyway the main objective had been to recover the contents in order to gain an advantage over Sam Deans.

Each speculation had led to so many alternative solutions and actions that the pointlessness of the exercise had been demoralising and began to detract their attention from the matter in hand.

Max eased open the office door and as soon as he entered Mary stood in surprise and walked over to the door to meet him. She was faced by a beaming smile and she realised instantly that the news was good.

They left the bank the same way they arrived, unhindered and like a perfectly normal couple. They had of course declined the Manager's offer to arrange some security at least to their vehicle.

Max and Mary strolled as casually as they could through the streets of Boston carrying $50m of diamonds........it was unbelievable yet it was very true and very real to them both.

It was impossible to walk; they were virtually running like two school children who had raided the candy store and trying to escape without raising attention. They bumped into each other as they walked and stumbled on nothing at all until they reached the car.

Max's grip on the handles of the box was so tight that his knuckles had turned white. They had made the four blocks in seconds and were suddenly sitting in the car, staring at each other.

'Well what the hell have you got there......what was in the box. Tell me...why are you holding out on me? Now Max tell me NOW!!' Mary's patience had just expired.

Max was still staring and he simply said, Drive Mary! Let's go I will tell you as we drive'

'No ways my friend absolutely no way...you tell me now!'

It was incredulous to think that they were arguing, exposed to the whole world and *fucking* arguing.

Max's voice calmed a little,

'Mary, would you kindly start the engine and drive us and our 50 million dollars worth of diamonds out of here, before we attract attention'

'Diamonds??.... What the…'

Suddenly it dawned on her what he had said…

'Whoa!!' She screamed 'Whoa!! Lets hit the road…..'

Mary fired up the rental car and headed out of town.

The Ford Explorer pulled away just behind in quiet and discreet pursuit.

Chapter 19

As Sam Deans walked into the opulent and exotic reception area of his Boston Office he was converged upon by people with messages and documents to sign and all had adoring smiles. He loved the attention and insisted on being revered as the boss. It was a power trip for Sam Deans, the whole thing. He adored the power and the wealth and also the autonomy to be able to affect people's lives …..for better or worse but more than anything, he enjoyed the notoriety and adoration whether it was true or false, it mattered not to Sam Deans as long as it was obvious.

His loyal 'subjects' were already assembled as he would have expected and he was greeted at the door to the pretentious boardroom with a cup of black coffee, one sugar and a copy of USA today. Mr Deans was also big on routine and ritual, as long as he was the centre of attention all was well with the world.

Charlie 'C' set out the outline of the offer from Botha and everyone waited for a response from Deans before they dare make an observation.

'I want the dealership but I am not keen on the terms…too much for them and not enough for us, an obvious first offer and one which I find just a little disrespectful at best. I will get the Kruger set of diamonds anyway, of that I am confident, no need to worry on that score, but the dealership we need to play hardball right away…....Charlie?'

'Yes Boss, I will get right on it.'

'No you fool!' Shouted Deans

'Don't just humour me…I am asking what's your take on the offer?

Of course, humouring and obeying Sam Deans was just what he wanted, but he did enjoy watching what people did when they think that they had a say in proceedings….just a bit of fun, but sometimes it proved to be very revealing.

Charlie knew the rules to this game well enough and replied as expected. He was a survivor and he suspected that Sam was after someone else today. After he had summarised the offer in another way adding just the things that he knew Deans wanted to hear and then took a seat to watch the show.

'OK, Charlie I like the counter offer idea and I also think we should lean on Mr Botha's people to see how far they might go with this. Can we get directly to the diamonds without going through this South African imbecile?? Err…. Mac! What say you to that suggestion?

Deans pointed at Mac who was sitting directly opposite him, across the large oval meeting table.

It all went quiet as the assembled suddenly realised something was wrong. This was completely out of character and the tone of Deans' voice had completely changed the atmosphere in the room.

A fearful, anxious hush descended on the room patting each of the men assembled firmly on the shoulder as it formed a metaphorical cloud above the proceedings. Apart from the sound of nervous feet shuffling beneath the huge table and eventually, the uneasy sound of Mac clearing his throat squirming in his chair, there was silence.

'Don't even think about it Mac!' Sam Deans voice boomed across the room smashing the silence of the room into small pieces.

'Don't you dare try to make an excuse…I know!!'

The atmosphere in the room changed and it was obvious to all. Sam continued his verbal assault.

'Our esteemed colleague, Mr McDonald has been very foolish'

The uneasiness and unadulterated fear of 'Mac' McDonald, who knew better than to object or protest, cast a shadow over the proceedings. He just hoped and prayed for some small mercy from Deans and from his peers around the table.

'As we all know he was assigned to stay close to Mr Reynolds and he proceeded to lose him time and time again. A professional indiscretion you might think BUT my friends….. there is more. When he did catch up with Mr Reynolds he eventually decided to think outside the proverbial box and steal the very thing he was supposed to be protecting……maybe his intentions were good maybe he just wanted the stash for himself. Who knows….well I do! Sheer fucking stupidity!'

'The goods which he took were fake and useless to anyone outside the sting…….the very reason they were planted was a ruse to bring Max Reynolds and the real treasure to me'

'I only tell you this to make the very serious point that I have reasons for everything I ask you to do for the organisation and you have no place in my team if you want to know or believe you have the right to question those decisions'

Deans stood up and wagged an accusing finger in the direction of McDonald.

'This is precisely why I demand obedience. It's so easy… just follow the instructions and don't ask questions unless you are asked to do so. I am the only one who knows the whole picture…I make the fucking picture for God's sake!!! All I ask is obedience and loyalty!'

The veins in Deans' neck were standing proud as he yelled across the table. He looked into the eyes of every man around the table one by one. He held his stare just long enough to hit the message home before he moved onto the next man. They all knew that this was bad, very bad indeed. None of the men knew exactly what Deans was talking about….they knew little about the whole picture and it was so out of character for Deans to reveal so much and so publicly to the whole room. They were all a little confused and didn't want to know any more. Knowledge may well be synonymous with power, but knowing too much can upset the delicate balance of power in the world of organised crime which can only lead to big trouble.

'I have no intention of putting you all at risk by explaining the *rest* of my plan'

There were sighs of relief from around the room and Deans started to walk the long way around the table to where he had been pointing. He continued to talk as he walked round the table and although they were all expecting it to happen there was still an intake of shocked communal breath as Deans grabbed Mac and dragged him to the floor. He was standing over him with one foot pressing down on his throat. As Mac struggled to catch his breath Deans reached out his hand and a selection of weapons were presented and offered up for him to take.

He had a choice of hand guns, knives and even a baseball bat to choose from and amazingly, he chose none of these offerings and simply stooped down next to his ex colleague, placed both hands around his throat and began to strangle him with his own bare hands…..he squeezed and groaned until Mac could stand the pressure no more….Mac was dead in a matter of a few minutes which seemed like much, much longer. Sam Deans was panting from using up so much energy. He returned to his seat as if nothing had happened. His face was still red and flushed but his expression was filled with exhilaration rather than remorse, his body language was as frightening as his actions

The Price of Friendship

as he clapped his hands together just once to attract everyone's attention...then said.

'So! Let's get down to business!

Deans looked around the room and settled his stare on one man.

'George!' He called

He pointed at George Meredith who was a diminutive man with greased down hair and a small thin moustache. Meredith looked less like a thug and more like an academic than his colleagues and he sat bolt upright, trying to make the most of his small stature.

'Yes Boss, what can I do for you Boss' His small, un-rimmed glasses had slipped to the end of his nose like a professor who had been reading for hours and he pushed them forcefully back up to the bridge of his nose. He finally settled his eyes on the stare of Sam Deans after risking an involuntary glance around the room checking the reaction of his colleagues to his being summoned by the Boss.

'You will be taking over Mac's clients, his men and his position in the organisation'

There was a ripple of noise and everyone could sense the shock and discontent in the air.

'Please stay after the meeting and we will make the necessary arrangements'

It was incredulous to think that this was actually going to happen. Mac had been a fearsome character and everyone would expect him to be replaced by a man of similar stature in the circles in which he operated. George Meredith was a far more 'back room' guy. He didn't relish the limelight and he was in the group mainly for his financial contacts, IT skills and his high intellect. His contribution was invaluable but no-one had ever seen him as a leader of a team. All they could conclude was that, as normal......Sam must have a plan.....

The meeting between Deans and Meredith was short and sweet and at the end of it Meredith knew exactly why he had been chosen and what he had to do to achieve fortune beyond his wildest dreams.

George Meredith had been a loyal and reasonably contented man and now he was virtually skipping out of the building, into his very conservative vehicle and off he went…to the first day of work in his new job. He felt the old George was being left behind and a new beginning was upon him.

Sam Deans wasn't far behind him and although he was heading in a different direction to Meredith, they were as one in their mission…to make sure that the deal with Johan Botha did NOT go ahead.

The remainder of the senior membership of the Sam Deans organisation scattered in various directions. No wiser than before they had assembled except that they were one less in their numbers and they had been shown yet another example of what happens when a person crosses Sam Deans. There was no compromise and no way out but the rewards were immense if you managed to stay alive long enough to enjoy them.

There were so many comparisons to be drawn between Sam Deans and Johan Botha. Both knew how to be successful in a very challenging world of crime. Both had a very ruthless streak which enabled them to operate and run their respective organisations with a combination of fear and unquestioned loyalty.

It had been inevitable from the time that a share of the worlds diamond market had brought their worlds together that the two world renowned crime Lords, were about to clash.

Chapter 20

Many people had tried to describe the exhilaration and excitement directly associated with just finding out that you had become immensely rich but few have succeeded. Max stuttered and spluttered his way to an explanation as Mary drove through the western suburbs of Boston, taking an unusual but pre-planned route to Interstate four ninety five outer ring road. Mary was much more calm and composed as she negotiated the afternoon traffic staying no more than five miles per hour above the speed limit. Under the circumstances there was no need to attract the attention of the traffic cops. Max was once again impressed with Mary's powers of restraint but this time he failed to keep his observations to himself.

'Did you hear me Mary?? We have in our possession, forty eight perfect diamonds worth fifty freakin' million!!!' No response

Mary heard exactly what he said. She had heard it the first and the second time and every time since they had got in the car. All she wanted to do was get somewhere safe…quickly and in one piece and *then* she could at least look at the freakin' diamonds.

'Yes, Max I heard you….just calm down and shut the hell up! Let me concentrate on driving!!'

Max was taken by surprise, but she was right, of course she was, he hugged the aluminium clad treasure close to his chest and sat back in his seat.

Eventually they rounded the curve leading into the Centenary Road which would finally take them to the sanctuary of the motel.

The explorer took the same curve and found a discreet parking spot at the rear of the motel and waited. He radioed to a second car which pulled up at the front of the hotel watching the main doors. There was no way that anyone could afford to make another mistake.

The driver of the second car was George Meredith.

Max and Mary were in the room almost before the motor had stopped running as they raced along the motel corridor and disappeared into Room 1251.

Mary was captivated by the extraordinary beauty of the diamonds as they lay twinkling and sparkling at her from within the aluminium case. What splendour and perfection she whispered to herself, how absolutely perfect they are.

She couldn't hold back a second gasp of delight at what she saw and a tear trickled down her cheek as she began to cry very quietly and very sweetly more like a whimper than a cry. Max lightly placed an arm around her and very gently pulled her close to him. They both stared in wonder at the diamonds and it was obvious that this was the most amazing sight they had ever seen. They sat down together and Max pulled out the appraisers report just to make sure he had seen what he thought he had.

Mary was quiet and thoughtful as Max re-read the documents, this time giving them the attention they deserved. She wanted to speak but whatever she said would come out wrong, she knew that. She turned to look at Max and he could see the sadness in her eyes, the amazing eyes which normally lit up such a perfect face were without their normal splendour. Max was captivated by the change which had overcome Mary's face, the beauty was still there of course but the high cheek bones seemed a little less high and her gorgeous skin tone had just slightly less glowing, there was such a sadness in her eyes.

Mary took one last look at the diamonds and then she bolted into the bathroom just as the tears started to flow in earnest. Her reaction came as a complete surprise to Max and he called after her,

'Mary! What's the matter?'

The bathroom door closed heavily behind her and Max got no reply. Mary flushed the toilet to cover the sound of her crying but Max could still hear the sobs and cries and he could visualise her sitting on the bathroom floor, back to the door with her head in her hands.

'Mary, I don't understand, what's wrong…?'

It was a long time before Mary emerged from the bathroom. She had showered and freshened up and burst into the room with a beaming smile. The eyes were still a little sad but Max was pleased to see her sprightly and upbeat. He hugged her close and stroked her hair, she responded by kissing him very warmly on the lips and holding him tightly.

Mary eventually pulled away from the embrace and backed away to the small table taking Max by the hand and asking him to take a seat next to her. As they sat, she started to explain,

'I had no idea what was in the box but I did know it had to be something very special. I was overwhelmed and yet it brought back the memories of Chuck's death and………'

'It's OK Mary' interjected Max

'Its fine…really…Its been a lot for us both to take in…we just need to chill for a while and then we can talk about what we should do next'

'Max…It's not that simple, there are things we need to talk about, personal things which…..'

'It is exactly that simple' Insisted Max

All we need to concern ourselves with is what to do with these beauties. It's all that matters, for the moment at least.' Max was no longer listening to Mary. He was concentrating on the next step and what it meant to have the diamonds in his possession, and how he was going to use this new found advantage and…..

Mary looked away from him and tried to hold back the tears. There was something very important to tell him and he just wasn't listening, another time maybe, she thought to herself. The moment had gone and she would have to wait for another opportunity and it had to be soon.

Max had stood up and he was pacing around the room, thinking out loud. His tone was thoughtful and contemplative. He truly believed that he had the advantage now that they had the diamonds. He was becoming more and more convinced that they had the bargaining high ground but he had no idea what to do with it, how to use it. He was trying to go through all the options and as he slowly paced around the room carefully considering the options out loud, he was unaware that Mary had left the room. She strolled just a few yards in front of the row of motel rooms pausing beneath a huge majestic tree to light a cigarette. If Max could see her expression and look into her eyes, he would see a much different persona to the one he was growing to love. This was the face and the expression of a much different person. There was a little more coldness in the eyes and a look of resignation in the sad yet cynical smile. It was impossible to clearly identify what was going through her mind just at that time but if Max could see the expression he would have every reason to be concerned. Mary Moore looked like a very confused lady who was trying to come to terms with a course of action which she had no choice but to take.

Mary carefully tapped a text message into her cell phone and took a long hard puff on her cigarette as she awaited a reply. The reply was swift and she had a look of relief tinged with sadness in her eyes as she stamped out the cigarette into the damp ground and inched her way back towards the motel room door one very slow pensive and deliberate step at a time.

The Price of Friendship

She soon found herself staring down at the ground just outside the door, composing herself before she entered.

Max was sitting studiously at the small occasional table, he was writing a list of some sort and as Mary entered the room he was surprised to see that she had even left.

'Is everything OK? You should be careful going outside, showing yourself like that we may be being followed.

'Come over here would you; tell me what you think of this for a plan'

Mary approached the table grudgingly, hardly wanting to look Max in the eyes for fear of revealing any sign of what was racing through her mind like a speeding train. She was finding it hard to contain herself as she prepared to sit beside him putting her arm carefully and delicately onto his shoulder as she lowered herself into the small functional chair. It could be anyone who had just sat down next to Max he was completely absorbed in the development of his plan, he didn't even look at Mary he just directed her attention to the written explanation of what he thought they should do with a wave of his hand he sat back in the chair apparently satisfied with his work.

'I think we should find a secure place for the diamonds, maybe a safety deposit box of our own and take the authenticity documents only on our trip to see Deans..'.

Why do we even need to go to Deans, we just run.....just take the diamonds and run?? Interjected Mary. It was a strange thing to say, she even had to admit that to herself, an empty gesture at best, but as the words came out of her mouth, at that very moment, she really, genuinely meant them. If only things were different.

'But they will never leave us alone? We need to secure our safety.....I reckon we could trade some of the diamonds for our 'release' and keep the rest. You know they will never stop looking for us Mary we need to do a deal'

Mary was looking out of the window, anywhere but into Max's eyes. She was neither, agreeing or disagreeing with his idea. It was immaterial anyway she thought, it just didn't matter because soon it would be over…she felt like she had sold her soul but now she just wanted it to be over, she pleaded under her breath to anyone who was listening.

'Mary! Mary! Are you OK? You seemed miles away then…' Called Max

Although he spoke quite softly he startled her and she began to cry, quite involuntarily but once she started she was soon into a full scale weep. Max was simply confused. He had no idea what had gotten into Mary and couldn't seem to get through to her. He reached across the table and hugged her tight, there was something very vulnerable about her now, that self confidence and assuredness was in tatters as she wept on his shoulder and all the emotion and pent up frustration came flooding out.

Suddenly and without warning the door came crashing open.

They instinctively pulled each other closer as they fell to the floor screaming as one still in a tight embrace. As they hit the floor they protected each other by wrapping their arms around the other's head. It all happened so quickly that they had no chance to see the masked man who had charged into the room and was making his way directly to the diamonds, which were still inside the case but the case was exposed, almost asking to be plucked from the surface of the table. The thief went directly to the case as if he knew where he was going and what he was looking for. He swept the case from the table and turned quickly and efficiently back towards the door he had just slammed open, climbing over Max and Mary who were lying statue-like and motionless on the floor.

He spun out of the door, clutching the case closely to him and pointing a hand gun directly out in front of him as he lurched towards his car which was parked directly outside the motel room.

The Price of Friendship

Max sprang to life and dumping Mary from his arms, he lunged for the door and when he saw the man just getting into the car, he leapt towards the car door in an attempt to stop him from escaping.

He heard a gun shot which appeared to come from somewhere to his left and he dived to the ground to avoid being shot. His hit the gravel surface of the ground very hard and he could feel the sharp stones digging into his skin through the light material of his thin cotton shirt. In a split second he found himself lying against the front wheel of the car and looking up he saw a car screaming away from them and out of the parking lot. Through the confusion and shock he could sense that the danger had passed and he risked picking himself and as he knelt against the car, he could see the thief slumped against the steering wheel of the car. There was a huge hole in the side of his head and blood from the open wound had splattered onto the roof on the car, all over the seat and there was a large splatter of fresh, scarlet, shimmering blood on the inside surface of the windshield.

Max spun around in the parking lot, looking for the other car, but all he could see now was a cloud of dust where it had been. He spun back around to see the case containing the diamonds lying on the floor, unopened and undamaged. It was like an extract from a dream…a nightmare which lasted only a few seconds….what had just happened?

Max carefully collected up the case brushing it down and cleaning it off as he backed away from the car, the dead body and the evidence of what had just happened.

He walked slowly back into the motel room to see Mary still lying face down on the floor arms still covering her head. He stooped down and as he got closer he could hear her crying softly and submissively to herself, no movement just a quiet whimpering noise coming from the bundle of arms and head rigid with fear.

He placed his arm on her shoulder and nudged her very gently and carefully but sufficiently hard to bring her out of her frightened trance. It seemed to have no effect and she remained very still and if anything, she began to cry a little more loudly.

He nervously called her name softly at first and then a second time a little more urgently,

'Mary…MARY! Its Ok…they're gone…It's over'

He got an instant and unexpected reaction as Mary rolled over and sat up in the same motion staring at him in complete shock, her eyes wide and surprised.

Max was taken aback and physically startled by the response and although his mind leapt to the conclusion that she had snapped out of the trance like state she was in his instincts told him otherwise.

'Mary. Its me…Max…what's going on are you OK?'

She threw her arms around him and began sobbing, avoiding eye contact and holding him just a little too tightly. Max was perplexed and bemused by this reaction and as she clung tight to him he knew that something wasn't right.

He gently eased her away and held her at arms length but still she cried and avoided his stare, looking away from him and down to the ground.

'What the hell is going on Mary…Do you know something!!!'

His voice had an edge of panic to it and he tried to turn her head to face him before she answered.

'Mary!!'

This time, a little louder and more forceful.

'Oh! Max I am so sorry I don't understand…I just don't understand…'

The tears were streaming down her face streaking black eye make-up down her beautiful skin. The tears were very real and she was visibly shaken and shocked.

Max closed the room door leaving the outside world behind and positioned Mary on a chair facing him as he stooped down in front of her. He looked into her swollen eyes and wiped away the tears with his sleeve. Mary was staring at the diamonds case and shaking.

How could she even try to explain the lies and the betrayal to this sweet, sweet man? How could she even begin to tell him about the plan which was supposed to have taken the diamonds from them?

Her thoughts and reflections were racing through her mind as she prepared her brain to put them into words, but they never settled long enough in her conscious mind to be converted into words because of what her eyes were seeing.....They were still here! The diamonds were still there...They were supposed to be gone, no-one was meant to get hurt and the diamonds were supposed to be gone.....

Max grabbed Mary by the shoulders and shook her with just enough vigour to get her attention.

'Mary! Listen to me....a man has been shot right outside our motel room, there *will* be people coming to find out what happened. I have no idea what just happened, but...what I do know is... that we need to get out of here and fast....'

Max started to throw clothes into bags and collect up their things, Mary sat motionless staring at the diamonds and only when Max grabbed the aluminium case, did she snap out of her trance

'Are you coming? Or are you staying?

They fled from the motel room and as they ran to their car they noticed motel room doors cracking open as people risked a look outside, obviously thinking it may be safe to venture outside.

Max shielded Mary's eyes from the sight of the dead man slumped across the front seats of the red Chevy as they ran past it and as they screeched out of the parking lot and into the night, it was already becoming a distant memory.

They drove for some miles before either one of them spoke. Max was staring straight out in front of them, his eyes transfixed onto the road and Mary was looking out of the side window, following each passing car with her eyes hoping to find the courage to speak and tell Max what was supposed to have just happened.

'The main thing is that we are both still alive in one piece and we still have the diamonds' Max made the first attempt at conversation and after his opening statement he waited for a reply. But none came.

'I can only guess at what might have happened back there' he continued ' It makes no sense and I know that you know more than you are saying. Hell! You gotta know more than you are saying!!!'

Mary recognised the token attempt at humour and she humped her shoulders in recognition. She closed her eyes tight preparing to speak, preparing to tell all when just as she had gathered the courage she felt Max's hand on her thigh. Max could sense that she was really struggling, that she couldn't summon the courage to tell him yet and he provided her a lifeline.

'Leave it Mary.......lets just leave it for now. Answer me one question…'

Mary tensed and prepared for the interrogation…

I know what went down wasn't what you expected, so maybe we are both in the same place now…maybe we are both being taken for a ride and all I need to know is ….

They rounded a curve a little too quickly and as Max righted the car they both shook from side to side in response to the shift of the car. Mary grabbed for his hand and as the car settled down he could feel her squeezing his hand for all she was worth.

He forced her hand away from his as he continued…

'All I need to know is, Are you with me or against me?

I need an honest answer and I need to know now'

Mary steeled herself for the answer and dug deep for the courage to say,

'I though I could take the diamonds. I thought I could trick you without hurting either of us'

She sniffled and tried to hold back the tears

'I had my reasons and although I don't expect you to understand, it would also make you free from this curse that has haunted me for so many years'

She was grabbing for his hand and her voice was harsh yet pleading.

Max tried desperately not to show it but, he was seething with anger. He gripped the wheel so tightly that the veins stood out on both hands and his entire body started to twitch from the strain of his muscles tensing.

Now she was on a roll,

'I arranged for the thief to come and take the diamonds, but I swear no-one was to get hurt and it was not for me it was for......'

'But it all went wrong.....I have no clue why he was shot or who shot him or....how would anyone know what I was planning...It makes no sense Max I have no idea.....'

'I can't believe you would do it Mary....after everything we have....What next eh? What the hell next?'

Max was shouting and his angry voice reverberated around the inside of the car.

Mary covered her ears and shouted back at him.

'Stop it Max.....I can't think...let me finish...Stop shouting!' She screamed 'I have to tell you why!!!!'

Max swerved the car aggressively off the freeway, almost missing the off-ramp and skidded along the damp road braking quickly, he brought the car to rest in the middle of small side road alongside the freeway. He turned angrily to look at her, banging both hands down on the wheel,

'Just pull over somewhere safe and I promise I will explain... everything...' Mary was strangely calm and submissive as she gestured towards a gas station, pleadingly.

Max pulled into the gas station and parked outside the convenience store next door. He turned off the engine and turned to look her directly in the eyes expectantly and there was a nervous quiver of anger on his lips

'Well? Go ahead, lets hear it. Another lie I suppose. The whole 'us' thing was a lie also!!!!!'

Mary reached forward towards him but Max arched away from her like a cornered animal, not quite ready to submit or pounce in retaliation. He had recovered the case of diamonds from the floor of the car and was gripping them tightly on his lap as he waited for the miraculous explanation.

The vehicle which was following them almost missed the turn off from the freeway but had eventually found them and the black Ford Explorer rolled quietly past the gas station and took a position close enough to see but not too close to be seen.

Mary explained the dilemma in which she found herself as clearly and concisely as she could in the circumstances. She was anxious and uneasy but still managed to articulate her reasoning in a way which seemed to placate Max just enough to calm his mood…slightly.

Max was still waiting for the 'big reason' why she would plan to mislead him so blatantly, for so long. She had explained what had happened and how she had planned it, she had tried to justify her actions as a way of getting them both off the hook but how did it all fit into the Botha, Deans and DuPreez triangle? It was almost understandable if she wanted to run with the diamonds but she insisted that this was not the case… It still made no sense but Max was becoming more and more accepting of the fact that she was as confused as he as to what had happened outside the motel.

It was only when she showed him the photograph which she produced from her purse, that Max was forced to take a sharp intake of breath. The colour drained form his face and he stared at the photograph for several seconds in sheer amazement before plunged his head deep into the relative sanctuary of his hands, while he a deep controlled breath to alleviate the pain of the cold hand which was crushing his heart.

The helpless young eyes which looked back at him from the photograph were a younger version of Mary's. They were sad and scared and full of panic. The gag around the small, beautiful mouth was pulled tight and the sickening sight of a gun barrel being pressed hard against the tender cheek of such a vulnerable face brought instant tears to the eyes. There was no place for a small child in this picture. One so weak and defenceless should never be exposed to the sheer terror of the man who was on the other end of the gun barrel…..Sam Deans' face stared back at Max as if he knew that their eyes would meet in exactly this way at some time. The vitriolic sneer across Deans' face completed the vision of repulsion and horror and the fat cigar drooping from the corner of his mouth just seemed to add insult to injury.

Mary had broken down into a shivering wreck. She was staring to the heavens and banged the side of her head with clenched fists in a fit of frustration and iniquitous rage. Max grabbed her arms and pulled her towards him. He was feeling physically sick and the tears were welling up in his eyes. They held each other close weeping as one, tied together in a desperate embrace.

Once again in this twisting, turning ordeal for Max Reynolds, a simple photograph had changed everything.

Chapter 21

George Meredith was making a cell phone call to Sam Deans and the news was good. They were both confident that the matter in hand was under control. .Meredith was less than one hundred yards away from the diamonds and he believed he had all the angles covered. He had a second driver in a second car standing by who was patched into his cell phone waiting for instructions. There was one more task to perform before the situation was as under control as he had made Deans believe. He needed to get one step ahead of his prey. He was getting increasingly frustrated with the cat and mouse game which Deans had insisted upon.

'I want them to come to me….. unharmed and of their own accord', was the specific instruction

Deans must have his reasons but it seemed like such nonsense to Meredith. He was struggling to contain his rebellious nature and his preference to simply pull them in, wrap them up and deliver them on a platter to his boss. He knew as well anyone that this course of action was simply not an option and he would honour his task to the letter, come-what-may. He was also not prepared to fail and for this reason he had to know what they were thinking and what they were about to do *before* they acted.

Meredith had to be absolutely sure nothing could go wrong and he would not rest until he had made his delivery......it was as simple as that so there was no room for error or misjudgement. If he needed more information to make sure he would damn well have to find a way to get it.

It seemed like an age before Max and Mary finally broke away from each other. Each had been comforting the other and neither wanted the simple act of hugging to end. Eventually it had to and Max had to start thinking quickly and clearly. It was obvious that they needed to get the diamonds to Deans to save Mary's daughter. It was equally obvious that they were only safe as long as they had the diamonds. It seemed impossible and Max could see no obvious way out of this mess other than to head for the inevitable confrontation with Sam Deans. The rules had changed and so had the priorities. They needed to rest for few short hours and then they would confront the man who held all the cards.

Max was too nervous to check into a hotel and he urged Mary to try and get some sleep in the car. She was completely drained and burned out from the emotional roller coaster which had been her life for as many hours as she could remember. Max reclined the seat back for her and carefully covered her with his jacket. Mary cried herself to sleep within minutes. Max slowly drove the car around the back of the store and turned out all the lights as he prepared for a long night and as the role of protector.

It was a routine task for such an experienced individual. Even in the dark and on hands and knees it was easy to attach the position transducer to the underside of the rental car without being seen. The difficulty would be to find a way to be able to hear what they were saying as well as know where they were going. Meredith's man tried to open the trunk of the car without making any noise. He had done it many times and under many difficult circumstances. It was imperative that the recording device was situated inside the vehicle. Ideally inside the passenger compartment but inside the trunk would suffice under the circumstances, they would be able to hear what was being said, maybe not as clearly as they would like but the man crawling under the car didn't care a bit, he had a job to do and he would place the device wherever he could and report back.

The trunk lid make the slightest 'click' as it freed itself from the constraint of the key lock. The man froze for a second, just making sure he hadn't been made before continuing. Deftly and expertly he attached the magnetic device to the rear bulkhead of the trunk compartment and covered it with the vehicle lining.

Max had heard the 'click' but decided not to move in response. He would wait it out, hoping and praying that it was nothing but knowing in his heart that he was wrong. He knew the noise was coming from the rear of the car and he steeled himself for something to happen. Nothing did happen except for a second 'click' and then silence. Max switched the interior light switch to the off position so that it wouldn't illuminate when he opened the door and he shuffled his feet into a position from which he could ease out of the car with minimum effort and noise. He adjusted the mirror and as he checked outside he could just see a shape crawling away from the car. What the......? Shit!! Maybe he had frightened the man away and maybe he had planted something on the car...shit! Maybe it was a bomb!!!

Max got control of his 'mini' panic and decided to just sit tight. If there was a bomb he was probably dead anyway!!! If he tried to leave the car would it help? He doubted it somehow and it was much more likely that they were being followed and if this was the case he could maybe make use of the information as long as he didn't let them know he knew. He settled down and prayed quietly that the 'bomb' theory was wrong. The next few hours were very nervy and Max twitched and craned his neck at every, slightest noise. By the time it got light he was completely exhausted.

Mary awoke from her uncomfortable sleep and stretched out on the seat rubbing her face and neck as she stretched. Max watched as she uncoiled slowly and exotically into the stunning beauty that she was. He couldn't help smiling for a split second at the predicament they found themselves in......at that very moment there was only the two of them and they were relying on each other to stay alive and he kinda liked that, they were joining forces to protect the most precious thing in Mary's life.

Chapter 22

Sam Deans had been waiting for the call from his South African counterpart and he had been waiting patiently for some time to speak directly to him. A number of deadlines had passed and the two heavyweights were bound to come in contact with each other sooner or later, it was the only way to really know whether the deal was worth the effort. The bigger the deal, the higher up the pecking order it was elevated. Both men relied on their underlings for much of the day to day stuff but now and again it was necessary for a negotiation to go straight to the top of the organisation, and as they say, Privates can never get audiences with Generals. So the generals were to meet at last.

Deans was polite and relaxed as he explained that the terms of the deal would certainly seem to be unacceptable but he was willing to discuss some alternatives. He knew that the alternatives would be in his favour and he would make sure that there was little room for his opponent to manoeuvre.

Botha seemed much more agitated and his manner was curt and typically South African. It was a fact of life that those who professed to be superior to their peers couldn't hide the arrogance in their voice and certainly not in their eyes. Deans was looking forward to the meeting with great anticipation, he loved a tough opponent and he prided himself on the fact that he excelled in the skills of negotiation and when negotiation couldn't settle a deal he had the ruthless streak to be able to seek, shall we say, alternative ways of settling a disagreement. In fact he was a little surprised that the South African was happy to travel so far for nothing. He allowed himself a chuckle at the thought. Deans was confident that he could bring this to a suitable conclusion with the minimum of effort, after all he did have the upper hand…the diamonds were already on the way to him so all he needed to arrange was the terms of the distribution agreement…simple…like shelling peas. He laughed to himself as he made a note in his diary…… marking down the day and time that he would finally meet his new partner.

Deans couldn't believe his luck that the Botha entourage was travelling to Boston for the meeting, not unknown but very unusual for a person such as he to agree to meet outside their own patch and this was an indication to Deans that he was indeed in the driving seat. It was also a little unnerving. It could be considered a very bold and brave declaration by Botha. He had demonstrated no fear and he was certainly no fool so Deans did have a certain trepidation about the reasoning behind Botha's agreement to travel. The meeting would be held in a conference room at the Red Sox Baseball Ground.

However, it had to happen somewhere and it sure was better for that 'somewhere' to be in his own back yard than that of the other guy……….

Botha travelled from Johannesburg via the office in London where he de-briefed with his team of advisers and collected a number of associates together to join him on the second leg of his trip to Boston. There was little time to pontificate or present any alternatives to the big mans strategy and everyone realised that this would be futile anyway. If there was any risk, Botha would have covered it somewhere in his plan if there was even the slightest chance of coming second out of the deal, he would have that covered also. They agreed with all and any suggestion for the sake of harmony and they all knew the role they had to play in the negotiation. It was just simpler that way and also much safer.

Deans felt so confident that he planned an evening of celebration with a select few friends and he wasn't ashamed to let the whole town know. He wasn't at all sure that Mnr. Botha would be staying for the festivities. His arrogance and confidence was intoxicating for all those around him and there was a sinister buzz about Sam Deans which created an air of excitement. The scene was set and he was ready and waiting to become even more wealthy. Sam Deans had ceased to be attracted by wealth but he never looked a gift horse in the mouth. Oh No! Sam Deans was motivated by power, status and recognition and he was driven by the exaltation which comes from shouting 'Look at me!' from the highest rooftop. No-one could ever accuse him of humility or subtlety…not Sam Deans.

Johan Botha was also in a confident and positive mood as he relaxed in the back of the limousine on the way from the airport to the hotel. The weather was good for the time of year and the traffic was unusually light. He had travelled business class on the transatlantic crossing from London and he felt fresh and bright as he looked out of the smoked glass windows of the large vehicle at the busy Boston streets. His entourage of associates were less comfortable having travelled in coach class but they were still ever grateful and fully prepared for the next few days. There was an air of excitement and anticipation circling the entire party and they seemed focused yet relaxed about the whole ordeal. It was a good day and they all carried a feeling of impending success.

Chapter 23

Max Reynolds and Mary Morris had spent what seemed like many hours debating and deliberating over their next move and they had decided to make a special delivery to a certain person and although they were tired and nervous, they were in a very determined mood. They were a little dishevelled and uncomfortable after spending the night under less than ideal sleeping conditions and it was certainly necessary to make a stop soon to use the bathroom and freshen up for the considerable ordeal which was facing them.

After a brief refreshment and bathroom stop, their purposeful journey continued towards the town of Newport, Rhode Island.

As Max drove the rental car south from the city, Mary fixed her gaze on the road ahead, a mental picture of her precious daughter securely positioned in her minds eye. Her stare was stern and her mood could only be described as controlled anger. They had a plan and it had to work……it just had to. The diamonds had become currency rather than the prize and Mary felt a little closer to her daughter with every mile that passed by.

Max was way past angry.

He had been through so many switches and changes of emotion and his life had been at risk for as long as he could remember it seemed. He had to focus on the immediate task in hand but it was difficult to suppress the feelings of anger and fear which had become so much a part of his life. They had to get the girl back, whatever the cost…it had suddenly become all about the child and it was much more personal than at any time throughout this whole ordeal. Max touched Mary gently on the knee and she took his hand with a firm grip, squeezing and holding the squeeze in a knowing show of emotion and feeling. They were in the same mental zone and they were determined to succeed together, failure was not an option for either of them from this point forward.

Mary would have her daughter back and she knew that there was much more to that than even Max could imagine. Max would have his life back, well something like the life he remembers.

Sam Deans was casually tracking their rental car every single mile of the journey from the comfort of his luxurious office in Newport. The journey which would lead them to his door like a diamond delivery service…He roared with laughter as that very thought passed through his twisted mind. The big man took a long draw on the large Cuban cigar and waited patiently for their arrival.

Max pulled up the car outside the large house of Sam Deans and he had a 'Deja-Vue' moment casting his mind back to a time not so long ago…the last time he came here. Much had happened since then and Max felt more prepared and more angry than that day. There was much more riding on the outcome of this visit and at least he knew what kind of reception he was about to receive. They had decided to hold back the diamonds until they were sure that Mary's daughter was safe. Max would go in first to see Deans and as soon as he was satisfied that the girl was safe, he would send for the diamonds, not much of a plan but they had the element of surprise, or at least they thought they had.

Mary was leaving nothing to chance.

Max walked towards the huge gates as Mary drove around the back of the property and waited. Max had insisted that she was armed and he had convinced her that she would need to shoot anyone who came near her as she waited. It was a major achievement for Max to persuade her that she would have to wait for his signal before storming into the house demanding her daughter. Mary was on auto pilot regarding meeting her objective which was the return of her daughter safe and sound and that was all. She had considered various ways of achieving this goal in recent months but since Max was prepared to help then so be it. There was still much that Max did not know about the situation and she was sick to her stomach with guilt that he was being kept in the dark…but it had to be this way, she knew that if she was ever going to see her daughter again.

Mary left the car in a small clearing between two groups of high trees and grabbing the diamonds she set off on foot to the waiting car which was just pulling to a halt less than 25yards away.

As she approached the waiting vehicle which had crept to a stop and was stationary with the motor still running, there was a vitality and purposefulness to her step which seemed out of place in the circumstances. The door opened as she approached and she climbed into the car.

'Hey! Mary fancy meeting you in a place like this' the man's voice was casual and friendly.

'Listen George! Things have changed a little since our original arrangement…' Mary was talking to George Meredith as if they were long lost friends.

'It sure has doll….' sniggered Meredith. 'The diamonds please…' He gestured towards the case which Mary was gripping firmly against her chest. It was obvious that there was no way out for her now. She had agreed to the diamond heist plot way back before Deans had taken her daughter as insurance…but now everything had changed everything.

She drew the gun swiftly and professionally from the rear of her pants and in one easy motion and in less than a second it was delivering a well aimed bullet directly into the chest of Mr George Meredith.

The silencer had reduced the noise to a loud thud and as soon as the bullet had left the barrel, Mary had reached out to stop his limp body from falling onto steering wheel and she was forcing his body out of the driver's door onto the road. She stopped the motor and ran around the car to recover the dead body, dragging it to the rear of the vehicle. She opened the trunk of the large car and with an extreme effort fuelled by the adrenaline rush she managed to force his bent over body onto the edge of the trunk opening with the top of his torso reaching into the opening. The rest was easy, just swing his legs into the trunk and the task was completed.

Mary instinctively recovered Meredith's weapon from his holster before closing the trunk and then returned efficiently and without a moment's hesitation to the front of the vehicle. It came so naturally and she even surprised herself at the ease with which it had all come back to her…she was sickened and excited at the same time but most of all she was concentrating on the task of saving her baby.

She knew that Meredith would have a back up and he would also have to report into Deans on a regular basis that was just how things were done in a Deans style stakeout and she should know.

Any security breach would be advised immediately and directly to Deans. She couldn't allow that to happen before Max had finished making his pitch. She needed them both to be unaware of what was happening outside the house for as long as possible… She needed to move fast.

Finding the back-up car should be easy but she had to do it before Max sent her the signal to bring the diamonds. Mary shuffled through the undergrowth between the trees which bordered the property looking out for the second vehicle. She moved hurriedly and effectively between the huge trees still carrying the diamonds close to her as she ran. The other vehicle came into view on the other side of the property. This would make sense because the two vehicles were covering entry and exit points in and out of the house and also keeping a watch on her vehicle.

Mary approached the vehicle very deftly from the rear avoiding being spotted from the windows or the mirrors. She was willing to kill again to save her daughter and if it turned out to be necessary she would not hesitate. Creeping slowly alongside the vehicle she prepared herself to attack the driver drawing long deep breaths silently, poised to attack. She stood upright and spun towards the drivers window with the gun held out directly in front of her held perfectly balanced and aimed directly into the driver's compartment of the car. There was no-one in the vehicle and she cursed and scanned the surrounding area for any movement…nothing.

There was no time to lose and she knew that she wouldn't have time to search for the driver.

She felt a glancing blow to the side of the head as a man attacked her from behind. She moved just in time to avoid a solid blow which would have knocked her out cold for sure. Spinning around and hitting the ground in one easy movement, she fired a single shot without thinking and the man hit the ground like a lifeless sack of emptiness, still holding the tree limb in his outstretched hands.

Mary recovered her senses instantly and swiftly fired a second shot into the man's chest before dragging him from view. She ran back to her own car holding her head trying to stem the flow of blood which was seeping from the wound. Her head was pounding and she was beginning to lose composure as she felt the tears welling up behind her eyes. She finally got back to her car and after slithered back into the driver's seat like a wounded animal retreating to its den she sat shaking and shivering as she contemplated what had just happened.

Max Reynolds and Sam Deans were standing toe to toe in the drawing room like two heavyweight boxers, silently sizing each other up.

'Well, Max we meet again and so soon…' Deans began the exchange.

'Look Deans, I have no intention of getting into any small talk or even conversation with you. I want the girl and I want her now…….' Max was so angry that he could hardly control the tone of his voice.

'Well, well, direct and to the point, I like that. We shall do business Reynolds just as soon as you produce the diamonds'

'I need to see the girl before we even consider an exchange, where is she, you fucking animal?'

Deans began pacing around the room and for an instant Max couldn't believe that he was here in this room again arguing with the same idiot, it was so unreal that he was caught off guard as Deans threw open a set of double doors to reveal another room to the rear of the drawing room. Max heard a whimper which sounded like that of a small child and he almost fell as he ran over to the doors and went inside the small room. As could be expected two huge men stopped his passage into the room and he came to an abrupt halt as they each held out an outstretched arm barring his way. He peered over the huge pair of arms and he could just see the girl tied to a chair just as he had seen her in the photograph.

A sudden thought leapt to his mind….there didn't seem to be any element of surprise, Deans was waiting for him and he had the girl bound and ready for the show…..it was just too unreal…..

'And now Max…What now? Have you really thought this through?' Max's head was spinning and he was finding it very difficult to concentrate.

'I walk out with the girl and you get the diamonds... simple...' explained Max

'Why don't you just call the beloved Mary now Max...it will be so good to see her again. We can party together like the old days...'

The plan was in tatters thought Max. The bastard knows everything, please don't tell me he already has Mary prayed Max as he closed is eyes and tried to collect his thoughts and emotions.

'No girl...No diamonds that's the deal' exclaimed Max as he turned and headed towards the door. As he turned he pressed the 'send' button on his cell phone which was in his pants pocket and was set to send the 'come and get me' signal at a single key press.

Deans motioned for the two men to bring the girl into the room and he picked up a phone form the huge walnut desk to make a call.

Max turned to see the girl being carried into the room still strapped to the chair and crying. She was still bound and gagged and Max ran over to remove the gag from around her mouth. He was stopped by the two men but Deans allowed it and Max began to tear away the gag and all three men started to release the restraints releasing the girl from the chair.

A frown began to appear on the forehead of Sam Deans as he realised there was no response from the number he was attempting to call. He dialled a second number and eventually sent one of the bodyguards out into the main house after whispering an instruction to the huge man before he left the room.

Mary was driving towards the huge gates and as she approached they opened automatically, which is exactly what she hope would happen. She slammed her foot down on the gas and the wheels spun sending gravel and dust into the air before they took hold of the surface beneath and the car jolted forward and sped down the long drive. A single shot into the mechanism which operated the security rendered them disabled in the open position should they need a quick getaway and Mary Moore was on a mission…….. Once again.

The car screeched to a halt at the main door and Mary opened both front doors before grabbing the case of diamonds and storming into the house. She had one hand gun in her right hand and another tucked into her pants at hip level. The weapon in her hand was loaded and cocked and she was ready and waiting to save her daughter.

A single shot floored the bodyguard as he was attempting to leave the house, too pre-occupied with carrying out his most recent instruction to notice Mary as she rushed into view…he just happened to be in the way. They all heard the shot and Max threw himself on top of the girl to protect her. Deans seemed to still be in shock as Mary launched herself into the room and marched directly towards Deans, gun held high and pointing straight at Sam Deans, ready to fire at the slightest movement.

'Woah! Woah!! Hold your fire!!!' Deans let out an involuntary scream as he saw the gun barrel approaching.

Max looked up from the ground still holding the girl tight to see a wild and powerful alter ego of Mary Moore who was pressing a gun barrel tight into the temple of Sam Deans.

'Ok….. Let's all calm down……Calm the fuck down…. everybody…….' The big man pleaded with everyone to stop and think.

'Max! Stop staring and bring my daughter over here…Come on! Come on! get moving'

Max took a moment to regain some composure and looking nervously around the room he gathered up the small girl in his arms and did just as he was told.

'Now then….' Mary was in control 'I will be taking my daughter out of here and just so that there is no hard feeling I will leave the diamonds on that small table over there' She pointed at the table with her left foot '..And if anyone has an alternative plan speak now and I will take great pleasure in blowing Mr Deans' brains all over this stunning room'

She stared directly into Deans' eyes and also pressed the gun barrel a little more forcefully into the flesh surrounding his left temple as she whispered, 'and you know I will…..you know how much pleasure I would get from blowing you away right now!!'

The talking was over.

Everyone was in a state of shock, everyone that is except Mary Moore. She marched Deans out of the room at gun point, followed by Max still carrying the young girl and the bodyguard who had one hand on his revolver ready to draw the gun at the slightest opportunity. In the hall way they were met by three security guards and another of Deans' goons all in a similar state of readiness.

'Get in the car Mr Deans…NOW!'

Despite a pathetic attempt to object, Sam Deans got into the passenger seat of the car and Mary got into the rear seat behind him, the gun still pointing at his head. Max bundled the girl onto the back seat next to Mary and got into the driving seat ready to drive them away form this incredible situation.

'Drive Max! We have a meeting to go to………' Max duly obliged and he glanced across at the furious Deans with some satisfaction and a great deal of hatred.

The other members of the cast in this amazing scenario just stared in disbelief from the front steps which cascaded down from the huge wooden doors at the front of the house. They had no idea what to do next, any attempt to free Deans would surely lead to his death.

As they drove along the drive towards the security gates, Deans began to speak for the first time since his abduction,

'There is no way you will get away with this….even if the diamonds turn out to be real I will hunt you down until I find you and I will have my revenge'

A quick flick of the wrist brought the gun butt down on top of Deans' head and he let out a scream as a the weapon made contact with his massive head and a gash appeared immediately producing a stream of blood which he attempted to wipe away with his sleeve. Another blow stopped him from raising his arm and this time it was an arm from Max which came lashing across Deans' chest.

'This is a simple exchange' said Mary 'You of all people know how this works',

'The diamonds - for my daughter. I am disgusted that you would stoop so low to get the diamonds but I should know what you are capable of. You are a monster and you know it, if you keep your big mouth shut and do exactly as I say you will stay alive long enough to enjoy your latest acquisition. If not and you still have ambitions of retaliation…I will kill you and you know that I can and I will…So what's it gonna be ….do we have a deal or do you want to die right here, right now

Deans said nothing, just gave a sickly grin and started to shake his head very gently. Enough movement to deliver his sarcastic message and wind up his assailant but not enough to make the gun go off which was still pressing against his head. He was a cold calculated gangster and a stupid broad wasn't going to ruin his exterior image on the world, not even one he had trained.

'Stop the car Max….right now…stop the damn car' Mary was starting to lose her composure. Cracks were starting to appear and in her present state of mind that could be very dangerous…

She reached forward and jammed the gun barrel right into Deans mouth. She was leaning right across the seat and her face was right next to his as she spoke calmly to Max without averting her stare from Deans' wicked eyes.

'Max! Please just do as I say…take Sophie for a walk outside. I want to talk to Mr Deans in private'

Max was amazed at everything he was seeing and hearing.….. *leave them alone in the car? Less than a mile away from the house and what sort of chat was they going to have? Who were these people?? What was happening here?*

He felt very vulnerable and feared for his life once again and of course that of the child……

His protests fell on deaf ears but the instant he left the car he wished that he hadn't given in to her this time. They had walked less than 20 paces before he heard the first gunshot which was swiftly followed by two more.

They raced back to the car, 'Mummy! Mummy!' the little girl cried and Max felt his heart stop. Sam Deans was lying sprawled on the ground outside the car with blood all over his chest and there was a small hand gun on the ground next to him as if it had just fallen out of his hand. Mary was slumped down next to him, her back leaning against the front wheel of the car and there was no noise and no movement…everyone was silent. Time stood still for an instant and then Max instinctively kicked the gun away from Deans' open hand and dumped himself on the ground next to Mary, lifting her head to gently towards his own he looked at the cold, lifeless face and saw no signs of life.

'Mary! Can you hear me…are you alright?' There was no reaction and he felt a surge of panic as he slapped her face with both hands, trying to get some reaction. Then he felt for a pulse….nothing. He couldn't see any blood….what the…he threw her down flat on the ground and started pumping her chest…the little girl started to scream as if a delayed reaction had just kicked in. Max pumped Mary's chest and tilted her head back ready to blow good, fresh air into her lungs…I must clear the airways…he chanted to himself trying desperately to remember his CPR training…come on! Come on! He chanted….Come back to me Mary….

All of a sudden, she arched her back and lurched forward coughing and spluttered, flinging her head sideways, she spat blood all over Max's knees and stomach as he knelt beside her.

He grabbed her and spun her over into the recovery position as quick as a flash. She coughed and spluttered again until eventually her eyes rolled down from somewhere inside her head she opened as she blinked wildly she could see two panic stricken pairs of eyes staring back at her. She was alive.

Max slumped next to her hugging her tightly as she tried to catch her breath…she was trying to push him away but he held her tightly and then there were three of them as the little girl joined the celebration.

They sobbed and squeezed each other and dragged each other from the ground still holding tight as could be. As Mary raised her aching body up into a kneeling position, they rocked backwards and forwards on the ground like a human tepee blowing in the wind.

There was a groaning noise coming from Deans and at the same time they could hear footsteps running towards them in the distance. It was obvious that Deans was still alive, barely but alive all the same and once again they had to move fast.

'Where are you hurt Mary…can you move?'

'We struggled and we both fired a shot…I must have been thrown into the car and knocked out…..'

She was frantically patting her body for a wound, for blood but all she could feel was the bloody mess on the side of her head which had been there earlier….it was amazing she had no significant injury, a massive headache and she felt like shit but she couldn't see or feel a bullet wound…

Whilst she examined herself, Max had recovered the two guns and he placed one back into her hand and the other he was checking for bullets.

"We have some company", Mary, he announced and they both took a position behind the car looking back down the road in the direction of the running footsteps.

It was a young couple who had seen the incident whilst driving past and they had pulled over and come to check if everyone was OK. How fucking stupid thought Max…keep driving, always keep driving... They had no idea what they were doing. He pushed Mary and the girl down behind the car and slipping the gun into his pocket, he stood up and raised an arm as he walked towards the couple.

'Its OK we're fine. Thanks for stopping we will be fine...'

"Are you sure, Sir, Is there anything we can do", the voice of a young man in his twenties, if that, came back at him and Max shook his head.

"We're fine honestly, just a little accident no harm done." The couple stopped dead in their tracks as they noticed the blood all over Max's clothing and the handle of a 9mm gun protruding from his pocket.

They looked at each other and backed away defensively.

'Look' said Max, if you want to help I suggest you turn around, go back to your car and pretend that nothing happened.

They started to back away for a few step and suddenly, grabbing each others hand they turned and ran stride for stride back to their car. Max let out a long slow breath and walked slowly, backwards towards his own vehicle, scanning the area as he did so. It suddenly occurred to him how bizarre this was...maybe it was a set up of some sort...maybe not.

Mary had managed to raise Deans into a sitting position and she was patching his wound with her jacket. There was lots of blood and Deans was barely alive. Having removed her jacket her back was visible and Max could see a thick red line passing across her shoulder blades, more like a graze than anything as if something had whistled past her taking just enough skin to burst a blood vessel or two but nothing more....like a bullet just missing her on the way past...he suddenly went weak at the knees as he realised how close it had been from imbedding in her sweet gorgeous body. There was some blood but not much so he decided not to mention it, not right now, there was too much to do.

'He's still breathing Max we have to get him to a hospital…'

'And say what? Oh! I just shot this man but I think he might make it!!! You are crazy woman!!! He's a fucking gangster …let him go!'

Max exploded in a barrage of sarcasm…which Mary chose to ignore a she reached for a cell phone. He snatched the phone from her as she prepared to make the call…

'What are you thinking? Its just too late leave him and lets get out of here, we can send an ambulance back for him but we have to move and right now!!.'

'I can't leave him Max…He is Sophie's father….

She put her free arm around the small vulnerable frame of her daughter and pulled her close….Max's knees finally gave way and all he could see was the monster holding a gun to the head of his own child…It was revolting and nauseating and Max heaved and threw up as he stumbled to his knees in an involuntary reaction to the horror of that mental picture and the news he had just received.

Mary Moore. His Mary……and the monster Sam Deans. It was horrific and so very sickening but it did start to make sense of a few things which had happened along the way. Max's mind was racing and so was his heart rate, he felt his heart thumping away as if it was trying to climb out of his chest. Max got to his feet and glancing quickly at the scene of carnage which was assembled alongside the rental car on his way past the car as he started to walk away from the scene.

Mary jumped to her feet. Laying Deans' head carefully on the ground she followed Max down the narrow road and into the trees.

'It seems such a long time ago Max, I….'

'Save it Mary! The girl cant be more than five or six years old……you have played me and everyone else…people have died Mary!!!'

The Price of Friendship

'I don't know who you are anymore so much has happened......I just want to get away and stay alive...'

Mary grabbed his shoulder and spoke calmly and in such a manner that Max was forced to listen. There was coldness in her voice,

'The only way to get away in one piece is to keep Deans alive, if he dies his people will never rest until they find the person who killed him....' Her tone was serious 'I know this Max, because I used to be one of them'

The revelations just kept coming...Max were stunned yet again...

'We get him to a doctor that I know and he will be looked after...all I am asking is help me get him to the doc's or just go and leave me to do it alone. We never need to see each other again...'

'It's your call....' She turned away and was making her way back to the car when Max grabbed her by the shoulders and threw her to the ground...

'How dare you! How fucking dare you!' He forced the words through clenched teeth and all he could see was the stunning beauty of this amazing woman lay underneath him and he could not stop himself forcing a huge kiss onto her voluptuous lips. To his amazement she responded and their lips and tongues squirmed and twisted in unison as they kissed each other passionately rolling on the ground like a couple of teenagers. The energy was electric, the passion vibrant and wanton.

It was the most bizarre situation...incredible and bizarre. They ended the kiss simultaneously and started to scamper back to the car as if they had been caught in a hay loft by the farmer. Sophie, Deans...the horror of this mess suddenly came back to them and as they regained their senses, they knew instinctively that they had to stop this before it went too far.

Mary allowed herself a wry smile out of sight from Max despite the pain and panic, inside she was in control, the training took care of that and it never leaves a person once it was there.

Deans was desperately struggling for breath although he was unable to move, his face was contorted as he lay alone in the dirt. Sophie was huddled against the car her knees tucked tightly into her body and both arms pulling them tighter and tighter in towards herself. She was in shock and was it any wonder.

They loaded Sophie into the rear of the car and Max decided to take charge.

'Mary, tell me where this doctor is and I will deal with Deans, you take Sophie somewhere safe and wait for me'

'Nice ideas Max, but it won't work…….The Doc will not open up to you it has to be me. There is another vehicle about 200yards around the curve, its between the two rows of trees and the keys are in it ready to go…I will take Deans in this car and you take Sophie…I will meet you at….erm…at the motel on 495…tomorrow morning…make sure Sophie is safe please I have to trust you on this.

Max took Sophie out of the car and they began running towards the other car, as if it was the most normal thing in the world to be doing…running through the park playing ball on a summers evening…Sophie was somewhere else, she had been through so much that her mind had gone to a safe place…. some other place and some other time, where she was happy and contented.

The ran to the car ad Max drove out of the residential area, on to the freeway to the intersection with 495 and headed towards the motel.

Mary was back into character and weaving the rental car through the narrow streets looking for the address which she had not used for so many years, she hoped it was still valid although she knew that the Doc was still on the payroll or he was dead. Not much choice but to take the chance after all she

The Price of Friendship

did have the head of the organisation, bleeding to death in the back of her car.

She came across the large metal gates as much by accident than design; she crashes the car through the gates setting of the alarms and screamed down the winding driveway to the small country style home in the woods. She was met by the Doc standing at the doorway pointing a gun directly at her. She called out...

'Doc! Its me Mary....I have Sam Deans, he is hurt pretty bad...'

She threw open the driver's door before the car had even come to a stop and rolled out onto the dirt holding both hands outstretched

'I am not armed.... we need your help!' She pleaded as she rolled to a stop and faced him up

Whether he recognised her or not he pointed the gun directly in her face and rushed around to the rear door of the car and then he saw Deans outstretched on the rear seat, blood was seeping from the coat which was strapped across his chest...

'Jesus! What the Hell!!!'

He looked back at Mary and shouted.

'Come on! Help me get him inside, Come! Quickly'.....

They dragged him across the driveway and into the house; the Doc fetched a young woman who was presumably just waiting for such an occasion...

Deans was stable within an hour. He was laid out on a stretcher bed with a saline drip in one arm and he was wired to an array of monitors and machines. The young woman was checking his vital signs regularly on the heart monitor and loading another hypodermic needle ready to administer more medicine as soon as required. Mary sat nervously in a small lounge chair watching the emergency medicine activity.

As soon as she knew he was stable she interrupted the doctor...

'I need to speak to him Doc, when will I be able to speak to him?'

'Go and get something to eat and drink. I will call you as soon as he can talk' replied the Doc all calm and collected and sympathetic.

Mary duly obliged and shuffled out of the room into the corridor. She saw a kitchen at the end of the hall and she suddenly realised that she couldn't remember the last time she had eaten. Maybe she should get some food and a drink. The Doc could handle things and she was so tired a short rest may be in order. She found a cold beer in the fridge and some crackers. As soon as she sat down to eat them she noticed that her hands were shaking and there seemed to be blood stains everywhere.

A short time later the 'nurse' arrived with a change of clothes for Mary and also a towel

'Take a shower and get cleaned up…the Doc insists, there is a shower and somewhere to change at the other end of the hallway.' She was curt, yet pleasant enough, very proper and formal, almost business like in her manner. Mary hadn't noticed how pretty she was when they first arrived. She was tall and slim with short blonde hair, probably in her late twenties and although there was a formality about her every action and movement, she had a very beautiful and expressive smile.

Mary hadn't appreciated the extent of her injuries and as the warm water hit her back she squealed and spun around to see what was causing the pain. The scar on her head had now erupted into a large bump and a purple and blue bruise was appearing as big as an apple almost closing her eye, she looked like a boxer who has gone 10 rounds of a title fight and then lost…

As she carefully examined herself she was more than satisfied that the wounds were superficial and she had been very lucky. Now to turn the screw on Mr Deans and his adversary Botha she thought as she looked into the cold calculating eyes which stared back at her from the bathroom mirror. She had all the knowledge she needed directly from the Deans inner circle and such was the plan when she decided to conspire and collude with Meredith…How she hated herself for that but it had been necessary…the end justifies the means she told herself over and over. There was no way she could confide in Max he was too fragile and he simply didn't understand the workings of the underworld, why would he? He was good man a sweet, successful and dependable man who was good to the core. Why would he want to understand the world in which his good friends Mary and Chuck had operated for as long as he had known them? She despised herself for the deception over the years but now it was even worse, she found herself torn between her old life and the love of an exceptional man……. How in God's name did she get into this mess?

Sophie was safe, that was the only thing that had mattered and she had to make that stick; for everyone's sake she had to live. It wasn't in her plans to ever tell Max about Deans being her father but it had become necessary to complete the plan. She was sure that she could get over all of this if only the last part of the plan comes together……please God! Let me finish this and lead a normal life.

Chapter 24

Sophie sat on the huge bed resting her head against a pile of large pillows. She hadn't spoken for ever it seemed and Max had no idea how to comfort her she was distant and aloof and he just couldn't make any progress with conversation. He decided it was sufficient to make sure she was safe and he would watch over her just as Mary had asked.

Where Mary was he had no idea or for that matter when if ever she would return...It was incredible to think that he was here with the child of a gangster and his lover protecting her from God know who and he had no idea what was going to happen next. He didn't even know the child existed and now he was the baby sitter!!! He paced the room silently considering his options over and over trying not to alarm Sophie...she stared blankly at the TV clearly oblivious to what was showing on the screen.

Max considered calling her cell but that might create further problems. Who was this woman anyway? He thought he knew her and he though that she knew him...nothing seemed real anymore and he just wanted this all to end. It was inconceivable that she had been in any way connected to Deans. But what about the shootings and the kidnapping and...Hell she was awesome. Just like an agent or a spy or whatever they call these people. She certainly saved their lives so far anyway, he had no choice but to trust her until it was time to get the hell out of this incredible life. He had been forced into a life of subterfuge and crime just to stay alive….what was Mary's reason… to save her daughter in the first place but now? What was going to happen next was a complete mystery and Max was powerless to do anything but wait……

Sophie managed to get some sleep and Max became nervous more than once wondering if she had stopped breathing like a small baby in a crib, he checked her again and again during the night.

The knock on the door was like a bomb going off in Max's brain, as it shattered the silence of the night. Mary appeared at the doorway like a vision, she was clean and presentable and absolutely stunning in the glow of the dimmed hallway lighting.

They embraced and he pulled her into the motel room trying to shield her from danger… as if she needed it he thought to himself, but it was an involuntary action and it made him feel better.

'Deans will be fine…really,' announced Mary

I left him across town at the Docs but I have to go back as soon as it gets light I just wanted to make sure you were both OK…

She rushed over to Sophie and hugged her tight, the tears began to flow uncontrollably, and the serious and almost sinister veneer which had overcome Mary was at last showing signs of weakening. Max smiled and joined in the hug but Sophie made no such gesture. Mary backed away concerned and worried that it had all been too much for her, she looked into Sophie's eyes and they didn't look back at her. as she held Sophie at arms length she could see the glaze over her eyes.

She looked frantically at Max and then back at her beautiful, helpless daughter, the vulnerability of them both was plain to see and Max tried to calm the situation,

The Price of Friendship

'She will be fine Mary, she has been through so much it will take some time but I am sure she will be fine….if we manage to stay alive that is…'

'What happens now?' He continued. 'I need to know, this waiting is driving me mad I feel so helpless, lets just get out of here I can arrange travel to Europe within the hour , let's just get the fuck out of here…'

'We can hold up with my folks in London…no problem they would probably even be pleased to see me…' Max was beginning to rant….

'Max! Max! Stop…It has to be finished. We need closure on this or it will never end for us. Never! You just have to trust me on this.'

Max was close to throwing a tantrum like a spoilt child but he managed to contain himself.

'Mary how the hell can I trust you? It just isn't possible…I don't even know you anymore!'

'I came to you to help and now I have been sucked even further into a web of killings and children I didn't know existed and the fucking mob are still after me…'

'It has to end Mary whatever needs to be done I will do but I just want out…do you understand?'

His voice was urgent and raised but he was trying to muffle the sound to avoid attracting attention. If Mary could find them anyone could he hadn't even given her the room number and there is no 24 hr desk at this Motel he made sure of that…

'Well, Max! You still have the option to walk away…there is the door.' She pointed to the motel door and turned away. 'I have to see this through and I need to know where you stand.….If you leave then fine…...I can't protect you any further…'

'Protect me!!! I have never been in so much danger since you came on the scene…' It wasn't entirely true but Max was so annoyed that he could slap her face for even suggesting that he needed her…

The argument was interrupted by the sound of crying coming from the bed.

They both broke off in mid argument and rushed to the bed. Sophie was staring at them and crying, her red swollen face still looked sore and bruised and now the tears were flowing down of those perfectly formed cheeks as she cried out...

'Please stop! Please...I need you Mummy'

Mary comforted her baby and they cried together. Eventually she stood up, tucked her baby in under the sheets and announced that Mummy has to go away now she will be back soon promise...

Max was livid and he decided to object.

'Before you say a word Max, my sister is on her way over and she will take care of Sophie until WE get back...'

'Are you running away or are you prepared to help me end this...I need your help Max. I hate to admit it but I do need your help to end this......'

Sophie was gone and safe and Max and Mary were driving again, heading for the Docs house and as soon as Deans was well enough...to a Red Sox Baseball Game...for a date with destiny.

Chapter 25

Johan Botha was a little annoyed that the meeting had been postponed for a couple of days and he considered returning to Jo'Burg at once. The offer from the Deans people to stay in Boston for the holiday weekend and enjoy the sights all expenses paid was as good as the first points scored in the negotiation and he decided to accept the offer. It wasn't the money, he could probably buy the hotel he was staying in a few times over it was just a matter of one-upmanship and he felt good about having the upper hand before they had even started.

The Doc worked long and hard to 'repair his patient and they had manned the temporary surgery with the best that money could buy. Money wasn't the problem, but time was. Deans was doing well and with the right care and attention it was felt that he would make a full recovery......he was not ready to be moved as the Doc explained to everyone and anyone that asked, including Mary.

'He needs to be at a meeting in town in two days time Doc....Its a matter of some urgency...It's essential that he is there....' she explained.

Max had taken up residence at yet another motel and he was waiting patiently...yet again for the signal to pick Mary up from the Doc's residence.

'Its impossible Mrs Moore, he won't be ready in time. He has some internal bleeding and it will take time to heal…Its just not possible…'

Mary had already asked when she could talk to him and the best guess on this was in a few hours time, she decided to use the time to persuade the Doc that Deans had to be ready.

Sam Deans lay in the 'hospital' bed oblivious to all the goings on and there was a time not so long ago that he was convinced he was dead. His mind was ticking over and all his mental and physical energy was being used up trying to stay alive. He knew he could make it if only he could concentrate all his effort and focus on getting well, he could make it for sure.

Deans had been conscious for at least twenty four hours before the Doc allowed Mary to speak to him. She had been in and out of the house several times and all to no avail. The Doc had made all those who needed to know in the organisation that he was recovering and they all knew what they needed to do. A net of secrecy was thrown over the issue and to the outside world business continued as usual. It was fortuitous that there was a holiday weekend during the main period of recovery and although the life of organised crime never stopped, it did slow down sometimes and this was one of those times, less awkward questions to answer. In the deepest background of the organisation candidates for his potential successor were throwing their hat into the ring and it would not be long before the world knew that there was a problem….It was amazing to think that the momentum never stops and can't be allowed to stop, too many people made too much money for that to happen.

When Mary entered the room she was surprised to see him looking so well, the drugs and medication, both legal and otherwise work wonders at a time such as this.

She knew that the Doc would have primed him and that he would have been told everything that had happened before

The Price of Friendship

she even got into the room so there was no need for small talk or explanation.

'My dearest Mary, the scars of conflict don't suit you at all, no wound should ever be seen on such a beautiful face…'

Mary automatically lifted her hand to stroke the large bruise on her face. The lump had subsided but her face was still a mess with cuts and scratches across her forehead and bruising all over.

'I suppose I ought to thank you for saving my life but then again you did try to take it in the first place..' He tried to laugh but it caused a searing pain in his chest and the nurse rushed to his assistance 'and of course the fact that you have been so eager to see me means that you have a deal to offer…I guess you just wanna stay alive…that might be a start eh?...'

'I do believe we have the diamonds although we left in such a hurry that I never got to see them…I am told they are absolutely stunning and what is more they appear to be genuine…My dear I am disappointed that you didn't try to cheat me!!! You are losing your touch…'

'We had a deal and I honoured my side of the bargain…… How could you be so cruel to our daughter… even for you that was a low blow….'

Deans was under instruction to stay calm and it was all he could do to do that right now. He knew she was right but he didn't care, he had plenty of sons and daughters out there somewhere, none so valuable he would have to admit but his plan had worked and now he had the prize…the diamonds. There was no weakness in the mental armour of Sam Deans he was a ruthless individual and proud of it.

'Low blow or not, it worked…I have the gems and you have the girl……done deal…'

The matter of fact nature of the statement was no surprise to Mary and she had known he would check the diamonds every single one of them that is the very reason she had played that particular card in that particular way.

'I want a piece of the action with the South African and I want your assurance that Sophie and I will not come to any harm from your people....'Mary got straight to the point and sat back to await the big man's response...

I could do with a spokesperson at the meeting for sure, I am sure that they don't allow hospital beds in there...and I do owe you for not leaving me to die.......but I thought you wanted out, you have been so quiet for so long.....why now?'

He had taken the bait and now she had to start to reel him in.

'I need one more big payday then I am gone for good' she continued

'There isn't any 'big payday' with the South African deal...just a distributorship to operate and probably a little government extortion to make sure the deal sticks...'

It was going exactly as she had planned but the next suggestion would tell whether it was going to work or not, he had to go for the next suggestion...

'I can make sure you get the whole operation for yourself... no shares with both...no profit splitting...all yours. I know you think that in time you could do this yourself but I can make it happen day one....'

Deans was interested she could tell. His tired and pained eyes lit up just a little, he shuffled uncomfortably in the bed as he mentally constructed his next statement....

'Well, you have been busy...I suppose it's a woman thing this solution that I can't make happens but you can...' He allowed himself a small chuckle, just stopping it from turning into a laugh just before the pain hit home and the nurse ran towards him again. 'I don't suppose you would care to explain?'

'No!'

'Thought not' replied Deans

'Here's then deal, If you pull it off, get me 100% guaranteed with no associated risk, I give you a one time 10% pay off and you disappear for ever...I mean for ever....'

'That should make you a cool couple of mil and you get to live…..'

'If it goes wrong the risk is that they will pull out and I will be left in the cold…it's a big risk I am taking here Moore so you better be on it….I will want some collateral of course…..a little insurance…

Mary's elation turned sour in a second…she hadn't considered collateral…it couldn't work this way the bastard had second guessed her.

'I will stay with the organisation if it fails and I will work for you on a salary like the guys at the bottom…I will pay you back for everything you would have lost in time and effort….'

A chuckle was no longer sufficient and Deans laughed out loud, groaning with pain at the same time…

'A modern day slave eh? Whatever next my dear…you must be crazy….'

'What makes you think I want you? A little confident in your own abilities aren't you?'

'Don't answer that…..the one thing I do know is that you must have a foolproof plan to offer yourself as collateral, I remember the way you forced yourself out of the organisation, ruthless and very risky. I am sure you don't want to be back with us….and of course it would be good for my image to have you killed for trying to take my life……..'

'I will make the necessary arrangements and then you might have yourself a deal. You better be sure of this you pretty little thing…..because you will be publicly executed if you fail….and I will find a way to get my 50% of the deal from Botha………It is all I can offer…..succeed or die…. and like you, I will keep my end of the deal whichever way it goes'

It was not quite what Mary had in mind but at least she was in the game. It felt good to be back in the game and they both knew that she would have to die if she didn't offer him a deal anyway; it was just the way of things. At least this way she had a chance and so did Sophie…

They shook hands and Mary left the room, she hoped she would never have to see his face again.

She drove like a mad woman to the motel and burst into the room hardly allowing herself time to open the door.

"Max, we need to move, we need somewhere to stay in the city. We need to pick up some of your contacts at Fenway Park and….."

"Whoa! Calm down, stop and talk to me. What happened……?"

'The game is on, Max…we need to get moving now. Deans has asked me to represent him at a full scale meeting with a big fish in town in days. We need a plan and we need it fast…'

'So he's alive then? Asked Max, stating the obvious but a fact that she had forgotten to mention.

'Of course he's alive I made sure of that….!' Her answer was short and impatient. Mary had forgotten that Max knew nothing of her plans and she hadn't even brought him up to speed. She settled herself before explaining what she was planning to do next. Max listened intently and although it all sounded a little far fetched and like something out of a spy novel, he had come to believe over the last few weeks that if Mary Moore had a plan then it had every chance of coming off and a person had better pay attention or be left wondering what was going to happen next.

Chapter 26

'Max Reynolds!!' said the tall slim and extremely fit looking Chad Myers.....'How you doing' Man, long time no see! How you been..?'

Max was pleased that Chad remembered him with such enthusiasm, he really needed his help and that was a great start. They were in the same restaurant at the same time and to Chad it was a pure coincidence but to Max it was all part of the plan.

'You know this and that...working and playing' He replied 'I've been out of town for a while spending some of my money..... hahaha'

Chad Myers was another in the long list of ex professional sports men which Max had managed to help a little along the way and had formed a good relationship with. He was an ex Basketball star with Boston Celtics and now he ran a corporate hospitality business in Boston. Entertaining the rich folk and feeding the poor he liked to call it. Myers had been a household name in the nineties and he had retired a wealthy man. He wanted to put something back into the sport an he used the money from his hospitality business to fund junior development programs, building courts and gymnasiums in the poor areas and doing free appearances for schools and colleges to help fund raising. An all round nice guy and he and Max had got along well in all of their dealings together.

The two men chatted a while and eventually they agreed to meet up the following day to discuss a deal which Max said was going to be really big and would be a great way to put a little money into all their pockets and a substantial amount into the coffers for the local kids.

Another piece of the jigsaw was in place and although Max hated to use his friends for his own gain, it was a necessity and he knew it.

Mary was spending her time just waiting for the call from Deans; she needed confirmation of the exact time and location for the meeting, although she knew it was at Fenway Park she needed to know the precise timing and which room was to be used and who the caterers would be. In fact everything there was to know about the arrangements. There was no room for error and every detail had to be meticulously planned and understood.

She was also making sure she looked a million dollars for the meeting, it was very important that she looked her best it may all come down to that.

The second task was easy but the first one was frustrating and annoying in the extreme. It was still amazing to her that Deans was allowing her to represent the organisation and she was sure that there was more to the agreement than met the eye. She was aware of the people who were following both her and Max but she was equally aware that they would make no move without the go ahead from Deans.

They had both got used to being followed and it came as second nature now…just ignore it and get on is the only way to deal with it they had decided. Both Max and Mary focused completely on the plan; there was no time or attention spare to consider anything but the plan.

Max met with Chad the following day and he established the time and location of the current bookings under the name of Sam Deans Holdings Inc. and interestingly enough, Chad had been asked to appear as one of the special guests for the evening function. Max was amazed at how much Mary actually knew about Deans, she had predicted that there would be several nineties sports personalities on the guest list and one would definitely be a basketball star. The others all coming from the same era but representing Baseball, Football and strangely enough an Olympic track star, track and field was a particular favourite of the big man and he could indulge his own preferences as well as those of his business guests.

The evening function was very likely to be cancelled due to Deans' ill health but Mary seemed obsessed that it goes ahead and she was planning on that being the case. The more activity and the more people around the better…It all helps with diversionary tactics should they prove to be necessary.

Max discovered some of the other guests names and also what entertainment and catering was planned. He had no idea how Mary was going to ensure the event went ahead but he had a job to do and he was doing it. He discussed a finance deal which he knew would never come off but it was all part of the plot. They agreed to discuss the matter further at the function and both agreed that it would be good to have a beer together again as soon as possible

Next stop for Max was an inside contact at Fenway Park, home of the Boston Red Sox and one of Max's most favourite places in the world. He had been brought up on soccer in London and he had been to many of the stadiums in the English football league, his father had taken him to Wembley to watch the English team play when he was 5 or 6 year old and from that point on he was hooked on sport. The amazing attraction which Fenway provided, the history and the age of the stadium was so much like the way English football clubs used to be, it had been good to Max when he started out in sports promotions career in the US. He knew Fenway Park inside out and many of the people who worked there from the hot dog salesman to the owner of the Sox…Max would certainly be playing on his home turf when the day of reckoning arrived. He certainly had the edge over Deans if he needed it at his beloved Fenway.

Max managed to get a meeting with a number of influential people on the inside track at the Park, easy really if you know the bar to go to and the time to be there…he 'bumped into' plenty of people and just to let them know he was looking for an opportunity to mingle with the big boys……get close to some new faces at the stadium and maybe cut them into a deal…the word was out and Max was back into 'his' game. He was well respected and considered to be a fair agent…many aren't and some of the people in the bar were doing just the same as Max but with altogether different motives. He would get his chance to meet the up and coming stars and also some of those looking for a 'retirement' idea…the only problem was she needed to move faster than the normal speed of things in this game, he needed an IN right away, a good reason to take temporary residence at the ball park and today wouldn't be too soon.

Eventually after too many Bud's and a lot of persuasion he got a breakthrough. Because it was very early in the season the team is always looking for more than one agent to help out the new rookies in all aspects of their development, not too much money in it initially but if the player likes them then the agent gets the chance to develop the relationship. It also takes some of the strain off the team officials.

Max was in like a shot,

'I will meet your boy tomorrow' he announced, 'See what I can do to help…., No promises mind, lets just see how it pans out'

Max was trying not seem too eager, but inside he was jumping for joy…..this was just the opening he was looking for, it meant he could come and go as he pleased, at least for a few days.

As he headed for his car he decided that he had been drinking for most of the day and it was probably best to walk the few blocks to the hotel and collect his car the following day.

He could easily walk to the hotel which Mary had chosen as their base, so he turned his collar to the cold snap in the air and headed off towards 'home'. It might have been his imagination or the effect of the beer and shots he had consumed but he had a prickly feeling that e was being followed. He was getting more and more nervous as he got closer to the hotel and he even considered not going to the hotel at all...maybe he was bringing trouble to Mary. The cold air and the fear was heady cocktail and although he was feeling quite alert he knew that he would never be able to take anyone in this state if they chose to attack him.

His stride got longer and his breath got shorter as he tried to lose whoever it was.....he rounded the corner leading to the main entrance of the hotel and the footsteps behind him got quicker as if they were starting to run....he ran towards the hotel entrance and as he threw himself into the revolving door he heard a voice in his ear

'Good night Mr Reynolds, Mr Deans sends his regards'
Then nothing.....

Max was waiting for the blow to the head or even the shot to the stomach....basically the pain, but there was nothing. The man passed him by and kept walking.

When Max told Mary of his encounter she showed no surprise.

Just making you aware that they are out there and close', she eventually said as if it was perfectly normal...and of course it absolutely was. For Max it had become a way of life and he sensed that although it was new for him it was not such a new situation for Mary.

He lay on the couch exhausted and slept for three hours before he was able to explain the details of his day. Mary had just waited patiently for him to wake or recover....

'Great news Max…Way to go!' She clenched her fist in a victory salute, 'We are getting close Max…very close'

Max knew that there was still a ways to go before they got to the end of this nightmare but he had to admit the signs were looking good and the first stage of the plan was setting up nicely.

The morning came and Max was off to the ball park. He had all the correct passes and identification documents and it was much like a normal day at the office except that the next few days could well turn out to be a matter of life or death. As he made his way across town, he prepared himself for the list of tasks he had to complete as soon as possible. He had to find out as much information about the arrangements which were in place for the Deans meeting as he could. He would also have to make sure he didn't arouse any suspicion; Mary's life may depend on it. He knew all the right people at Fenway and he was confident that he could get the information in no time at all. It was the second part of the plan which had him worried. How on earth he was going to convince Chad Myers to help them, he had no idea. It was imperative that they had someone in the room Mary had explained, to create the diversion. Max had tuned out from the detail of what was going to happen once the diversion was created, he had too much to focus on to be worried about the next phase of the crazy woman's plan.

He walked briskly to the stadium and swept passed the security guards like the regular visitor that he was. The Park was an eerie place when empty; Max had always found it that way. Built in 1899, Fenway Park remains the second oldest baseball park in the country and although it had old world charm in the true American sense of the phrase, it only really came to life when full of fanatical cheering Red Sox fans, then it was an awesome place to be. Max had great memories of his childhood visits to see great World Series winning teams and great, great players. His father made every effort to bring Max up as an all American boy and he was proud of what his son

The Price of Friendship

had achieved, would he be so proud of what Max was about to do, he was sure he wouldn't and as he made his way around the park and through the empty seats to the bull pen on the far side of the field. His boy was an up and coming pitcher and he was watching the pro's practice, an honour and a pleasure for any newcomer to the team and Max had arranged to meet him and his colleague's right there in the middle of the action.

The early discussions seemed to go well and although Max was pre-occupied he managed to convince the rookie coaches that he could help with TV and Radio interviews and guide the youngster through the pitfalls of dealing with the media. They all seemed happy with the arrangement and Max agreed to leave then to practice for a while and he would meet later that day to get through some video clips he had prepared.

He was IN and the boy seemed pleased to have a friendly face around. All the new starters wanted to do was play ball and learn all about playing ball and Max knew just how to take the pressure off them to allow them to do just that.

He left them on the field and started to circulate amongst the offices and meeting rooms, taking care of the real business of the day.

He left for the hotel at the end of a long tiring day with almost all the information that Mary required. It had been easy to get the details of the meeting and he also discovered that all of the hospitality was being taken care of by a single supplier which made things much easier especially since Max knew the company Deans had chosen very well indeed, in fact he had been used himself on many occasions. He would have no trouble getting an invitation for his friend to the evening festivities; all he needed was a disguise and maybe a date. He was uncomfortable about being there as someone else but Mary insisted he was present and incognito and what was more, she knew a man who could make him look like anyone he wanted to look like, of course why wouldn't she know such people!!

Max had collected his car earlier that day and moved it to the 'employees' parking lot just outside Fenway. As he inched forward in the heavy city traffic he noticed something out of place on the dashboard. A small piece of notepaper folded in half with his name written boldly on the outside in large capital letters.

He reached for the note and unfolded it whilst keeping one eye on the slow moving traffic.

'Meet me at the Millennium Hotel bar at 8.30pm and come alone'

That was all, no name, no explanation and as Max looked down at his watch he realised that he had hardly any time either. It was 7.45pm and he was heading out of town. The Millennium was in the centre of the business district and he would have to double back and find parking and…then it suddenly occurred to him. What was he thinking? Why was he even considering going to this meeting? It could only be bad news…..who would go to the trouble of breaking into his car, planting a note and leaving no indication of who they were or what they wanted? No-one he would want to meet with that was for sure…

Just as he had convinced himself that he would get back to his own hotel and ignore the note completely, his cell phone rang loudly in his ear piece.

'If you turn back now you may just make it' the voice said

'Who is this?' Stupid question Max thought but it just came out.

'What do you want?' Another stupid question….

'Only one way to find out…' The phone went dead and Max was no more informed than he had been before, except that they knew where he was and that he was alone and presumably, where he was heading.

'Shit! Shit! Shit!' Yelled Max as he slowly started to shift lanes and waving apologetically to the vehicles he was pulling in front of. He began to make his way back into town and he had no clue why he was taking the bait, but he was and it bothered him.

Max walked into the modern lobby of the hotel and nervously made his way towards the bar area. He had been there before but couldn't remember when. He took a left through the lobby and as he approached the bar counter he could see that no-one was seated at the bar. He quickly scanned the seated area which opened out into a large conservatory with picture windows and a combination of leather sofa's and wicker seating with bright coloured upholstery and large throw cushions. Still he saw no-one looking his way and before he knew it he was standing right next to the bar and the bar tender was asking him what he would like to drink. He ordered a Jack and Coke, believing that he would need a stiff one for whatever was lying ahead and he pulled up a wooden bar stool.

It was difficult to see the entire room from where he had chosen to sit and so he motioned to the bar tender that he would be moving to the far end of the bar. As he stepped down for the stool he almost bumped into a large burly man who was passing by almost knocking the glass out of the mans hand... An uncomfortable feeling came over him and he stood motionless for more than a few seconds before he regained some sort of composure and carried on walking to the other end of the bar.

The man he had almost collided with took a seat in a large leather sofa and stared directly at Max, his piercing green eyes drilling directly into his own and the frightful stare was quickly accompanied by a slight nod of the head and a subtle wave of the hand.

Max looked around the room and noticing that no-one was responding to the gesture, decided that this was it. He wandered as casually as he could towards the man who sat almost 'Buddha-like' in the middle of the large sofa, taking up almost all possible seating area.

As Max got closer the man shifted his large body a little to the left offering a small part of the sofa towards him to sit.

There was barely room for him to sit but Max managed to perch precariously on the arm of the sofa and stuttered an uncomfortable greeting.....

'Max Reynolds...........you wanted to see me?'

'I do have someone who would like to speak to you', said the burly man and he offered Max a cell phone inviting him to put it to his ear and listen to the message.

'Max. It's me....you need to do exactly what they say'. Mary's voice sounded nervous and scared.

Max was stunned. He gripped the small cell phone tight as he clenched his fist in shock and anger. Before he could respond he heard the deafening 'click' in his ear followed by a constant buzzing as the line went dead.

He held the phone at arms length and stared at the slovenly form beside him.

'What the fuck is going on!! I don't understand......Who the hell are you people?'

The man calmly prised the cell from Max's hand and introduced himself,

My name is not important but I represent Johan Botha. We just want a little insurance that we will not be screwed by Deans and we stumbled upon a good idea.....Mr Deans has a soft spot for your Mary Moore and so do you so that seemed to be a good plan all around...don't you agree??'

Agree? He was supposed to agree?

Max felt sick to his stomach and the guttural South African accent didn't help.

Trapped AGAIN...How many times was this going to happen? His mind raced as he tried to comprehend this latest dilemma. He felt as though he had been slammed against the wall and pinned back by the horror of yet another ultimatum..

What now? Mary sounded OK but what if their plan included taking everything and killing them both should he go along with the plan or try to find Mary....

He was working out some options as if he had a choice!!

Mary had agreed to represent Deans at the up coming meeting and now she had been kidnapped. It didn't make any sense...what could they gain from taking her out of the picture?

'Well we should get going Reynolds.'

There was the disgusting voice again.

'I am going nowhere until someone tells me what is going... Max suddenly realised that these were the first words he had spoken since the shock and they came out form his mouth as a whimper. He cleared this throat and spoke again

A huge arm reached out towards him and the paw like hand grasped his throat in one quick movement.

Don't think I wont kill you right here and now Reynolds...... You will do as you are told.…..no more …no less….Verstand Yeh? He was checking that he was being understood.

The man had made his point loud and clear and Max realised that very quickly, as he struggled with both hands to loosen the vice like grip around his throat. Eventually the grip loosened and Max was led away from the hotel spluttering and choking.

Chapter 27

Two days later Max Reynolds was standing outside Fenway Park looking across the road at the ball park wondering whether this was going to be the last day of his life. The sun was bright and the sound of the traffic and trains filled the air. Max was more than a little nervous and he prayed inside that he could channel the nervous energy and fear into constructive and focused activity.

It had been three days since he had seen Mary and it seemed like a lifetime. They had spoken briefly on the phone every day, just to prove that she was still alive and always with one of Botha's men in attendance at both ends of the phone.

It still amazed him that Botha believed Deans would give up the diamonds and the contract just to save himself and Mary. He did feel that Sophie was safe and that was some comfort. That was the only condition that he and Mary had managed to negotiate. Botha's men had snatched her and had her stowed away somewhere in Boston, Mary had spoken to her and had relayed to Max that she was safe. That would have to be good enough for the time being.

Max's palms were sweating and he felt very uncomfortable in the new suit which had been purchased for him. The jacket hung form his athletic frame like a coat hanger and it had been a long time since Max had worn a suit which hadn't been made for him. At that moment, he had no difficulty remembering why he insisted on that small luxury.

The craziness of the situation in which he found himself had Max thinking about anything but the reality of it all. He hoped that Mary had a plan because he sure didn't and he was sure that this would all go horribly wrong. Nothing else made sense. He had convinced himself that, even after all he had been through, and unless a pure fluke of an opportunity presented itself…he feared the worse. He had also convinced himself that he was not going down without a fight. It was almost liberating to know that he was so close to success or failure and the next few hours tell.

The black suburban pulled up in front of where Max was standing and Mary was escorted out of the back seat by two characters that looked like they were straight off the set of the movie, 'Men in black'.

Max strained to read Mary's face as she walked towards him, searching for a clue in her expression, anything which might just save them both. Did she have a plan?....was she trying to tell him something?......but the more he searched the less he saw, she looked straight ahead and cast only a fleeting glance in his direction.

His heart missed a beat and then caught up just as quickly, too quickly if anything and he found himself trying to catch his breath as he joined the entourage heading towards the main entrance of the building. It was as exhilarating as it was frightening and Max was beside himself with fear and expectation. He was entering the meeting as part of the Deans organisation and yet he knew when the signal came he would have to switch sides and also he assumed, would Mary.

All he could concentrate on was the role he had to play and trying to concentrate on a way out of there when the shit really hit the fan. It was a crazy plan and he could only ever see it going wrong, especially for him and Mary. They seemed to have been through the same briefing and for the sake of Sophie at least, he hoped that they could play their parts well enough to get Botha what he wanted…everything.

They had taken no more than four steps towards the building when Mary just simply stopped in her tracks. She stopped then she turned let fly with two expertly crafted karate kicks one left and one right which floored the two men alongside her. Before they had time to react she had floored them and she was gone. She bolted from the group and headed back the way they had came over the road and away. Max froze for a split second then instinctively ran in the opposite direction. It made perfect sense to him at that moment in time and he ran as fast as he could. He could hear the three men behind him getting to their feet and at least one shot was fired. It never hit him and he hoped it hadn't hit Mary but he ran as if his life depended upon it, dodging in and out of doorways and alleys hardly looking where he was going. He heard tires skidding and loud voices behind him and he knew they were close. If his heart was beating fast before, it was pounding out of his chest now as he almost lost his footing as he barged through a group of people

'Coming through! he yelled as he spun around and headed left across the street. He knew he would never get away on foot and he looked frantically in all directions as he ran, searching for anything which would help him get more speed. The screeching tires were getting closer and Max darted towards a street mall entrance. He ran through the tiled floor of the mall slipping and sliding as he avoided shoppers and carts. He noticed a security guard looking suspiciously in his direction and he took a left through a coffee shop and out the other side, back out into the street.

As he re-entered the street there were plenty of people coming and going. He saw a young man roller blading towards him and he wished he had roller blades or a small moped or anything to help him get out of the city. Maybe he could get a tram or a bus, but then he would be trapped even for a short while inside the vehicle with no control. No! That wouldn't help. The fear gripped him as he decided to mingle for a while, try to look inconspicuous in the crowds. That would give him chance to catch his breath and think. Think Max think! He had run away from the ball park on pure instinct. He had no idea what made him do that and even if it was the right thing to do. Maybe he thought that Mary was giving him a sign to go when she bolted, but all he knew now was that he had to survive the next hour or so. She would never have ran if she thought that life would be compromised so he was glad that he wasn't the one left behind to deal with the anger of Botha and Deans. Jesus! How had he got himself in the middle of such a mess? He had long since lost interest in the diamonds. It had all become about the girl and of course, Mary. His plan to come clean and save himself and the girl was also gone from his mind as he shuffled along the busy street looking for some refuge. He decided to make it back to the hotel. As he walked briskly yet cautiously he could hear footsteps running behind him. He risked a backward glance to see if he was still being followed and he saw one of the men in black. Max began to run again, pushing away the young couple who were locked together arm in arm. They both stumbled and fell to the ground. People gasped all around him and he knew they were staring in disgust but he had no choice, he ran. Out on to the road in between the cars he ran and across into street into a multi story garage.. His lungs began to burn again and he was so glad that he was a fit and healthy, he knew the burning would pass.

He ran up the ramp of the garage ignoring the stairs and the lift running and he found himself running against the cars which were exiting the garage.

The screeching of tires broke his concentration and as he dodged to the side to avoid the on-coming car he heard his name being called out,

'Max!! Max! Quick! Get in the car....'

The Price of Friendship

It was Mary……...Jesus it was Mary!. Max was in a panic now and he spun around and around looking for the men who he knew were chasing him and he saw no-one. It was bizarre. They were gone! No-one appeared to be chasing him……… How did she get there and how did she get a car so quick….. Something was very wrong about all of this.

He stared at her for a brief moment as she leaned out of the passenger window of the black suburban and he knew that something was definitely wrong.

Max turned away from the car and sprinted back down the ramp, back across the street and down an incline into a subway deep beneath the crazy city streets.

'Max! Come back!'

'Damn you Max Reynolds! Damn you!' Mary banged frantically on the dashboard with the palms of her hands as she cursed the man she loved. A straight arm forced her back into the seat and the suburban sped away in pursuit of Max Reynolds.

Max was sick with panic now. His legs were weak and wobbly and his mind was racing faster than he could ever imagine. He knew something had gone horribly wrong but he didn't know what and he had no ideas what to do next. Why was Mary trying to get him into the car and why did he choose not to get in? He was relying on intuition and gut feeling and he prayed that he was doing the right thing.

He emerged from the subway and made his way back onto the sidewalk delicately and warily like an animal trying to evade a predator. He had discarded his jacket long back but still his white shirt was soaked with sweat. The tie was also gone and he decided to try to make it back to the hotel to get a change of clothes. Maybe Mary would try to make it back there if and when she could. Maybe he should have got in the car, he pondered. What the hell!, He was where he was, and that was it. He needed to get away from there as quickly and discretely as possible.

The hotel was only a few blocks from where he was and he figured that they would never think that he would go there… surely not. Decision made, he started to jog as discretely as he could towards the hotel.

He heard a gun shot and he threw his hands to his head. The jog became a sprint again and he was off again running through the streets. It couldn't have been a gunshot, probably a car backfiring or something else but surely not a gunshot, in the middle of the day in open public. Not worth thinking about though Max, just keep going. He knew he was running for his life and if they were so close he couldn't risk going to the hotel. But there was nowhere else to go so Max headed for the hotel. His head was spinning and his heart was thumping. Beads of sweat were streaming into his eyes and stinging against his skin as he brushed it away with one hand and pumped the air with his other hand trying to keep a rhythm as he ran.

In a moment everything changed.

Max stumbled and fell against the wall and was immediately found himself looking up at a large man dressed in black pants and a black shirt who was pointing a gun directly at Max's head. The man looked flustered and he was panting hard as the people around them scattered screaming.

Max lifted a leg and kicked as hard as he could at the man's groin. At the same time he rolled to his left and covered his head in case the gun went off. The man cried out and crumpled in a heap dropping to his knees next to where Max had rolled. Max grabbed the gun and fired a shot into an outstretched leg. He leapt to his feet and backed away, adrenaline had taken over and Max felt a surge of energy rushing through his body..

He tucked the gun inside his belt, pulled his shirt out of his pants to cover it from view and he ran. The commotion had raised enough attention to attract the city police and the sound of sirens filled the air. Max continued to run a little more quickly now and with more urgency.

He knew that there was more than one person following him and he had to be vigilant. He had a gun now, that was an advantage but plenty of people could also recognise him after the shooting so he needed to find somewhere to lie low for a while at least.

He turned into an alley between two tower blocks and threw himself to the ground behind a line of trash cans. He was panting heavily and when he looked down t himself he was shaking and sweating.

He needed to find a way to get to Mary and Sophie and he also had to find out exactly who was chasing him, apart from the Boston Police…..was it Botha or Deans or both? Why did they need him now? It made no sense, his role was to facilitate the changeover of power at the meeting and them they would all be safe…but he knew that would never happen. Now he had no idea what was going on over at Fenway and what was he to do now? The shakes were getting worse as he contemplated the possible outcomes and he knew he needed to keep moving so as soon as he caught his breath he peeked around the trash cans and back down the alley looking for anyone following him. He may have lost his chasers for now and so he decided to carry on. Jumping over a metal fence and over a small brick wall he made his way between the large buildings and headed back towards Fenway. It seemed the only thing to do. Back to where it was all happening he couldn't run forever.

He needed to know who was chasing him and also he had to find Mary. The thinking was that if the trail was still hot then Fenway was the place to find an answer to all these questions.

He broke into a Laundromat from the rear door and found it easier than he would have thought to steal some clothes at gun point. Dressed in blue jeans and a long sleeved top, he thought it would be better to cover the large tattoo on his right arm anything to conceal his identity, he headed towards Fenway. He felt that he could negotiate the ball park quickly and without suspicion and he needed to find out what was going on.

Armed and feeling very dangerous, Max casually walked into the park from a side entrance. He made his way up the fire escape ladders on the south side of the main building knowing that would take him to the outside of the main meeting rooms and all had to do was find the right room by peering into the windows as he made his way along the metal walkways which surrounded the lower floor windows.

He saw nothing out of the ordinary. There was no game on, no people apart from a few cleaners high up in the bleachers preparing for the next game. He crawled underneath the first few windows and knowing them to be staff rooms and offices he made no attempt to see inside. He judged that the meeting room he thought was the xxxxx suite was the second window around the south corner turning north around the building. He could see the green monster at the far end of the ball park and for a second he recalled how he had sat looking at the huge green wall on the many, many occasions he had watched the Red Sox, man and boy.

Eventually he stopped crawling and stooped with his back against the wall just before the large picture window. He checked his weapon, released the safety catch and held the gun close to his chest with the barrel facing upwards. His grip tightened as he prepared to move in.

This was it… he peered around the corner of the window and shuffled his feet beneath him to get a better view. His mouth fell open and he almost lost his balance as he tried to take in what he was before his very eyes.

Sam Deans was standing not 3 feet away from him, shaking hands vigorously with the Johan Botha the huge South African. Both men were smiling and joking with each other.

Max dropped back down into a stooping position and threw himself back against the wall.

He tried to calm himself and telling himself to concentrate, he settled for a few seconds before it dawned on him that maybe, just maybe he had been set up all along. All he had been through was for this meeting. He sneaked another look and the two men were walking towards the window arms on each others shoulder and Deans was pointing out to the ball park. Max dipped back down quickly and dropped the gun which clattered onto the metal plates which formed the walkway. The noise was deafening to him and he froze hoping that no-one had else heard it.

After a few seconds he reached for the gun and just managed to grab it with the tips of his fingers and pull it back towards him without coming into view. The two men were staring out of the main picture window. At the perfectly manicured field below. Max had stopped breathing for fear of being spotted and he strained his ears to try and hear what they were saying. Deans had a concerned look on his face all of a sudden and Max could just hear him say,

'We should be getting back to the meeting, there are many details to go over and now that we should have got rid of the loose ends we are able to… ……' His words tailed off as they walked back into the huge room and away from the window.

Max allowed himself to breath again and tied to contemplate what he had just heard.

Am I a loose end? Are Mary and Sophie loose ends? It doesn't make sense…why are they going ahead with the deal and what the hell is the deal….it didn't make any sense…

Suddenly, Max realised that Deans had made a miraculous recovery……something stinks and it stinks real bad, thought Max as he scrunched into an even smaller ball and tried to become invisible outside the huge window.

He needed to find Mary and he needed to find Sophie quickly. He decided that there was nothing he could do here.

He managed to evade capture as he craftily left the ball park and headed back towards the city centre.

The hotel may hold a clue to what was going on and by now the heat may have died down there so that was his next port of call. The hotel lobby was buzzing with guests arriving and leaving and Max found it relatively easy to make his way to the room unnoticed, or so he thought.

He knocked on the door and rushed behind the door at the top of the stairwell, waiting to see if anyone would answer. There was no response and after a few moments he let himself in with his key.

There were no signs that anyone had been around for some time and Max was disappointed not to find anything or even anyone…it was a long shot but it had been worth a try. As he was leaving the room he noticed a face cloth draped across the bathroom door handle. He closed the door and removed the cloth…maybe it was nothing……but he was suddenly excited that this may be a sign from Mary. It sounded too far fetched but he was desperate and running out of ideas. Maybe she planted the face cloth there just before she was snatched and now he had to work out what it meant, if indeed it meant anything. He could only think that it was a sign to check the bathroom again.

Max stooped down on the bathroom floor passing his hand over the tiled surface looking for something, anything. He looked in all the nooks and crannies beneath the toilet bowl and the sink. There had to be something…but the bathroom seemed clean and the more he searched the less he found. There weren't many places to hide anything in a hotel bathroom but if she had planted anything for him to find then find it he would.. Then, sure enough there it was.

Max recognised the curled up business card immediately as he removed it form the cistern and dried it off with a white hotel towel. He instantly knew that this had to be a clue to the whereabouts of Sophie. Mary would have known that they would keep moving her but to keep moving them both was tricky and risky. It had to be Sophie, it made sense to keep her close, in the city and maybe Mary had even been allowed to see her, who knows. But Max knew exactly where he was going next and suddenly he had a renewed purpose in his stride.

The Price of Friendship

Max allowed himself a little reminiscence as he tried to remember the last time he and Chuck Moore had taken their partners to the Shanghai Chinese Restaurant and it almost brought a tear to his eyes. Chuck was dead, Mary was in considerable danger and Sophie was held hostage….and he was running for his life…….life had a way of changing everything he thought…everything had changed.

Max sneaked out onto the street and flogged down a passing cab. He called out his destination to the driver and felt for the gun in his belt almost at the same time. This time he wasn't going to fail. He would find Sophie alive he convinced himself and if there was the slightest chance he would also find Mary. He stiffened his body and steeled himself for the next challenge as the driver expertly negotiated the narrow downtown streets. He specifically asked to be taken to the rear entrance of the Chinese Business Centre building and although it was not the easiest route through the city that was exactly where the driver had dropped him. In the alley. The property was deserted for most of the day because the apartments were mainly used for long stay business guests. The restaurant on the ground floor was extremely popular in the evenings and Max made a mental note that the evening was fast approaching.

He wandered into the concierge's office as though he was supposed to be there and before the concierge could object, Max hit him as hard as he could as many times as he could until he could pin him down without any resistance. It was crude but it worked and Max changed clothes, tied him up and wandered out into the main building as the concierge. He didn't know exactly where Sophie was being held in the building but he had decided that the disguise would give him a better chance of moving around.

It was not necessary to move too far because as he started for the elevator, he saw two women and a small girl walking towards the far elevator a little too quickly and quietly for an afternoon stroll. He recognised the frightened face of Sophie at once.

They got into an empty elevator and Max waited to see what floor they got out. He thought he may be able to beat the elevator up by taking the stairs but just as the doors began to close he realised that none of them would recognise him and he was in disguise anyway.. He walked quickly towards the elevator and slipped in just before the doors closed. He turned his back on Sophie and the women apologising a he did so and asking them which floor they required he pressed the button for 3rd floor and 4th floor and the doors closed.

Max was shaking and he could feel the nervous eyes of the women burning into his back as he tried to stand as still as possible as the elevator started to move.

They reached the 3rd floor and the doors opened. Max moved to one side as one woman then Sophie then the other woman left the elevator car. They were moving quickly and efficiently without turning their back on him. Well rehearsed and well executed. Max knew he would have to come up with something very slick to get Sophie away from them. But she was there and alive. He had found her just as Mary had intended.

Max slipped out of the elevator behind them just before the doors closed and headed off in the opposite direction not daring to turn for fear of raising attention. He stopped as soon as he thought he could risk it and knocked on a random door to cover his movement. The sign on the door said 'Storage Closet' and Max winced a little hoping that they hadn't noticed. From the corner of his eye he could see them taking a left at the other end of the corridor and he swiftly turned and ran in pursuit along the richly carpeted floor. As he reached the corner of the corridor he drew his gun and as soon as he peaked around the corner he was called upon to use it. A hand reached out towards him and tried to grab him by the throat. He struck the hand away from him with as much force as he could muster and pressing the silenced gun hard against the arm he fired a bullet deep into the flesh.

It was a knee jerk reaction and as the woman fell to the floor he kicked at her, his flailing foot made contact with her stomach and she let out a cry with the pain as Max cracked her across the back of the head with the butt of his gun. He hoped she wasn't dead as he dragged her limp body to an alcove which contained the chilled water dispenser which was close by. He tucked her into the alcove as best he could and hoped that she was 'one down' and 'one to go'.

There were about ten doors to choose from as he made his way back down the corridor. Amazingly, the gun shot although muffled didn't seem to have raised any attention. Max knocked each door one by one as he made his way down the corridor hoping that no-one answered, this would mean that Sophie and her minder were the only people in, on that corridor at least.

Max worked his way along the rooms with no answer from any one….now what? He had to find which room Sophie was in so he decided to wait.

What would Mary do? She was the one with all the bright ideas. She was the one who seemed to know what she was doing. She had been quite a surprise throughout and how he needed her now. But there was no Mary, in fact he had no idea where she was so he was on his own and he had to succeed.

The sound of the elevator soon broke the silence as Max waited in a position form which he could see both corridors. A UPS delivery man emerged from the lift and made his way down the corridor. He stopped outside a door about half way down the corridor and knocked. There was something different about the way he knocked as if it could be a coded knock. Two taps on the door followed by a gap and then two further taps and a louder knock. Max was mesmerised and he watched so intently what was happening that he must have attracted too much attention. The man turned quickly and looked in Max's direction and he knew he had been spotted. He began to walk towards the man as the real concierge would and passed by with no more than a nod of the head and a brief greeting.

As the door opened the man kicked it further open with some force. He leaned into the room and the shouting and screaming started at the same time as the man launched something into the room and began to run down the corridor away from the door. He almost knocked Max over as he sprinted towards the stairwell and disappeared through the doorway.

Max was taken aback and he stood staring at the man and then at the door. It took him a few seconds to move as he suddenly realised that this must be the room Sophie was in and she was almost certainly in danger… He spun around and ran towards the apartment door.

The dull sound of an explosion from inside the room could be heard all along the corridor. It wasn't a bomb or even a grenade thought Max…not enough noise. As he reached the apartment but there was plenty of acrid smoke belching out into the corridor. There were no flames and no flying objects as he flew into the room slipping on the tiled floor as he went inside. It was a smoke bomb and he covered his eyes and mouth instinctively with his jacket.

Sophie! He called in a very weak voice, 'Where are you?' He stumbled around the entrance hall calling frantically.

'Sophie! Shout out if you can hear me!!!'

Max almost tripped over a body lying on the floor but it was too big to be Sophie. The little girl ran straight into him as she was rushing to escape from the smoke, coughing and spluttering as she ran. There was no time to say anything and Max scooped her up into his arms and threw him and Sophie out into the corridor.

They ran down the corridor stumbling and tumbling along until they reached the elevators.

'No! Max called out, we must get to the stairwell' His voice was croaking and screeching as he tried to clear his throat as he called out.

The Price of Friendship

Sophie was crying and rubbing her eyes in panic as she staggered behind him, holding tightly onto is arm as they struggled to the end of the corridor. The smoke was making its way swiftly along the corridor and the sprinklers had come on spraying a water mist everywhere.

Max and Sophie reached the stairwell and quickly headed out of the smoke slamming the door behind them. It wouldn't be long before the fire Department arrived and he had to get her out of there fast. He and Sophie sat down behind the door holding back the door from the smoke; Max began to explain very quickly what was happening to a very frightened little girl. He turned Sophie's face to look at him as he spoke,

'Listen! Sophie', He croaked,

'Your mother Mary sent me to get you, I am Max Reynolds'….He could hardly get the words out as he gagged with the smoke.

'You need to do exactly as I say and we will get out of here…OK?' He waited for a nod or a reply anything. I need to know that you understand' He added and eventually Sophie looked up at him and nodded, the tears were streaming from both red blotchy eyes. She was in some pain and discomfort and Max felt that she would have agreed to anything just to get out of there.

They left the building from the rear entrance, passing the fire truck as it made its way to the incident at high speed with sirens blaring. Max called for a taxi and they clambered in.

'Just drive!' announced Max 'Head out of the city and I will tell you when to stop'

'OK Buddy! Out of the city it is', replied the taxi driver and he hit the gas.

They drove for no more than a few minutes when Max changed his mind and decided to stick around in town to try and find Mary. He had Sophie, it was unbelievable but it was true there she was curled in a ball next to him shivering and shaking but safe all the same. He couldn't believe that she was safe and he had to keep her that way. Now it was time to find Mary. If he was on a roll then it was now or never and although he had no plan and didn't really know where to start looking, he knew he had to try.

First he should make sure Sophie was safe and he decided to hide her at a friend's house it would be hard to explain but at least anyone looking for her would not think to look there. She would be safer than with him that was for sure and he wasn't sure what was going to happen next.

Max was once again alone and fighting against the odds.

Sophie was as safe as she could be and it hadn't been as difficult as he had expected to convince his friend to look after the frightened little girl. His face had said it all; everyone had rallied around as soon as they saw the unlikely duo on the doorstep of their home. They never asked why, they just saw a frightened and vulnerable child and simply had to help. Good, kind and honest folk thought Max, as he cruised back into town.

It was evening now and the sun had set some hours ago over the western suburbs. Max was driving as carefully as he could and trying not to let his frustration and state of mind take over him completely. He had decided to cruise by the ball park, as good a place as any to start, and then he would try contacting Mary's friends as a kind of long shot. He hoped that something would happen in between that would give him a clue, because he knew she would still be held and there would be no chance of contacting her friends. He still couldn't understand why she had tried to call him over to the car and he had even less understanding of why he had run but he still felt that this had been the best option.

None of it mattered any more really, Sophie was safe and sound and he would do his damnedest to find her mother. He had become accustomed to the fear of being hurt or even killed over the last few months and it worried him that it didn't seem all that important anymore.

The ball Park was in darkness. There had been no game that day and there were no signs of life. 'Strike one!' though Max as he circled the city roads searching for inspiration as to where to look next. It was a ridiculous strategy but it was all he had to go on. The hotel was probably the next option.

It wasn't long before they found him.

As he parked the Honda in the parking lot across from the hotel, he got a sixth sense that he was being watched. He felt for the small hand gun in his belt and braced himself for what was to come. His body tensed and he concentrated on walking straight and steady as he crossed the road and wandered into the hotel lobby as large as life.

The commotion had died down since the incident earlier and Max seemed to raise no more attention than any other guest as he wandered through the lobby and towards the elevator, where it had all started hours before. The expectation was electric and Max was back in the zone. Alert and scared yet focused on drawing them out, it was all he could do. Then, as had happened with the Sophie incident, he would have to act on impulse and do what he could.

Almost as if he had planned it, he felt the familiar shape of a gun barrel in his back and the warm breath of a person just about to speak, in his left ear.

'Just keep walking to the elevator' Max tensed then relaxed in an all too familiar pattern of response as he followed the instruction and made his way to the elevators.

His mind was racing and the game was on. Had this been a big mistake or would it lead him to Mary? They stopped at the elevators doors and a sharp nudge in the back was enough to persuade Max to take the two steps forward into the elevator as the doors opened.

As the doors closed all Max felt was the pain of a blow to the back of his head and he sank to his knees powerless to react. The second and third blow came in quick succession and Max blacked out.

The last thing he remembered was the doors closing on the people in the lobby and thinking that he must be close, very close to Mary.

Chapter 28

Mary stood over Max's body and waited for him to come around.

The room was spinning as Max finally opened his eyes. He felt like he had been run over by a truck and his hand immediately went to the back of his head to rub the place which hurt the most. All he felt was a damp patch of matted hair and a huge lump. He winced and cried out as the feeling came back.

As his eyes began to focus he could just make out the face of Mary hovering over him.

He called out to her but his cries were met by a slap across the face and a scream which he couldn't understand. The shock of the earlier blow was far outweighed by what he had just experienced.

'You fool Max……..' Growled Mary.

She was staring straight into his eyes and there was anger and panic in her eyes. He could see her but he didn't recognise her at all. There was wickedness in her eyes and her face was a picture of anger.

'You damn fool; you just couldn't let it be could you?'

This time she punched him and the pain shot across his left cheek bone. Mary stepped away looking at the others in the room and shaking her head.

Max was lost. He had no idea what was happening and he couldn't get free from the excruciating pain all over his body. He was lying down on a sofa of some sort and knew he wasn't retrained in any way, there was no ropes or ties on his arms and he was free to move, but he just couldn't move.

Mary began to explain.

'I had a great plan to come away with everything. Everything! The diamonds, the deal and the girl but you had to go playing the big hero.' She was ranting and Max could hardly make out what she was saying.

'Everyone has gone to ground now and we are back to square one. We had one chance and you ruined it you damn fool.'

This was incredible. Max was dumbfounded at what he was hearing. The pain and the words were just swimming in his brain as he tried to make sense of what was happening.

'Take him into the other room, I can't look at him' Mary gestured to another door and Max was dragged from the sofa, thrown across the room and bundled into another room. All he could remember was the slamming of the door as he blacked out again.

He was only out for a short while and as he came back to his senses, Max could hear voices coming from the other side of the door. He had no idea how long he had been out but he managed to pull his aching body up to the sitting position, resting against the back of the door. He winced as the back of his head rested against the door, but he was too tired to do anything about it.

He heard them arguing and shouting and Mary's voice appeared to be the one of authority. As he began to concentrate on the words and focus on what they were saying the realisation hit him like a brick.

It was Mary all along. What a fool he had been. Mary was playing him and maybe all of them, but how had he been such a fool and what about Sophie…So much of it made no sense but he was sure, very sure indeed that Mary was behind it.

The Price of Friendship

Max cursed to himself as much in embarrassment and anger as from the pain which was beating at his body, with no let up.

He just couldn't believe he had been such a fool and now what? What the hell was he supposed to do now?

As he contemplated the implications of this news the door swung open and he was pushed forward with the force.

'I see you are back with us Mr Reynolds, our boys must be losing their touch'. It was Botha! Unbelievable!

Max just couldn't take it all in. It was all so wrong that his throbbing brain could not even contemplate what this all meant.

Max found himself sitting in a bundle on the floor of a small room staring up at Mary and Sam Deans and they were smiling back down at him. It was so surreal that he thought he must be in a nightmare of sub-consciousness or just a plain old nightmare.

Deans pointed to his goons to lift Max up from the floor, brush him down and bring him back into the main room. It all happened so fast that Max hardly noticed the bag of diamonds on the table as he was planted down onto a lounge chair.

'We have one more job for you Mr Reynolds and then this will all be over' Deans had taken over the lead role from Mary and she looked non too pleased about it.

We knew that Botha would try something but it wasn't clear what until you kindly flushed out his plan. Mrs Moore almost succeeded in fucking the entire plan up for everyone by, shall we say, mismanaging her charge, namely you Mr Reynolds. You did prove a little unpredictable even for the very capable Mrs Moore.'

Deans was enjoying the whole thing. He was in charge again and loving every minute of the notoriety even in such a small captive gathering. He was brimming with confidence and looked back to the best of health, a miraculous recovery though Max as Deans came closer and closer to him with every word he spoke. He grabbed the bag of diamonds and flung them forcefully into Max's lap.

'In this bag is almost a quarter of a million dollars worth of diamonds a fraction of what you gave to me I'm afraid but they ARE all yours…..for a small favour…'

Deans too a breath for effect and then continued, 'OH! And the girl of course, we will need the girl, the precious darling.'

It made no sense to Max that they would offer him anything at all. The favour must be big and dangerous and what about Sophie…he had gone through far too much to give up on her at this stage of the game.

Max stared into space, a man with a big decision to make but there was no doubt in his mind what he had to do. His gaze eventually fell on Deans and then Mary and the two goons who were standing beside her. He couldn't concentrate his stare on anyone or anything as he tried to concentrate. He knew of course that there was no way out for him.

It seemed like for ever but it must have been only a few seconds before Deans started to explain what he wanted Max to do.

As he spoke, Max was still staring seemingly aimlessly around the room.

'Are you listening to me Reynolds ?. Deans grabbed Max by the hair and yanked his head up towards his own so that their noses were almost touching.

At that very moment the telephone rang and the sound seemed to break everyone's attention.

In an instant Max pulled his head back away from Deans' grip and then threw it back towards his captor's head sharply landing a sharp and forceful head butt across the bridge of Sam Deans' nose. Deans screamed and Max followed up with a knee to the groin. The classic defence.

The big man fell to the floor with a thud screaming and clutching his groin.

The Price of Friendship

Max launched himself from the chair and landed in between the two goons with his arms outstretched he knocked them both to the ground. He had noticed that only one of the men seemed to be carrying a weapon and he grabbed at the gun as they all fell to the ground. He had the element of surprise and although he didn't get a clean grab on the gun he had managed to knock it to the ground. Mary who had reached across for the phone and was caught unawares by Max's actions also reached for the gun. Max reached out and grabbed at the weapon. He just managed to get there first and he spun his outstretched body over and over coming to rest with the gun firmly fixed in both hands. Incredibly he had it…he had the gun.

'Freeze!!' He screamed as he got to his feet, waving the gun from person to person, left to right and back again.

'Everyone, Just stop….. Right now…I swear I will shoot anyone that moves'.

Deans was still writhing in agony and Max stepped over his huge body as he walked towards the back of the room. He stopped and turned as he passed over the big man and landed a well placed kick straight at Deans; head. He was in a trancelike state, and it felt like he could do anything. Another scream and Deans was out cold

Max was in control and he looked across the room at Mary and the two bodyguards who looked like they were about to burst with anger and frustration, fidgeting nervously and staring straight at him with venomous eyes..

He settled his stare on Mary Moore. There were no words he could say, nothing came out of his mouth as he opened it to talk.

She started to plead and as she rambled away incoherently he heard nothing, not a single word she was saying and he marched them all backwards into the small ante room. As they backed away hands held high, Max looked for a key or some way of securing them into the room whilst he thought out his exit plan.

Mary was still protesting and Max was still ignoring her manic ranting as the main door was caved in with a crash and a deafening bang. The sound of the door ripping from its hinges was immediately replaced by automatic rifle fire. The noise was deafening and everyone hit the floor and looked for cover. Max rolled towards the corner of the room and threw his arms up in front of his face. He curled up into a tight human ball and buried his head behind hid hands in shear panic and fear. He peaked through the gaps between his fingers to see the most amazing sight.

Two men were standing just inside the room they were firing indiscriminately at everything they could see. They were dressed in black coveralls and black woollen ski masks and they looked ever bit the executioners that they were. Max threw himself against the wall covered his head with both hands and prayed that it would be quick and painless.

Almost as suddenly as it had started, the resounding sound of gunfire stopped and the men were gone.

Max was still alive.

He uncovered his eyes and looked around the room. It was amazing how small a person could make themselves when it was a matter of life and death Max had curled up into such a small ball it was very uncomfortable to uncurl his aching body emerged and he tried to stand up. There was broken glass and furniture everywhere. The soft furnishings were all in tatters and the smell of gunfire still lingered. The bag of diamonds had been shot to pieces and Max could see small glistening stones all around the room.

In a state of shock, max patted himself all over jumping around like a madman, checking for blood and bullets but there was nothing. He found himself stumbling all over the room shaking and sweating, staring at the damage and searching for something and then suddenly it came to him……..Mary and the others……..

Sam Deans' deformed looking body was stretched out on the floor, his torso full of bullet holes gushing blood like some sort of macabre human fountain..

The two bodyguards were flatted against the back wall of the next room having met the same fate as Deans, their faces contorted in agony and shock.

Mary was curled up behind the door and as Max approached he just knew she was dead. He stooped down and removing the debris he gently turned her towards him

She had been shot repeatedly and there was blood pouring from several wounds. Although she had hidden behind the door, it had presented no defence against the automatic rifle fire. Max bent down towards her, already knowing that she was dead still he reached out to feel for a pulse.

All of a sudden a desperate hand reached out, she grabbed his hand and gripped it tight.

Max was startled and fell backwards. She was mumbling and gurgling as if she was trying to talk. He crawled towards her weak blood drenched body and held her close. He pressed his ear against her much to hear what she was saying,

'So…….So…Sophie….'.Mary was spluttering blood as she tried to force the words from her mouth.

'Please Max……. she… she's yours…your daughter……..
I swear' the words tailed off as the blood began to pour freely from her once beautiful, perfect mouth.

Mary's head drooped and fell as her body went limp, all the life had gone out of her.

Max fell backwards as some sort of chain reaction, skidding back on his butt away from the horrific sight. He couldn't think or speak or hear. His mouth was dry and his eyes were wide open in shock. He stared at the terrible scene all around him, the stench of death and destruction was everywhere. They were all dead and he had been left alive. It made no sense. Once again nothing made sense but this time it didn't seem to matter.

All that seemed to matter was that Max Reynolds had survived for a reason and he knew that he needed to be with his daughter. He quickly moved around the room frantically scooping as many diamonds as he could into his pockets.

Then he left, not daring to look back at the horrendous scene and hoping that he was putting the fear and terror and more importantly the people who had plagued his life for so long, well and truly behind him.

For Max Reynolds it was over.

Printed in the United Kingdom
by Lightning Source UK Ltd.
135419UK00001B/10-12/P